BETWEEN BODY AND SOUL

BOOK ONE

WRITTEN BY

J. SILVERSTONE

NEYTIRI PRESS

Published by NEYTIRI PRESS

www.NeytiriPress.com

Copyright © 2020 J. SILVERSTONE

All rights reserved.

No part of this book may be reproduced or transmitted in any form or by any means, electronic or mechanical, including photocopying, recording, or by any information storage and retrieval system, without the prior written permission.

Cover photo Subbotina Anna/shutterstock.com

Printed in the United States of America.

ISBN: 978-1-7352987-0-2

Between Body and Soul is a work of fiction. Names, characters, places, and incidents either are the product of the author's imagination or are used fictitiously, and any resemblance to actual persons, living or dead, business establishments, events, or locales is entirely coincidental.

BETWEEN BODY AND SOUL

J.SILVERSTONE

THRILLER

NEYTIRI PRESS

"Following our instincts
connects us with the creative,
the link to the spiritual,
a step closer to the angels,
God's messengers."

~ Carl Jung ~

TABLE OF CONTENTS

ONE	9
TWO	11
THREE	13
FOUR	17
FIVE	21
SIX	25
SEVEN	31
EIGHT	45
NINE	55
TEN	67
ELEVEN	86
TWELVE	94
THIRTEEN	101
FOURTEEN	106
FIFTEEN	116
SIXTEEN	133
SEVENTEEN	147
EIGHTEEN	157

NINETEEN	162
TWENTY	168
TWENTY-ONE	174
TWENTY-TWO	183
TWENTY-THREE	190
TWENTY-FOUR	204
TWENTY-FIVE	213
TWENTY-SIX	220
TWENTY-SEVEN	225
TWENTY-EIGHT	231
TWENTY-NINE	247
THIRTY	256
THIRTY-ONE	268
THIRTY-TWO	281
THIRTY-THREE	290
THIRTY-FOUR	292
THIRTY-FIVE	300
THIRTY-SIX	309
THIRTY-SEVEN	312
THIRTY-EIGHT	332
THIRTY-NINE	336
About the Author	343

Chapter One

When I hear the rumbling I think for a crazy fleeting split second moment that a train is coming. Then I'm pulled into a freezing embrace, heartlessly pushing me backward, upside down, sideways, away from the wide eyed look of the man who watches, frozen with helplessness.

Unspeakable power tosses me like a ball in the surf. There is no time to breathe, less time to think as I struggle against the turbulent monster trying to push me from life. Then suddenly its quiet. I'm no longer tumbling. By some miracle I've landed in a cloud of soft white.

"Get out! You'll die!" Crashes into the silence. It jerks me into action and I flail at my cold shroud.

"Stop panicking!" shouts the same voice inside me.

"You're squandering air. Without it, you'll die!"

Reality begins to filter to consciousness. An avalanche. A helicopter. Rumbling snow coming down. I try to move. Are any bones broken? I'm pinned by snow that will soon turn to ice.

Fear starts to race through my body. How much longer will I have till the oxygen runs out? I have to do something, I could suffocate or freeze to death. Will death be painful if I'm buried alive?

Chapter Two

O.k. Stop, I hear something saying. *Don't worry, you're alive, you're going to get out.* But which way is out? I can't tell the difference. Am I on my back or my stomach? Oh my God. I've got to dig out.

Menacing thoughts start circling inside me: *Prepare yourself, you're going to die.* Yet somewhere on the edge of that consciousness, a trickle of confidence is soothing my mind. I'm all right, I'm alive, I'm going to get out.

Don't kid yourself rushes into my thinking. *There's a fifty percent chance you'll choose the wrong way. What if you dig deeper, into the interior, in the opposite direction of fresh air and life?*

A big black wave of thundering, jolting terror threatens to rip me apart. I close my eyes and let myself take it. A trick I had learned as a child. But now I can't breathe, my lungs are tightening, the snow is hardening, it's turning to ice. Am I going to die? How much longer do I have here?

Please God, give me a sign, I want to survive. Nothing. I don't hear anything. I can't see anything. Nothing is working. Did I *ask the wrong way?*

The air is dwindling, I feel myself gliding, slipping away.

Will I live again? Is there life after life?

What's the meaning of all this? Why are we walking around?

CHAPTER THREE

For the most part, my life has been rushed, stark and special. Working as a supermodel I paid my own way. I was booked a lot and made lots of money. I was able to schedule classes at NYU and earned my Bachelor and Master's degree at the same time. Using satellite to study in planes, cars and hotel suites across the globe, I used the travel time to study for those degrees.

Does it sound glamorous? It's really not. I never cared where I was going till I got there, then changed my focus from study geek to glamorous model with two degrees and a lot of money.

When a cover story in "Vanity Fair" said I was *"THE ULTIMATE CHILD WOMAN"*, all the other social media jumped on the bandwagon to feature stories and photos about me. Everyone thought they knew the real me. They didn't. How could they? I didn't know who I was.

On social media I became a glamorous icon. At times I had security guards but usually I was able to duck the paparazzi, peel off the patina and be a comfortable nineteen year old at home, the butterfly morphed into a caterpillar to study.

People in my neighborhood are pretty cool. There are a few other public figures who live nearby and no one seems to care except for a possible cursory nod of acknowledgement.

This is New York. Within the mold of notoriety I'm another face that made big money because of lucky genes. But beneath that carefree pretty girl façade there is an arsenal of strong focus and discipline to accomplish whatever it is I need.

My agent, Catherine Pearl, said that kind of energy made me a superstar. Whatever it was, it was making me rich and I had the luxury of starting to feel secure.

Most thanks go to Catherine who was not only my barricade, but also my advisor who carefully built my career and future. Despite the offers we were receiving, she steadfastly held to my desire that I needed time to study. This I believe, built up the allure.

She did sign me up for a few select lucrative product endorsements that made me more money than I'd ever thought possible. I guess that's why I could giggle at the marriage proposal and offer of a generous gold dowry from a Sultan I never met or the entertainment executive who actually said he wanted me to be his trophy wife.

It was amusing when at a bus stop or taxi stand I'd be holding the hard copy of a magazine with my picture on the cover and no one noticed I was the same person.

When I attended classes at school I didn't have the time or the focus to be friends with anyone. I planned to stop modeling after I graduated, but lucrative offers kept coming in with numbers too big to turn down. With the amount of money I was earning, I'd have the freedom to do whatever I wanted and take care of my mother for the rest of our lives. We'd never worry again.

But now, just as my life is starting to take off, after I've been given a second chance, it's ending. Somewhere a clock is ticking, counting out the moments of my life. There's no way to stop it. No way out, as the snow is hardening and my heart is going to accept it's fate and stop.

It's quiet now. Kind of peaceful. I'm tired and my toes are tingly. My eyes close on their own. *So much to do is* in my brain somewhere. My heart feels heavy, I feel weighted with regrets.

In high school I was nearly six feet tall with a dancer's long legs and torso. I had no friends. When I asked one of the only nice girls in class why no one wanted to talk to me, she said I made them uncomfortable and the boys felt the same.

An untouchable. No friends, no real home with only voices in my head.

Almost from the day Daddy was buried, the voices came to me. They taught me to cook and do simple chores. I ran the house and worked hard to keep my grades up in school. By the time I was sixteen I was a full fledge new age Cinderella and had voices as my guides.

To add to the emotional turmoil, the more responsibilities I took on, the more my mother grew reclusive. I had to keep us away from Child Services. If they separated us it would have killed her. She'd never survive. Yet I may be leaving her now.

Depression is taking over. Hope is fading. I'm going to be buried in a casket of ice.

Chapter Four

It's my birthday. I'm seventeen. I had a dream last night that was so real I'm still not sure if it was true or not. That happens to me sometimes.

I was walking to the end of an icy chasm. When I looked down, I had a clear discussion with an anonymous entity whether to jump or not. The entity said to go on. Then I woke up. Is that weird?

I figure the dream is about not wanting to go through another year as bleak as this last one has been. I'm trying to convince myself that birthdays are no big deal. I shouldn't feel bad if no one remembers this one. But I can't help it. It hurts to be forgotten.

My mother is still sleeping as I leave this birthday morning. To add to my pity party, this is the day my classmates will be coming to Casually Elegant where I work. They're coming to buy their freshman year of college wardrobes.

Adding to a huge dose of self-pity I can't let go of the fact I won't be going to college because the scholarship I had been counting on was denied. My SAT scores were in the highest percentile, but I had neglected a lot of schoolwork and my grades dropped. I could blame my mother but there was really no choice. It wasn't her fault she needed my attention. I had to take care of her.

So caught up with myself I barely noticed the elegant couple who seemed to glide into the store and pause to look at a selection of Italian silk and cashmere shawls featured in the window.

The gentleman looked vaguely familiar and nodded at me when he caught me staring at him. Then I realized he was Ricardo Verruno, the famous photographer whose name is attached to some of the best fashion photography in the world. I had actually fantasized about meeting him some day when I looked at his pictures in Elle and Vogue. His work is amazing, and now he's standing right in front of me.

Unconsciously straightening, I instantly felt like melting, when Verruno pointed a long finger at me.

"Look at her," he was saying to his companion. "I can't take my eyes off her! She's classic – Ingrid Bergman, Charlize Theron – that young open innocence, the natural sophistication. Look at her bones. They're sublime! Those cheekbones were made for my camera, She's a find." He waved his hands to circumscribe my face. "I want to test you," he proclaimed.

I stopped breathing. *"Test me?"*

"Forgive us," Verruno's companion cut in. "I'm Mr. Verruno's assistant Eva. T*esting* means Ricardo wants to photograph you to see if you're photogenic."

Heaviness hit my chest and I felt tears threatening. I was mortified. "I'm sorry, I can't afford pictures."

Eva's face brightened into a smile. "No payment whatsoever. Ricardo thinks you have great potential and he wants to see how your look translates on film. Looks have different aspects. Some of the most beautiful women on film are not that attractive when you see them in person. Sometimes it's the opposite. Beautiful people don't always photograph well. So don't put your hopes on this. We all might be disappointed, but we don't think so. Our instincts and experience make us think you'll work out well. Then you'll need the photographs Verruno has taken."

"Oh my god!" I actually squealed. The light bulb was on. "Ricardo Verruno wants to photograph me!"

Eva laughed. "If the photographs work – it will be good for Ricardo as well as for you. Also, if they're as good as we think they'll be, we'll put you with a good modeling agency and you should get plenty of work. And if it doesn't work, you're beautiful and the world is waiting for beauty like yours."

Her words affected me so deeply I was afraid to look up and started folding a cashmere sweater to give myself time to think. If I made enough money I could go to college, I heard in my thoughts. I could even buy a sweater like the one in my hands. This is my chance. I won't have to sell clothes I can't afford or get people ready for parties or travel I'll never attend. If I can earn money as a model I can have a great life. These people are my birthday present. They're a gift from heaven.

"I'd love to test! Thank you."

Chapter Five

Test! This snow bound coffin is the biggest test of my life. If I fail I might never be found till thousands of years later - a Mummy freeze-dried in ice. I'll be a scientific find like the embalmed mummies in the pyramids to be dissected then displayed in a virtual museum of the future. I wonder If the cells of my mind will stay frozen and if later melted, will resume the consciousness I have now?

Tears are starting to freeze on my cheeks. Is gravity pulling them down? I remember climbing a tree as a little girl to hide from my mother. I hung upside down from a branch and my tears rolled backward. These tears are falling down on my cheeks. That's it! My tears are pointing to go the other way.

Thank God for the pain my mother caused me! It may have saved my life. So I'm going to dig upward in the opposite direction of my tears. I'm going to survive.

All of a sudden as I grab a fistful of crusty snow, I hear my father laughing at me. At three years old I'm trying to hit him with my version of a snowball. "Don't use ice," my father gently admonished me as he scooped me up in his arms and hugged me. "You could hurt someone."

I touched the sides of my potential tomb. If only I could bring my father back. I loved playing in the snow with him and taking hikes. Can I ever love snow again if I survive?

Nothing answers me. The silence is deafening, crushing. Panic starts churning, a partner I don't want to have. Trapped in a teensy patch of air, perched precariously on the thin line of life or death, I'm probably going to die.

Don't think like that, crashes into my thinking. *It's negative. Be positive. Look for the light.*

But there's tons of snow on top of me, I argue *silently.*

Your mind is the engine, the voice *answers. It will keep your body alive.*

My stomach is getting stiff, I can't wiggle my toes they hurt they're so cold. My physical senses are leaving me. What does that voice from nowhere know. I'm freezing to death. *Dying by layers. Jokes don't stop these bucking waves of fear. First one part of the body, then another,* insists that taunting voice in my head. I wish it would stay shut. Will only my brain be left, will it survive without the body?

Why won't these questions stop? But I wonder, is only the mental left? Will I still be thinking like this? Is this what's called spirit? What has fate written for me?

No, stop I don't want to know. Let me survive. I'm actually praying. Please God. Give me a new start!

You could be dead now, crashed that miserable voice again. Then it says, *People who don't accept their death stay attached to life. They're ghosts.*

Shit! Panic comes in like a punch to the solar plexus. *No,* I silently yell back. *I'm conscious alive, I'm not a ghost.* That calmed me. My mind is working.

Don't kid yourself, interrupts my thinking.

I'm not. I'll keep on going, keep digging. I'm going to survive.

Truth though I'm getting tired of the snow and ice falling on my face when I try to grab it. My body is giving out. I'm getting tired. I'm going to die.

I thought I would die of embarrassment the day of my first photography session with Ricardo Verruno. I was so excited till I saw myself in the mirror. Tight and short cut-off jeans and a huge diamond necklace that covered my throat and ended at the very tips of my nipples.

"This belongs on a stripper," I said with dismay. "I'm a High School student. This doesn't suit me at all."

"Don't worry honey," said the stylist. "Ya look terrific. This isn't catalogue, it's editorial, it's artsy." She patted my arm then draped a robe over my bare shoulders for the exposed walk from the dressing room to the photography studio.

I'm not sure what I'm getting into. Is this a pornography shoot? Verruno's work is sexy, but it's never off the charts and always in good taste.

When the stylist took away the robe and left me alone in the center of the seamless paper, I wanted to run.

But the familiar voice stopped me. *"Stay. Fulfill your destiny. This is a chance of a lifetime. You'll survive. The necklace is gorgeous. Do it justice."*

A warm glow starts to bubble inside me. The music grows loud and I forget where I am. I can feel the diamonds sparkling – almost as if they've joined my body, thrilled as the music fills my soul. The wind machine joins our movement and we partner in the air, my crimped hair blowing in a tassle of wild strands as I prance and dance, twirl and strut, let myself be taken by some latent interior force exploding inside me. My senses have been captured. I've never felt such freedom and power before. It's pure abandon. Totally exciting.

"Wonderful! Fabulous!" Verruno's throbbing baritone joins the music. "You're a natural! I knew it. You're going to be a star!"

A star. How I wished I could see a star, a cloud, anything. All I can see is white. Uncomfortable tingles start to go up my legs, now it's morphing to burning, it's growing to fire. I hear a voice screaming. It sounds familiar. Is it my own?

Chapter Six

The airplane engines seemed to be screaming as they brake to a stop. The door opens and I nearly fly down the stairs of the private jet to kiss the ground of Nepal, my adopted country. Maybe in this peaceful country I can ditch the nightmare of my marriage. I feel queasy, it's the excitement.

I had no clue this nervous rumbling is a warning the land I was kissing could be my final resting place.

Waiting at the foot of the stairs of the plane is a young American Embassy worker, Bill Farrow, who smiles at delight with my dramatic entrance.

As he guides me around the teeming hall of immigration and visa lines both natives and tourists have to endure, he asks if there's anything I'd like to do before or after filming.

"I'd like to stay on and trek," I tell him.

"Sure," Farrow replied. "It can be arranged."

"It's a belated graduation present to myself," I explained. "Actually, the first real vacation in my life."

"There's a remote region on the border of Nepal and Tibet called Mustang", he suggests. It's supposed to be very spiritual and there are caves where the monks meditate. It's a distance but I understand the magic is worth it. They have a small landing field so we can fly in and not have to trek too long.

"I can't believe this," my heart felt like it was actually leaping. "Mustang is my dream."

"So it's set. We have a journey to the top of Nepal and magic," Farrow grinned like an excited schoolboy who just made his first date. In reality this was actually my first date.

Now suddenly reality comes crashing into my brain. I may never see Mustang, I may never leave Nepal.

According to Buddhist philosophy this is my karma, my own *fault*. The trip for the commercial to film a trek to Annapurna base camp had promised to be exciting. I was thrilled at the chance to purge myself of my nightmare marriage, the broken promise of Camelot, the hell I'd been through this past year.

Funny but even in this freezing crypt I can still smell the pungent rope incense that had been burning in the arrival room of Nepal's International Air Terminal. Thick as a cloud the incense seemed to cling to the throngs of people dressed in a kaleidoscope of multicolored saris and blankets, a colorful counterpoint to the Westernized institutional decor.

Giggles and sobs, the echoes of unmasked emotions were like a wall of sound as the Nepalese travelers, their belongings in brightly woven sacks, were unaware their primitive bags were soon to be tested in the violent and brutal world of airport baggage handling. They were also oblivious to the commercial travelers wielding smart phones in various dimensions to photograph those impractical bags for urban designers to manufacture en masse for the gentler streets of the Fashionistas.

As a total stranger, my objectivity makes me feel almost out of body as I'm swept through customs and the mélange of Buddhists, Hindus and Muslims whose philosophy and religion encompass out of body phenomenon. Now they're about to expand those ancient beliefs into the contemporary reality of airplane travel. Entering a silver object large enough to be a shrine and heavy enough to leave a hole in the ground they will be leaving gravity for a new way of seeing life.

And here I am, a representative of the flesh and superficial coming to Nepal to enter the stark void of nothingness. Maybe this is an opportunity to learn spiritual abandon. To learn about death.

The schedule for the commercial had called for the production company and talent to spend three days acclimating to the altitude and climate in Kathmandu, the Capitol of Nepal.

Kathmandu is a place both foreign yet eerily familiar. As soon as we left the airport we were met with a wall of sound comprised of wailing car horns and reverberating temple bells. Cobblestone streets coated with decades of foot and hoof traffic, incense and animal debris, were crowded with traffic in front of ornamental temples and winding alleys leading to thriving markets and packed squares. Monks with shaved heads, their burgundy robes floating along the rim of three-dimensional reality pass street urchins hustling tourists to buy Eastern versions of Western designer drugs. The dusty streets of Nepal's capitol city hold a mix of the worldly and spiritual. Bombarded with crass materialism and spiritual reverence, this hodgepodge of the worldly and spiritual is ruled by the Himalayan mountains. Their power permeates everything, inscribing reverence and awe on those who live or visit here whether they are aware of it or not.

I had wanted to know these Nepalese people of the mountains and learn the truth about a people who were judged poor by Western standards, but spiritually are some of the richest people on Earth.

And now these all encompassing Himalayas have captured me, made me their prisoner, holding me for eternity in their icy cold folds.

I had believed this land has the power to change those who are open to receive its spiritual message, but I hadn't expected to learn it this way.

My lessons began the first day in Katmandu. Bill Farrow, the Embassy worker, took me to SWAI

BODHINATH STUPA, a huge pyramid shaped structure with the all-seeing eyes of Buddha painted on top.

Surrounded by prayer wheels, Bill instructed me to circle the pyramid and spin the wheels with a prayer. I walked behind an old Tibetan woman and asked for knowledge. The moment I finished I heard a loud peal of bells and horns like a parade. I searched for the sound and discovered the music was coming down a narrow road leading away from the Stupa. Inside a storefront was a small Buddhist temple. Chanting Monks sat on wooden benches lining the walls. Behind them were other monks blowing conches and ten-foot horns.

The head Priest motions me to enter. I take off my shoes and before I sit down I realize I'm familiar with the Tibetan words of the chants and I know when the horns and conches will blow.

I see myself sitting across the room on one of the benches, a blonde vision in travelling white clothes amongst the maroon robes.

"Why do you look like that?" I ask the blonde model type on the other side of the room.

The familiar voice answered. *"Because that's what you're supposed to be now. Remember what happens then teach all you know."*

The memory makes me ready to dream. I can tell I'm smiling because my insides are glowing, something I had never noticed till this moment in time. I'll take the voyage, the trip to the unknown.

"*Oh no you won't,*" jolts that voice inside me.

If I could I'd be shaking my head. "There's no choice. What can I do?"

"*Stay and donate the gifts of your knowledge. You asked for wisdom, now you've got it. Life is about learning. If you flunk out and leave Earth you have to keep returning till you graduate.*"

"But how?" I cry into nothingness, my breath raspy as my lungs push for air. The oxygen is going. I'm not going to survive. There's so much more I want to see and do. To experience life!

The image of the client getting off the helicopter and calling out to me suddenly materializes. "Hi Snow Princess" he shouts before my world caved in.

It would make a great headline I'm thinking as I sink into nothingness. *An incredible marketing tool:* HIMALAYAN HARMONY'S SNOW PRINCESS GETS ICED!

My body shakes. I'm actually laughing. It feels good. If I can laugh, I'll survive.

Chapter Seven

Survival was all I could think about the day my mother and I flew to New York to meet with the executive staff and agents of THE FACE MODELING AGENCY. I think I was trembling with excitement more than nerves. I hoped I had put together the right outfit. Thanks to the Internet I found affordable designer jeans that fit perfectly, a white Hanes t-shirt and a to die for vintage Rick Owens leather jacket that cost $50. - a rock bottom price that could probably re-sell for hundreds more. Admitting a feeling of relief that I was dressed much like the staff of FACE in variations of *not give a damn chic,* I cut through the pleasantries and started the conversation.

"Whatever kind of money you're going to talk to me about will be temporary," I told them. What's important is when I get too old and no one wants me I'll have to make sure I'll be covered for that."

I noticed an agent lifting a questioning eyebrow toward another who twitched back a smile as the rest turned their attention to Catherine Pearl, the executive director of the Agency.

"Well," the matronly CEO answered with a smile. "We're not used to young hopefuls taking the initiative. Your combination of independence and youthful naïveté makes you even more delicious and desirable."

As if on cue, her retinue smiled and nodded robotically.

"What I want," I interrupt, ignoring the compliment, "is to have enough time and money to get a college education while I work. I think that in the long run, education matters for my future."

I'd rehearsed that dozens of times before I got to the agency and had worried it could be cliché. But it seemed ok.

Satisfied, I took one of the untouched scones from the sterling silver platter and bit into it, ignoring the disapproving looks from the rail thin former models and starved wannabes who made up the agency.

Catherine Pearl tried to get my mother's attention who was gazing out the window, entranced. When she didn't respond, Pearl quickly switched her attention back to me.

"A college education is good," she agreed. "Your modeling and commercials will pay for it, and a lot more. But first you've got to see how it works. Remember, this is the peak time in your looks. We can work around your schooling as well as make lots of money. It's up to you and your discipline. My gut says it will work."

I didn't know what to say as she gave me a moment to take it in, then continued in a soft, almost singsong hypnotizing way.

"We'll advance you money for your college tuition and living expenses and schedule your photography sessions around your classes. We only ask you do not load up your schedule so you get stressed. That will make lines on a face that's paying for your education and our commission. And forget alcohol and drugs. You won't have much of a career if that happens. The outcome is in your hands." Her smile appeared sincere.

I hoped it is. Unable to catch my mother's approval as she's still fascinated by something outside the window, I take the pen Catherine offers me and sign the agency's contract a year before my 18th birthday. Trusting it's fair, I ask my mother to sign on the line that says *guardian*. She doesn't read it either and signs where I point.

FACE arranges an interview with New York University for Monday, got us tickets for two hit Broadway shows, sent a car to drive us to dinner and the theatre, and paid for everything.

The next day I went to the meeting at NYU with my college entrance scores and then went home to wait for a decline or acceptance.

The week I waited was nerve wracking. When the University letter arrived, the enormity of the decision made me afraid to open it, so I went to the small park near our home where there's a duck pond. I feel peaceful and calm there. Sitting by the water I closed my eyes and took a deep breath and prayed, "say yes".

Opening the letter, I forced myself to read from the top and look at every line of the letterhead, my name and address, the date, then reluctantly, the text. It didn't take long till I screamed, scaring the ducks and driving them into a noisy clatter.

"They want me!" I called out to the nearest duck. "I'm going to college." Sinking down on the grass I found myself thanking God. *Life is turning around,* says that beautiful voice inside me. *You were listening after all.*

"Time seems to be flying," I tell my mother as we sit together on the floor, trying to figure out a way to update my mother's wedding dress for the prom.

The phone rings and I gratefully snatch it.

"VOGUE wants you in Paris for the PRET A PORTER in three weeks," says the gravelly voice of Catherine Pearl.

"Three weeks?" My mouth goes dry.

"Do you have a passport?" Catherine is asking. As I pause to think about never having applied for one, Catherine interrupts my thoughts. "Never mind. Of course you don't. We'll get one for you."

"Uh, Catherine…" I try hard not to stammer. This is to be an important decision in my life. They're coming with frightening regularity since that chance meeting with

Verruno. It was he who connected me to this woman now so powerful in my life. The fairy godmother who will make my dream come true. She's so important I'm reluctant to tell her, "I have final exams, the prom and graduation." It sounds so lame. I cringe.

Sweet and comforting sounds coo soothingly through the phone. "Of course you do, Jenny darling. I totally understand. I know exactly what you're saying." Then her voice turns a bit gruff. "DO you understand what I'm saying? *VOGUE. PARIS COLLECTIONS - THE PRET!*"

I hold my breath. I can't breathe anyway.

Hoarse from years of recycled office air and cigarette smoke, Catherine clears her raspy voice. "This is a career maker." She's sharp. "Others would cut off their pony tails to walk the Pret. NO model would pass this up - no one!" Her tone shifts. "Don't get difficult Jenny, you haven't started yet."

"But, I'm n... not a runway model." The words land in a lame quiver.

Catherine's voice becomes softer, lilting. "Can you walk? This layout alone will pay for your first year housing and everything beyond the scholarship, probably more." Her tone is crisp and clipped. "My guesstimate is you'll pick up some ads and maybe an endorsement and come home with a minimum of fifty to a hundred thou, probably more. Easy. For two weeks work."

"A hundred thousand?" I was blown away
Catherine didn't answer.

I had read super models earned humungous amounts of money but somehow I never thought of myself making big money like that. I'm seventeen years old.

"This is an important decision," I told Catherine. "I think I should talk to my mother."

"Of course. You do that." Catherine didn't hide her exasperation, knowing full well the decision is mine. "But let me know quickly so I can get someone else. There is always someone else. Never forget that."

I didn't know what to say and was a bit relieved when she continued. "If you like I'll call your Principal and make arrangements for you to take the final exams earlier. You'll be ready won't you?" she asked a bit impatiently.

"Well, ye..." I try to answer, but Catherine interrupts again. "My dear," she says with a slight trace of impatience, "I can arrange to have you take your final exams early, I can also arrange for you to get your diploma without being at the graduation exercises, but I can't persuade you to disappoint your prom date. Make up your mind with what you want to do with your life and call me back within the hour." She hung up before I could answer, so I called right back then called my prom date to cancel.

To my surprise my mother objected to my decision. "You should have consulted me first. You won't have those wonderful memories," she mumbles as she goes to the bedroom and locks the door, making me spend the night on the sofa in the living room, again.

The next few weeks I'm in a frenzy studying for finals, starving myself for modeling, and keeping myself out of the sun to keep my skin fresh and clear. Surreptitiously I check myself to see if the changes I'm feeling are reflected on my face. I thought I could see the signs of my end of young womanhood and the beginning of a new way of life but I was probably making that up. I did vow however to the innocent image I saw in the mirror, that I would always stay aware of my gifts and honor them. But then I wonder if I'm making all these plans for nothing. Maybe I'm not *pretty enough, tall or thin enough. What if I'm a dud,* I ask the face in the mirror. And what if I'm the first model out on the runway? I've never seen a real fashion show except on the Internet, now I'm walking in the **pret!**

Fashion has always been my escape. When I was old enough I'd go to the shopping mall and browse through the clothing stores. It helped me forget the dismal feelings I had when I'm home with mom in that terrible apartment.

It also gave me a little boost of pride when many times I'd see my ideas about fashion realized either on mannequins or in actual merchandizing, like new colors and layering clothes with clunky shoes instead of heels.

Each mini conquest of style and perception made me feel good. And now I'm going to Paris to the ultimate fashion extravagance to experience it for real. To actually *WALK* the hallowed Pret-a-Porter.

The Pret was established to showcase new and established designers to the press and important world buyers and has become one of the most powerful and visible examples of not only fashion but the way we think and feel. It's emotional and extremely lucrative. Multi-millionaires can be made on a hem and a drape. It also spotlights the next superstars of the runway, affecting media to shape how the Western world looks and feels.

It seemed obvious the agency was pushing me to be one of those newcomer instant stars. It's weird to think you're about to be famous, but when everyone started to treat me differently it made me begin to think about myself, to be more careful about the way I behave and look. I hope I didn't abuse that fame glamour, especially now, when I'm about to die.

But I don't want to think about that. I want to think about the Fashionista universe of know it all, follow the leader, blue ribbon Pret. To watch the audiences from back stage and see stars positioned in the front row to capture the cameras streaming to thousands on social media was interesting and educational.

New trends, colors and shapes were gobbled up by millions waiting with their smart phones and computers to find the designs or facsimiles of what they're seeing on the runway.

Not sure I'm ready for this fully framed career Catherine has started me on, I'm excited and a bit terrified when I look at my first U.S passport in my hand and watch my brand new set of Hermes luggage disappear into the tunnels of the JFK international terminal.

Westy, the FACE agent accompanying me took care of everything. All I had to do was settle in the roomy First Class seat about to take me to Paris, that romantic paradise I had only known from pictures and movies, a city of dreams.

Nothing seemed familiar when I got off the plane at Charles de Gaulle Airport. I kind of laughed at myself for thinking *everything looked so foreign and awesome,* especially when I saw the Eiffel Tower on our way to the elegant Plaza Athenaeum where we were staying. With barely enough time to do anything more than splash cold water on my face, I had to wait to explore the unbelievably elegant suite the agency had reserved for me. It was so perfect it looked like a set for a movie. I kind of feel like a queen.

But instead of reveling in my new found elegance I was whisked into the crowded chaos of the backstage PRET where the fashion press lay in wait outside the entrance. I want to dodge the cell phones and tablets poised to make or break the models coming in, but Westy had warned me to smile and walk in like I owned it.

That was familiar territory. I knew how to send out an attitude and it was all I thought about as I navigated through the pushing pushy crowds of photographers as they crowded to take my picture and shout questions asking who I was and who I was wearing.

Holding my breath to control my nerves, I made it inside as to what should have been sanctuary but instead was a mass of foreign tongues and naked bodies that seemed to quadruple the chaos outside.

Stopping for a minute to take it all in, I was blown away by the feverish layers of people working to provide embodiments of perfection on models swathed in millisecond chic.

These designers and their models were to become the physical and creative expression of contemporary society. If they were successful, the world would copy them physically and conceptually, or worse case scenario, they would be ignored in the fashion press and their calls not returned by buyers.

The electric excitement of knowing on some level I was about to become one of them, to be a global statement in shape, image and cloth made shake inside.

Snaking through the sea of young woman with no fat on their bones, I consciously avoid contact with their eyes. I don't want to engage with them. I'll keep my cocoon. I learned that in High School. Like the corridors in school, I feel a multitude of shadowed eyes and multicolored lips discussing me in various languages as I walk through their space, sizing me up to see how they should deal with the new competition.

Impressions decided, they turn away and resume their previous gossip. I was used to being shunned for no reason other than the way I look and note the conversations I can understand had quickly reverted to speculations about who would be the first out on the runway, who will wear the bridal gown and who was sighted in the front row.

Prominent considerations flew through the air of this high stakes game whose purpose was to capture the millions of dollars resting on the outcome of those walks down the runway.

Fashion is serious business. Not only the monetary rewards but in terms of status and power. Jolted out of my reverie as hands touch me, I understand the general area of the subject a woman is asking me in French, but I didn't understand what she was actually saying.

I smiled and shrugged allowing my feeling of inadequacy to show. I turned to Westy. "I'm not ready for this," I told her.

She laughed. "Don't let them do a number on you. They speak English. Stay true to yourself. That will make you successful."

Westy spoke with such conviction, I used my *turning inward* trick to detach and go into what I call my white zone where I could detach from the reality as I'm stripped, combed, and brushed into blending with the look of the others.

In the time I worked with Verruno and a few other photographers to build a composite of photo shots the agency used to sell me, I learned not to voice opinions. Those thoughts and feelings were only to be manufactured for the camera and used as props for the image.

Detaching from the reality I grabbed glimpses of myself as I was draped, painted and pinned into yards of material to become a hardly recognizable vamp in denim, or a Japanese war bride for Comme de Garcon. Only my eyes confirmed I was the person behind those shielding layers of clothing.

And when my worst-case scenario happened, I was to be the first model out on the runway, I had to make a split second decision of getting rid of my nagging fear that I had never done this before, and figure out what to do.

So I went back to my first instinct in Verruno's studio on seamless paper and threw caution to the wind. Forgetting myself, I bounced on to the runway, slipping into my feelings as I slinked and strutted, bobbed and floated, reacting physically to the way I was feeling.

Indulging in the kinds of young womanhood fantasies that had initially set me free, I was having great fun and so were the hundreds of people in the audience and the thousands streaming it. Later I learned the Press wrote I was *new and exciting; a little girl with a grown-up sizzle with legs to carry that innocence to a new pitch in modeling.*

Almost immediately I was being called the Star of the Pret. Photos were taken for VOGUE editorials. I was photographed what looked like partially nude for a new perfume from an old design house. And much to my surprise I watched amazed as Catherine Pearl turned down a French Vogue request for a layout in red leather Gucci that bordered on bondage.

Not yet," Catherine told the editor. "You have to wait. We want to exploit the innocence for a year or two, then when we've had all that sweetness, you can use her for bondage.

"Bondage will be over by then," said the editor.

"So you'll bring it back. You always do. You'll be the first and only. Is that a deal or what?"

I was being discussed with little regard to the fact I was sitting right there.

The great editor folded, bowing his head. "All right," he consented, "For now we'll put her in one of those little Vivienne party dresses", he winked at me, "with lots of pink Kewpie-doll rouge on her face. We'll seat her on a silver platter and photograph her surrounded by cheap prostitutes and their clients in the salon of a whore house."

"You're terrible," laughed Catherine. "She's not going to parody Brooke Shields in Pretty Baby."

"I'm serious," said the French Editor of Vogue.

"Oh you are just too much," Catherine laughed and took me firmly by the elbow and led me out, pausing to lay a kiss on both cheeks of the preening editor.

Once again Catherine had proven her mastery at keeping tough situations friendly.

Near the end of the Prêt, I had made enough money to pay back the agency for the money they advanced me. I also learned many of the models bought some of the clothes they wore on the runway at a fraction of their wholesale cost. So I bought my mother some smashing scarves and sweaters and got a to die for coat that I'll love for years to come.

Modeling isn't as easy as it looks but the money is incredible. I felt like I was living in a total fantasy. In some ways, it was.

Chapter Eight

When I got back to New York, FACE was deluged with offers for me to do campaigns and films. Catherine said no to film. She didn't want that much time taken away from the various campaigns she arranged and there was also my schoolwork.

I was learning the fashion world was a fickle lover that could bring great highs and crashing lows. It's an exciting, exacting, and completely irrational universe with a fragility that makes it potentially disposable and financially compelling.

Never splurging on unhealthy or fattening foods, I was able to discipline myself to focus fully on whatever I was doing, especially eating. I always tried to determine if a calorie splurge was worth the fleeting satisfaction and edited my diet with high-energy low fat food.

Photographed as the quintessential All American Girl, my reality was that the moment I got home I'd collapse on the sleep sofa in my furnished studio apartment, nap for about an hour, then get up to study or write term papers most of the night.

Some times when school and work overlapped, I had lunch or dinner in the back seats of cabs or even the subway. Subjects that I was studying in Psych class like emotional disorders and sleep deprivation were in danger of being demonstrated in the laboratory of my life.

Like in High School, I worked hard to support myself and my mother while keeping top grades. I don't have one person I could actually call *a friend,* but again, that is no different than High School. I knew lots of people but they were all in the context of work. There was no time for parties and less time for dates. On social media I sold a glamorous and exciting life, but that was where the truth ended. The remnants of that life were left in dressing rooms of photography and film studios after the director or photographer called "cut".

Once in awhile my hermetic life was broken by a guest appearance at a fundraiser with photo opportunities. In the five years I attended NYU, I never had a date with a nice ordinary guy for pizza and a movie and I never lived the life I looked like I was having in the pictures I posed for.

Sometimes paparazzi stalked me and took pictures under the most inconvenient circumstances. I don't blame them, the more embarrassing, the "better" the picture and the more cash it was worth. But when I spotted them I'd buy them coffee and donuts, or manage to avoid them by putting on a disguise or a limp or something like that.

Much to the paparazzo's credit, they didn't stalk me at school after I treated them to a pizza party and explained to them that the University was my sacred territory and not to enter unless invited.

Luckily, by the time I was twenty and thanks to the help of well-placed financial counselors, I had built an investment portfolio that earned enough interest so I could buy my mother a mortgage free home with a trust that would cover her expenses for life. Neither of us would ever feel needy again.

Because I loved animals, I agreed to go to a gala for an animal rights organization with Martin Simmons, a potential donor who explicitly asked if he could escort me. Martin was one of the top three men at Crystal Films, an entertainment giant that had been built by Martin and his two partners and he and his company would be an asset for the organization, so I agreed.

The evening of the gala, Martin called from his Gulf Stream G550 to say they had run into turbulence and had landed a bit late. He told me he'd send his car to bring me to his apartment while he got dressed. Something about it made me hesitate, it didn't feel right. But I agreed reminding myself Martin's personal as well as his corporate endorsement could raise big money for the animals.

When I got off his private elevator and stepped directly into a white marble foyer, I immediately turned back to the elevator, to ask if there had been a mistake, but the operator had already closed the door. The foyer was stacked with gun cases and refrigerated boxes marked PERISHABLE.

"Martin?" I called to a closed door.

I checked one of the tags to see if it had his name and I was in the right apartment.

The sound of running water stopped. "Hey," Martin called out. "Make yourself comfortable, I'll be right out."

I touched a "PERISHABLE" box. "What's in the boxes?"

"Ducks."

I looked for air vents. "Are they alive?" I yelled to him again.

"Dead." Martin came out of the master suite wearing a terry robe, rubbing his head with a towel. "They're for my father. He likes them.

"Dead ducks?"

He took my hand and kissed it, looking at me with a glint in his eye. It made my skin tingle in a creepy way.

"We have to cook them because my father's building doesn't allow pets," he continued.

I pulled my hand away from his firm grasp. "Did you kill them?"

"Haven't you ever eaten duck?" he asked, his loosely belted robe making it obvious he was naked underneath. It was also obvious he was getting aroused.

I averted my eyes and tried to answer but he wasn't listening.

"Did you shoot them?" I smiled brightly holding my breath.

Yes," he answered evenly, without expression.

"It appears to be quite a few," my voice had taken over. *It's not wise to continue this line of conversation,* I heard in my head. *It's headed for disaster.* But anger had taken hold and it was in charge.

"Yes," he answered again, his eyes narrowing.

"What a victory! A planned attack?"

"Would you have preferred I wring their necks?" His tone was hard, his attitude annoyed. The Martini shaker shook with anger as he poured the contents into two chilled glasses and held one out to me.

"Thank you, but I don't drink."

Martin stared as if I had insulted him. Keeping his eyes on me, he took a big swig of his martini, poured one drink into the other, then turned abruptly and strode back to the bedroom.

I wasn't sure what to do. Should I leave or wait? I feel dizzy, confused. Stroking the soft glove leather of his Bellini club chair I try to quell the churning in my gut. I don't know what to do.

I'm struck by the view from his balcony fifty stories above Central Park. I've come out to get fresh air, and now my head is starting to spin. It's so awesome it doesn't look real. If I fell off the balcony, I wouldn't have to make the decision what to do.

What's wrong with you? I hear in my head.

I try to focus on the chair that had been designed by the Italian saddle maker Bellini. I'd first seen his chairs in the permanent collection of the Museum of Modern Art and wanted one from the moment I saw it. But when I tracked down the chair's importer and learned that even discounted it was way out of my price range, I vowed one day I would own one of this designer's pieces.

Yet I was thinking about turning down business offers that could give me the means to buy rooms full of Bellinis and whatever else I wanted. I just don't want to keep living my life as a model, I remind myself. There must be more challenging things for me to do, even though I'm not sure what they are. I have two college degrees and enough money not to worry. I want to find a way to give back for the opportunities I've had.

A bubbly heady anger starts growing as I fixate on the boxes of Duck coffins. *This is wrong,* but the thought sets off the kind of emotion that takes over and propels words out of my mouth before I can stop them. "Do you realize we're going to a benefit for the "Prevention of Cruelty to Animals?" came out of my mouth the minute Martin walked into the living room. Wearing a dress shirt, perfectly tailored trousers and gleaming black patent leather Gucci loafers, he holds out two ends of his tie.

"Do me a favor, I can't tie this. My fingers are too stiff from pulling the trigger."

"That isn't funny." I turn away from him.

That I can't tie my own tie?" He reaches for my arm and I pull away. His touch frightens me.

He senses my fear and backs off. "They're ducks!" he says in a voice modulated for the court or conference room. "It's not as if they're freeze dried orphans from some third world country brought here for a mad scientist to reconstitute. There are millions of ducks in the world, they're not an endangered species." He starts toward me, which makes me back up more. "I have a very large check in my pocket for your little charity this evening. Want to feel it?"

Keeping my temper under control I turn toward him. "Do you enjoy killing defenseless little ducks? All they do is swim in ponds and skim plankton for nourishment which prevents harmful bacteria from building up. They save your life and you kill them."

"Thanks for the science lesson my dear. But this is business. I go shooting with congressmen. They like to kill."

"So that justifies it." I try unsuccessfully to stay calm. It isn't working. "You go out with government officials elected by citizens who hope they will be safeguarding their homes and country. And all you do is go off to kill defenseless innocent creatures. You probably write off the bullets as a business expense."

"That's right. Smart girl," his lips smiled, his eyes did not, "You're lucky you're beautiful, otherwise you'd have a lot of trouble in life."

His quickly switched his charm back on and took my hand, gently caressing it like a prize possession. "Jenny," he smiled, "we only shot a few pheasants and ducks, not Bambi or Gentle Ben." He arranged his face to look helpless. "Please - if I say I'm sorry will you tie this?"

No." popped out of me immediately, hoping he wouldn't notice my tears threatening. "I'm disappointed. One of the reasons I agreed to come with you tonight was because Crystal Films had brought me joy when I was a little girl."

Actually that had nothing to do with him. He had been a corporate lawyer who took over after a bankruptcy.

"You have ice in your veins and a calculator for a heart. Your drive is to conquer and control."

Martin claps his hands in mock applause and turns back to the mirror to tie his bow tie. "There's a bill coming up in the Senate a few months from now that's important for overseas distribution," he says. "I also have to clear the way for our new park. We're getting harassment from your save the planet types. When I shoot with those guys it makes our problems easier."

"Why?" I asked lightly. "Are you planning to practice on ducks before you shoot the protesters?"

"Right. We need practice. Fairies can fly."

I've had enough. The park is opposed by naturalists for ecological reasons because it will destroy thousands of indigenous rare trees and displace wildlife in an area that is becoming increasingly urban. Quite simply, the animals will go the way of the vegetation. Pulled from their roots they'll starve and die. Why am I staying here to participate in a charade, I ask myself.

Closing my eyes for a moment, I remember the park close to my home where I would go for refuge. The place that sheltered me and let me think things out. The park and its ducks had given me the peace and calm that protected me during the chaos of my young life. I was indebted to that little haven that gave solace to a shattering life I wasn't sure I could hold together. It was in this park with the ducks that I got the courage to open the letter from the University.

"Long ago my Grandfather told me Nature could be my greatest teacher. I could hug the trunks of large trees and receive comfort as well as shelter," I told him. "He also said I should rest in the grass, inhale the beauty of wild flowers and listen to the symphonies of birds and insects blending with the wind. It's the harmony of our world."

Martin smirked. "Lovely"

My anger took hold. "Now I'm with the CEO of a company who, according to a viral email is about to send armies of bulldozers to cut down the tops of mountains and fill in the valleys with cement. Condos and hotels will crush the flowering hillsides around your projected amusement park, and to make that happen, you kill defenseless birds."

Martin's face was turning red and strangely looked as if it was blowing up. Signs of anger. I better get out. I should no longer stay in this apartment.

"Visions of those dead ducks stacked in refrigerated cartons in your foyer is too much. Keep your check. Use it to dry your hands when you try to wash off the blood," I toss over my shoulder as I head for the elevator.

Chapter Nine

I think about the incident with Martin and his ducks now that I'm in a struggle for my life with Mother Nature. I don't think any human could be as unyielding as this blanket of snow and ice.

I had been so happy when asked to do a commercial for the new diet soft drink, HIMALAYAN HARMONY. I hadn't worked in modeling or commercials for quite a long time and when I was told the commercial would be filming in Nepal's Annapurna Valley, I was thrilled.

I had shot a fashion layout near Annapurna three years before and loved it. So much had happened since that time and something resonated when the offer was made. Maybe I could re-kindle the strength I had felt when I was there. Perhaps the Himalayas would soothe my soul.

But I hadn't figured on an accident. I always thought I was invulnerable. Now I'm vulnerable but I'm not ready to die!

The night before the film company was to leave Katmandu for the town of Pokhara where we were to start our filmed trek to Annapurna base camp, the production team met for dinner at Boris's Yak and Yeti Hotel. Spirits high and poised for the 4000-meter high hike, we washed down Boris's famous Stroganoff with his equally famous Borsht and pure Russian Vodka.

Someone in the group suggested I join the crew traveling to Pokhara by bus and I thought it was a great idea.

The production manager didn't. "The bus journey is long and arduous. "Jenny has to fly to Pokhara so she'll be rested."

"We can pick up local color for inserts," I interrupted. "Let the executives have the plane. It will be good to have me on the bus. We can do some pickups for local color."

Harry Hanson, the director, sent me a seething glare which I ignored. This meant he had to forgo the private plane and be bounced around for hours on an ancient bus.

"We'll be lucky if the bus makes it to Pokhara on time, if at all," he growled, throwing in a last shot.

I hugged his arm to placate him. "It's a chance to experience so much more of this enchanting country instead of looking down on it from a private plane. This is the best way to capture Nepal."

"Uh, it may not work," he warned. Then seeing my disappointment he relented. "Ok. But remember, we want you to look like you're having fun even if you're not."

"Don't worry, I will." I kissed him on the cheek.

Seven thirty the next morning, fuzzy from the time change and last night's vodka, we met at a brightly painted red and orange Nepalese bus that looked like something out of Ken Kesey's Merry Pranksters' road trip.

Cameras immediately started capturing the Nepalese and Tibetan passengers with their cargoes of chickens, goats and pigs strapped on the luggage rack on top of the bus. There was a big fuss when a young calf they had been trying to board refused to go up the steps. It would move only in reverse and it couldn't be lifted. But when the crowd saw me, the calf was forgotten. With the lack of help, the calf's owner tugged on its chain and led him away. I hope I had helped him escape slaughter.

Once the bus got moving I started passing out bottles of Himalayan Harmony.

The director shouted, "I love it, get this Sam," yelling to the cameraman who started filming the Nepalese passengers and crew toasting each other, the country, the King, and even the goats and the pig with Himalayan Harmony.

Seven hours later with an hour's stop midway to find and replace luggage that had fallen off the bus's roof, we stepped off the bus into Pokhara's main square. Although from my point of view the scene was exotic, I imagine the reverse scene was what made traffic stop in the market square. A tall European looking woman with long blonde hair flowing over an ankle length alpaca coat made an impact. We were immediately surrounded by a cluster of Tibetans and Nepalese who helped to make a wedge through the marketplace as we headed toward a sacrificial alter dripping with an animal's fresh blood.

The entourage drew back and waited respectfully as I approached the alter and bowed my head and pressed my palms together and touched my forehead.

"UH...Jenny...Jenny. That isn't going to work," Harry Hansen called to me. "It's weird. The client won't like it."

I ignored him and kept my head bowed as everyone else waited in respectful silence. Only when the hollow sounds of horns reached my ears did I look up. I guess my eyes were gleaming because once again the director was shouting, "Yes, yes, I love it, love it, get a close up Sam, get it."

As I went to explore the stalls in the market place the camera crew and entourage ran backward in front of me to capture every move I made.

Suddenly, an ancient barefoot Tibetan man, a threadbare blanket wrapped around his skeletal shoulders, approached the entourage as I clanged together temple chimes to listen to their timbre.

Acknowledging the old Tibetan in front of me, he opened his blanket to reveal a magnificent turquoise and silver necklace around his neck. Gesturing he let me know he wanted to sell it to me. But as much as I admired it's beauty, something inside me resisted the option to buy.

"He's probably worn the piece most of his adult life," whispered Bill Farrow, the American Embassy attaché who was accompanying the group to Annapurna base camp. "It's more than likely it's been handed down to him through generations."

I looked away, thinking of the American Indians in Gallup New Mexico pawning their beautiful squash necklaces and handmade Indian blankets for a bottle of cheap alcohol.

"When a Tibetan is ready to die, he gives up his necklace," Bill added.

As much as I would have liked to help the man as well as have the piece, I couldn't say yes and shook my head no. The Tibetan hesitated, waiting to see if I would change my mind. Resolute and firm I forced myself to shake my head no again.

Tears threatening I abruptly turned and walked away, unaware of the cameraman tracking me till the director shouted, "Slower, let's see your face."

I stopped, my eyes meeting the director's. "Don't use this, Harry." The camera was still going so I turned my back. "Please don't," I started to walk off. "That was private."

I have privacy now. So private that if I move too much I could bring down tons of snow on myself, unless that already happened.

I close my eyes and think about the old Tibetan. I wasn't sure what passed between us, but I know that in some way it must have been a warning. Perhaps I should have helped the man fulfill his destiny by buying the necklace. Maybe it would have protected me. Or maybe it would have done the opposite and I would now be dead.

I learned in the short time I spent in this part of the world, that little was to be taken for granted and most coincidences were actually lessons.

The Himalayan Harmony commercial was an odyssey. It was a reality spun from some unrealized fantasy that a story board artist in the solitude of a blank computer screen, tapped on keys to create and satisfy a personal dream: "*All-American girl takes a trip to the holy mountains and finds a new-age nirvana - HIMALAYAN HARMONY - the new diet soft drink*".

This was some Nirvana, I think, surveying as much of the icy tomb as I can. Where are the Sherpa guides, the cook and the kitchen boy? I wonder. How about the dozen or so porters that had made up the small army escorting the production team up the mountain? Had they been caught in the avalanche too? And what about the client? Were they all killed or missing? Is the rumbling continuing?

Risking the squandering of air, I take a deep breath and try to bring back the glorious memories of the path through the mountains that had revealed vistas of brilliance I never dreamed existed. We walked through blocks of light in the jungle filled with hundreds, possibly thousands of butterflies that were separated and delineated by color: pink, blue, mauve, yellow. No color crossed into another area. Striped walls made a stunning and strangely mystical experience as we walked through the rainbow of colored butterflies.

My resistance is starting to grow thin. I'm getting tired. Very tired. I want to sleep, but force myself to go back to this morning when I thought I found perfection. Rising before anyone I left my tent to look for Annapurna, the second highest peak in Nepal and where we hoped to reach base camp. The gray streaks of dawn were painting the sky and were accompanied by a far off bird singing the dawn's arrival possibly from Tibet, *that* mystical country on the other side of the mountain silently waiting for redemption and resurrection.

Grateful I had taken the time to put on the bulky hand knit sweater I had bought at the Pokhara market stall yesterday, it was keeping me warmer then my flannel nightgown would have.

I had layered quite a few items over my nightdress this cold morning. Having taken a moment in time, could now mean the difference between survival or death. I had to smile at this irreverent thought that despite everything, fashion is significant.

Through the streaks of dawn I saw the great Annapurna, known as the Goddess of the Harvest, the Goddess of Wealth. The sun had thrown a gauntlet of thin clear light that caused the coy mountain to throw off her incessant drape of clouds and stand bold and revealed in the early dawn light. It was the first time I had seen this holy mountain beyond pictures and it was awesome. I accepted the vision as a blessing.

Though it breaks down to minerals and vegetation the overall mass is inspiring, more compelling than any art or architecture I'd ever seen. Mesmerized I now know this incredible mountain is not *to be taken for granted.* But why is Annapurna my assassin? Why am I to be forever cradled in its apron of ice?

I had heard the rumbling. Or had it been the helicopter breaking through the quiet valley that made the ground rumble with the helicopter's pounding vibration? Would a helicopter be allowed in these narrow canyons and thin air? I had seen the diet drink logo on the side of the helicopter as it came into view. The right officials had been paid off for permission.

"How's our Snow Princess?" Glen Smith, the client, had called out as he stepped from the helicopter, like a poster boy for the WALL STREET JOURNAL. Smith's handsome Anglo-Saxon face, lean frame and graying blonde hair reminded me of my late husband, Tim. Wrapping his affable outgoing manner in the latest designer rugged wear for this mountain trip, Glenn was a prototype for corporate America. Most likely, when he signed his employment contract he understood that as long as he played by the rules he'd be guaranteed lifetime security. He rarely, if ever, would make decisions without first weighing company policy. His superiors knew he could be counted on as a solid gold corporate game player and was richly rewarded for it.

I remember answering his wave with a nod and smile just as the earth started to tremble and the rumbling grew loud and menacing.

The memory makes me tense and I try to relax my wheezing lungs and pounding arteries, begging the white walls of the tomb to spare me it's dark potential.

As my emotional roller coaster zooms into a nosedive, an out of space thought suddenly comes to me; there's no proof that anything written or taught about death may be true.

Who can prove the dead are conscious once they're not here? My thoughts taunt me. There are libraries of books about near-death experiences, clinical resurrections, and bright lights at the end of a tunnel. There is ecstasy and euphoria, dead relatives appearing, angels, Christ. All who remembered their out of body phenomenon say they had a reluctance to return to life.

But now, faced with this frightening moment in time, I toss out my own belief that death can be like waking is to sleeping. I'm not sure it's true. I feel so much dread. I could die!

It's getting harder to breathe. I'm not ready for heaven. I'm starting to panic. I don't want reincarnation. I want life. I don't want to die.

White light starts to turn everything whiter around me. Snow cakes my eyelashes so I can barely see. Is this really happening? I fall into the shroud of filmy white.

Yes, comes that voice in my head. *It isn't a dream.*

Cold fear stabs me. Everything has volume and substance. I'm cold, so cold that I would wake up if I had been sleeping.

The vacuum of silence weighs heavily on top of me. Able to draw into a fetal position I give myself warmth and protection.

The sound of a sheet of ice cracking in the tiny space reveals a tall stick-like figure coming through the wall. Coated with silver like a sprayed on film of Lurex, it's saucer shaped eyes glitter and cover half its face. For some unquestioned reason I feel compelled to give it my trust. Immediately healing energies begin to pour through me. This creature is going to save my life.

Feeling as if I'm spinning on a disk, I feel charged with blue/violet light, sizzling and crackling, filling me with energy. No longer able to tell where my skin leaves off and the air starts, I become formless, without structure. I think about the people I know with their ready-made lives. Why is my life so difficult, I hear myself asking.

For expansion, experience, whispers that voice in my head.

But the ready-to-wear route is easier, I counter.

"When you get your skin back, you'll decide."

My skin? I look down and see a frozen body beneath me. It's my body but I'm no longer in it. It remained behind, a small lump of pink flesh that looks like a rock. A huge knot of pain appears in the spot where my throat has been. Did the stick figure pull me out of my body? Am I dead? A pastel rainbow hovers overhead and I jump on to it and hold on as other figures, plumper then the stick man and wearing looser clothing and parkas, yell and pull the body out of the snow. Covering it with silver sheets they quickly load it on a stretcher and run to the helicopter that had started this all.

I can feel myself falling through a totally silent tunnel. I can't hear my own heart beating or feel my lungs moving. There's only awareness of a total stillness, a void.

My head is cold. Someone is pulling on my shoulders. I can see bright lights and hear clanging noises.

Shuddering, a wail begins to rise from my spine, uncoiling through my body till it comes out my mouth. Air begins to surge through my body. A slippery hand holds my forehead as burning drops fall into my eyes. A tube is pushed into my nose and everything is burning.

I'm choking. A warm cloth is wrapped around my newly exposed body and I start to feel loose and relaxed. Clenching my eyes tightly I suddenly feel terrible loneliness as I swim through the unknown. I fear leaving my senses and being pushed into a void. Then suddenly I'm free, floating and unfettered. Am I dead?

A high-pitched siren pierces the rainbow, sending diaphanous colors smearing through my head. Then they solidify into what I know are the walls of a hospital room and voices near my bed

Chapter Ten

I try to open my eyes but I think they are taped shut. My body is prickly, like it hasn't moved for a long time. I want to turn my head, but I can't.

Someone is nearby. I can feel their emotions radiating through the material of their clothing, seeping from nerve systems that are motivated by ideas coming from thoughts.

I'm not in the avalanche anymore but in a coffin of my own flesh and blood. My senses are so acute I can feel other people's feelings as deeply and as intensely as my own. There is no clear separation.

I wish they could know how much I'm hearing and feeling. Sometimes people look like a cubist reality when they come close. It's beyond maddening no one is aware this being on the bed is a thinking, feeling person.

I think I complained of a headache when they first brought me in, but I'm not sure they heard me. Maybe I just thought I did.

Someone said I had hypothermia and another that I suffered delayed contusion. They discussed Ph balances, acidosis and gas in my blood then a chorus of voices concluded I was *"irreversible"*. Athough I had been saved, I was going to die.

Right before my first trip to Asia, Roger my makeup and hair stylist was chattering about his visits to church because so many of his friends were dying from AIDS.

"SO you go for insurance?" I teased him.

Measuring out dabs of glitter into colored powders he shrugged, "Of course…"

Giggling I told him he looked like a mad scientist as I relaxed into the reality of the past.

Finals in school were over, my thesis had been approved and the only thing that was wrong with my perfect picture was that I was going to miss my graduation from NYU. Another walk down the aisle in a cap and gown deleted for the same reason I didn't go to my high school graduation – a job I couldn't turn down. History goes round and round.

"You're a princess and you're going to glow," Roger interrupted my reminiscence as he stirred more sparkles into the powder.

"Did you make everyone shine in Washington?" I asked, loving to banter with him. This is what I'll miss if I give up modeling.

"Of course!" Roger bragged. "I did the makeup for the VANITY FAIR cover story, Washington's Movers and Shakers."

"The President and cabinet?" I asked

He shook his ponytail back and forth. "Guess again."

"The money people."

"Darling," Roger squinted his eyes tightly and leaned in close as he applied eyeliner to my lower lid. "I can give you lists of places to go, where you can be seen or not, what to eat, who to talk to and who to shun. But there is one important piece of information that wipes all the others away. Despite headline and talking heads, there's only one power that runs the show. Actually two."

"What is it? I was actually holding my breath.

"Two men." Roger answered, nonchalant. "They run it all - from Capitol Hill to the White House."

"Who are they? I want to know."

"Read the article. Maybe the writer will mention them."

He turned and started rummaging through his meticulously custom fitted Vuitton Cosmetic trunk.

"I'd like to meet them." I was surprised at my request. It was as if my voice spoke for me.

"Jenny," Roger's face turned serious. "These two people and their staff have run every campaign that has won the Presidential election for the past twenty years."

"Well, can you arrange it?"

"They started as assistants and God knows what else for John Kennedy. They traveled with him throughout his Presidential campaign and learned a lot from the group that controlled the marketing and media that sold the young Senator to the American people."

Roger choked up. "I still get emotional when I think about Kennedy. It's been so many years, but it's still the pain of a dream shattered. I can't get over the regret for what could have been."

I hadn't been born when Kennedy was assassinated but I was moved by Roger's pain and his passion. The Kennedy legion had captivated and inspired me as it had for so many millions of people in so many ways and no matter their age.

"I'm talking about the number one political Public Relations firm in the country," Roger was saying. "They coined the word *Handlers*. Those who want to be in politics bow to them because it is through them they receive not only their public image, but also the validation they need to get party backing and financing."

"Will you introduce me to them?" my more aggressive self took over and asked.

"Washington is," Roger paused dramatically as he pinned an ankle length silver braid to a platinum crown on my head, "BERNSTEIN and KALMAN." He stepped back to appraise me. "Ta Da! God you're beautiful." He clasped his hands together, swaying with ecstasy. "I love my work!"

"Just a mortal palate for your inspired talent," I laugh with him. "But come on," I took his hands. "Tell me about Kalman and Bernstein."

"Bernstein and Kalman," he corrected me. "Don't get it reversed. Big NO NO. Placements of names are just as important in Washington as they are in Hollywood. Bernstein started the company so he's first. Then Kalman. Don't forget that."

"Okay, Chief," I saluted him.

"Remember BK - it's easier and don't touch your face!" He took my hand and put it firmly down on the armrest then lightly blew powder on my face. It sent shivers down my back.

"BK is the most influential power source in politics - probably the country, maybe the world. They're the ones who create the Presidents."

He leaned over in a theatrically conspiratorial way. "And they can destroy them. If a politician BK elects doesn't keep their word, they'll use every inroad built to destroy them. It's happened." He winked knowingly

Metal clattering on a tray startles me into the hospital, my frightening present reality. If only I could have jumped at the sound maybe someone would have seen me. I wish the medical practitioners were more sensitive. I don't know what to do. Does everyone feel abandoned at some time in their life? Are they as afraid as I am right now?

"We're waiting for her brain waves to go flat," Someone is saying. More shivers go through me. If only they could see how I'm feeling... *They're going to re-cycle my parts!* They're keeping them on hold for a certain amount of time, hooked up to a ventilator with an EEG machine and a pulse oximeter on my finger to monitor my vital signs. Gotta keep the parts alive with tubes bringing nutrients and removing wastes from the organs host. This life support machine is efficient. It gives people a second chance at life. Except me.

The only sensitive companions I have are these machines that keep me alert with their lights and sounds. I wish I could get one to tell someone I'm conscious and don't want to die. My organ donor contribution was to be used when I'm brain dead and not conscious. But I am conscious. I just don't show it and all my wishing and praying has no effect. Those malevolent machines that keep winking and blinking, senseless sophisticated robots that mock me with their life and death power they have.

When I'm not time traveling, I watch a slanted version of people in uniforms under my taped eyelids. Stethoscopes hang around necks, a symbol of honor, as they ritualistically circle my bed, lift a cover, pinch an eyebrow, then read the machines to evaluate my body like a used car.

They have no more feelings or compassion for me than they would for a horse they wanted to race or a cow to sell for slaughter. Evaluating my living flesh against lists of standards and criteria, I'm not seen as a living being with feelings or needs but merely an organic container of body parts.

I guess that sums up my modeling career. I loved the nurturing and the comfort success gave me, yet I was always aware I had to do what was necessary to make a living and survive.

Philip Landfield didn't change any of that.

The photography studio and Roger with his compelling words about Washington was the gateway to Phillip Landfield.

"I want to meet Bernstein and Kalman," I told Roger again, holding his hand and giving him one of my best compelling smiles.

"Right. They'd like that." He smiled indulgently extricating his hand and stepping back to appraise me. "God, I'm good. You're a goddess!" He peered at me critically. "But I think you're too pink."

"Politically?"

He ignored my question as he concentrated on testing various colors on the inside of his wrist. "You're made of crystals from the heavens. You're captivating, compelling."

"I'm lucky," I interrupted.

"If you don't want to be a goddess you'll have to take plain Princess. No other choice. Your beauty is your power."

He made me giggle. "ROGER! You're crazy!"

"Right," he dusted thin iridescent triangles of silver glitter on my cheeks and blended them carefully. "I'm painting moon dust on your face to proclaim your dominance and success.

"Roger, seriously, tell me about Bernstein and Kalman," I shivered as he brushed the silver onto my neck and blew on it to spread it.

"They're expensive and effective."

"That works," money buys power. And Roger, I'm freezing."

Roger nodded solemnly, ignoring my shivering. "Everyone in politics knows them." He picked up a can of Diet soda and dramatically sipped it. "Representatives from their firm are present at party nominating committees, national and local," he added.

I remembered reading about the Kennedy/Nixon Presidential debates. It was the first time they had been televised and it was at that time political powers learned how essential it was to have a charismatic, photogenic candidate.

"They usually start with someone early, hands on, from the beginning," he nodded for emphasis.

"How do you know so much? This is exciting. The molding of a President."

Roger smiled enigmatically. "They give potential candidates the political equivalent of a screen test before they sign them for representation. They want to make sure the candidate and family will photograph well and sound informed in every situation. If not, they fix it with plastic surgery; personal stylists, diction lessons and tutors, whatever is needed before any of them are allowed near a camera. MGM contract players in the thirties didn't get that much training and fixing. They hire me to do the makeup and hair for the times it counts." He takes a sweeping bow.

"So it's marketing national leaders, breakfast cereal or automobiles. Little difference. What about morality?" I ask.

"They sell it. A personal brand." He snorted. "This is politics. Marketing ideas for power. Politicians talk a lot about taking care of things, but once they're in office they begin their campaign for the next term. Their decisions are predicated on their moneymen, public image and the next election. Who is going to be in the administration so they can retain their power. That's why there are rarely substantive gains for the public.

"Politics is the art of posturing and photo opportunities for Teflon, sound bite Presidents with herd bound administrations. Individual thinkers are not allowed. I wonder if we will ever have a President like Washington or Lincoln or even Kennedy again?"

"I hope so." Roger leaned against the edge of the make-up counter looking older and wiser despite the ponytail and the hoops of earrings lining the rim of his ear. The front claws and teeth of a snarling Black Panther tattoo peeked out under the rolledup sleeve of his black Hanes T-shirt.

"You have to give the public what it wants," he was saying, "because if you don't someone else will."

"The public isn't stupid." I protest.

"I didn't say they were," Roger sounded patronizing. "I said give them what they want. They want to believe that those in power will take care of them and that elected officials are looking out for their good. Few people question a public person's positive rhetoric. Politicians get in trouble when they point out problems they might have. They never point toward themselves if things are bad. But they do raise their arms and jump around a lot if things turn out well. That's what they do best." Roger brandished a large body brush dipped in silver powder and flipped it over my face and hair.

"It doesn't matter who's in office. They're all actors. Reagan was a prime example. The people behind the public faces are the ones that count. They're the ones who call the shots. Like Bernstein and Kalman. He dramatically took another sip of diet soda and continued to expound.

"Reagan's first supporters were the KITCHEN CABINET. Remember them? They made millions from de-regulation, an idea they had for more than twenty years. They got together and decided to run Dick Powell, the movie star, for Governor of California. He was to serve two terms then run for President. Powell was very popular. He also had Howard Hughes' money behind him."

"Then why didn't he run?" I ask.

"Powell got cancer and died before the campaign started. This left the group with a lot of money and a strategy and apparatus to launch a political campaign. Nancy Reagan stepped up to the plate and convinced the multi-millionaires that her husband would be the best replacement. She argued that Reagan had high visibility as the General Electric spokesperson on television, had been President of the Screen Actors Guild and looked Presidential. He could play the part. So they replaced Powell with Reagan."

"How do you know all that?" I asked him.

"My dear - don't let this young handsome face and tight leather pants fool you. I've been around. And when the plain are made to look beautiful, they lay open their hearts and spill out their entrails. They tell me their secrets because I know how to hide theirs." His brows lifted like a Satyr.

"Could it really be that cold and calculated?" I ask.

"Can you really be that naive?" Roger threw his arms into the air, showering himself, the floor and make-up counter with silver powder. "Look at Reagan." Roger carefully blew the powder off his leather pants with a hair dryer. "No pretense. Totally obvious. An actor and actress were President and First Lady. The Kennedy administration could have been like that, except John Kennedy and his brother Robert made the mistake of believing he had power and they could use it. So they were assassinated. A President of the United States should not have grand illusions."

I was smiling. "You're so cynical..."

"My dear, politics is the business of selling belief. Vote for one side or the other and then pretend you got what you wanted. If anything ever succeeds it's the roll of the dice. The government is so huge, so vast and tied up with red tape and protocol that by the time an administration has been in power four years, barely a dimple can be developed let alone implemented. The only change for the most part is style."

I shook my head sadly.

"Sorry to burst your bubble Pollyanna, but it's been this way since the beginning of the Republic," Roger said. "Most probably it will be the same in the future. There won't be a revolution. The public is too sated and complacent. They'll do what they're told to do through their Twitter accounts."

"Oh Roger. You're such an elitist. You have no hope or compassion."

He continued. "It's about money. The higher you go, the more connected to the top. The greater the profits when their candidate wins. Think about it," he added strongly. "Airlines, banks, communications. The only difference between the U.S. and a banana republic are the sophisticated techniques used to obfuscate the reality."

He put the body brush down and squinted at me. "Like it or not Jenny, you have been making vast amounts of money from pretty much all of that. They use you to sell hopes and dreams. If someone buys what you're wearing or what you're fondling they're made to believe they will look like you and be as sexy and happy as you appear to be. Every time you do that, Ms. Princess," he made a final adjustment to my ankle length braids, "you manipulate people. Your modeling is part of the hoax to dupe people into thinking what others want them to believe. And I'm one of the conspirators!" He smiled his Satyr smile.

I don't want to think of that. I want to think about Bernstein and Kalman. "I should work with them," I blurt out. "I could work as a handler."

Roger laughed. "Ridiculous. But keep the thought. Intensity makes you look amazing." He snapped a picture with his phone.

"It could be a great opportunity. I said, ignoring his picture taking. "Shape policy, the future, history. I want to do that."

"Do what?" Roger stared at me. "What could you do? Model for posters? Hand out advertising sheets?"

"That is so rude and disrespectful. I'd be very good at public relations." I tried hard not to feel hurt, but I did.

"With Bernstein and Kalman?" Roger repeated, shaking his head. Making me fight back tears. "Honey, you're craaazy! They don't need a model!"

"How about a smart, motivated person. You are so sexist!" I wanted to keep my cool but I was shaking with hurt and anger. "I have a Master's Degree in Communications from New York University. Do you think that's easy to get - especially with a full and successful modeling career. I've been working for something bigger, something that can make an impact that will help people live better lives. Like Oprah. I know the world of images inside out."

"But this is Washington my dear. You wouldn't have a clue how to start…." Roger protested.

"Everyone has to learn whatever they do at some point in their lives. You weren't born a makeup artist, I wasn't born a model. I could be a brain surgeon if I learned how to do it, so why not a publicist? I already have an edge. I know how to work with cameras and image. Look Roger," I grabbed his hand away from my face as he was about to blot my lipstick. I quelled my urge to treat his movement as a way to shut me up. "I'm good with the camera. I have tricks that can help candidates and their families use these tricks for their public images."

He shook his head. "You're also one of the most photogenic women on this planet."

"Roger!" I wanted to scream. "I have TWO Masters degrees! I should be doing something significant. Anyway, think of the parties you will go to as my escort."

"Well, now it's a whole other story." He pulled up a chair and threw a leg up on the counter.

"I can build confidence, I know how to do that. I can help create candidates' public images and,"

And what?" Roger asked, amusement on his face.

"And I can help guide the public sensibility to think for themselves. To maintain their personal individuality and integrity."

Roger's ponytail bobbed as he shook his head. "Here you are in the middle of the advertising world talking about going to the citadel of mind manipulation to make people think for themselves. Don't you think that's a huge contradiction?"

"No. It's about insight. Enabling people not to think like others, to encourage them to think and respect their own ideas. People need to follow their hearts and that insight in their head that's called, truth."

"Wow. You're out of my league. I don't understand a word of what you're saying. It's too heavy, too deep." He shook his head as if to clear it.

"Don't you think we're always searching for truth whether we know it or not?" I'm relentless.

"Maybe you do - but not this happy camper. I want people to tell me whatever I want to hear, not truth. Another person's truth isn't necessarily my own. Why listen to anyone else?"

"Wow, you're right," I gave him a hug. My giggles stop when someone knocks the hospital bed and rushes me back to the present.

I wish I could tell the doctors and nurses circulating in the room how much I want to live. They're discussing which organs would most quickly deteriorate and how soon they can use them. Someone says a helicopter is on its way to pick up my heart. My heart!

There are people waiting for my brain waves to go flat. Then they can remove my usable organs and disseminate them to different parts of the planet, like the corpse in a Tibetan funeral ritual that is put on a high wooden platform, its body slit open and skull smashed so the circling Vultures will ensure the completion and continuation of life's cycle. Death bringing nourishment to life. Now it's the doctors who are medical vultures.

"Remove the feeding tube," someone says.

NO! I try to scream.

From another dimension comes the sensation of something being drawn from my throat. How many people, besides suicides and condemned prisoners, the sick or the elderly know when they're going to die? How will it feel? Will I starve to death, will it be painful, will I suffer?

I want to calm myself, make myself ready, but something won't let me. If only I could close my eyes totally and blot out the glare of the fluorescent lights. I want to sigh but it feels clogged in my chest. The respirator is controlling my breathing.

A rustle of starched material moves around me. "This too?" a woman's voice asks.

"Might as well," comes the bored, matter of fact answer of a person who doesn't seem to care. He's not interested in a terminal patient without hope. It's the ones who live that concern him. I know he tried in his book bound protocol way to save me, but he didn't look beyond the bounds and I feel his disappointed heaviness of failure.

A whoosh heralds the familiar sound of the respirator stopping. Air is no longer being pushed into my lungs. Hands not too gentle pulled something from my throat. Did I wince as they pull it out? If so, did anyone notice?

It hurt. But they think I'm an empty pelt and can't feel anything.

There is none of that panicky feeling that comes when I have trouble breathing. My lungs and heart are holding out.

I used to work out daily but now my muscles are mush. At times I leave my body and go up to the ceiling and look at myself. But I'm not sure the skeleton I see curled into a fetal position isn't just a delusion. I really want to think positive thoughts, but I can't find anything to take this doom and gloom away. I'm too scared of what is about to happen.

There have been times when a new nurse or intern alerted the medical team that there are stronger bleeps and arcs indicating activity on the monitors. They're told that the signals are not significant because they're below acceptable levels. Probably gas.

If only I could have communicated to those people and encouraged them to stick to their observations. If only I could have told them they were right. Now all I can do is wait with the other members of the medical team for my lungs to stop pushing and my heart to stop so they can harvest my organs.

I'm so angry with this helplessness. It's the way I felt as a child when everyone older had the ability to control my life. I wish I could accept that and make my anger go away. I need to stay positive, to be grateful for the life I had before the avalanche.

The clock ticked again, reality stabbing deeper. The Serpent of Doubt gloats. Death is coming closer.

The books I studied had given me promises that this transition should be a culmination, an opening to eternity filled with joy.

I don't feel joyful. I'm scared. I don't want to die. I have more to live for, I don't want to lose that.

The small hand of the clock dropped another minute from my life, my hopes and dreams careening into a major nosedive.

"She still has a pulse," said a very young voice.

"Well of course she does. She's not going to die the minute you turn the machines off. She'll go at her own time."

"But the helicopter is due in."

"What do you want me to do? Put a pillow over her head? Just shut the fuck up," yells the same angry voice.

Chapter Eleven

I retreat to cozy thoughts about my coveted graduation from NYU. Catherine had found me a lovely two-bedroom condominium on East Sixty Second Street and Park. It had been furnished tastefully and all I had to do was hang up my clothes and settle in.

"I guess this means I'm living here," I had said to Catherine when she handed me the lease with my name on it. Tears welled up. "You do so much for me. I don't know how to thank you."

"Then don't," Catherine shrugged dismissively. "An agreement has been drawn up if you want to purchase the apartment. It has a 2.5% assumable loan that's been approved, which I co-signed. Or you can buy it outright. Ask your financial guys."

My stomach flip flopped, conflicted by Catherine's kindness but resistant because of a sudden thought. "You bought it didn't you?" Catherine avoided my gaze and looked out the window.

"This probably cost over a million dollars. I don't know where I'd be if I didn't have you in my life."

"Oh yes you do," growled the tough New York agent. "I cash my commissions. All I've ever done was open doors, you did the rest. There are thousands of pretty faces that come to New York hoping to do what you've done, and they don't make it because they lack the discipline, the smarts and your very special character. You've got a purity and an honesty – you have it all. I didn't do anything but cash in on a good thing. If you're going to thank anyone you should be thanking God."

I had been surprised when I learned Catherine went to church every morning and Mass on Sunday. I knew she wore a cross but it was always hidden under her designer tops.

Swarms of guilt started to overtake me. I hadn't wanted to model forever and thought there would be a change when I graduated and got my degrees. The apartment was terrific, but it was situated in the middle of a concrete canyon of artificially generated light and sound. I don't know what I want to do, or how I can repay Catherine for all she has done for me, but I do know I want to use those college degrees as well as my creativity to impact the world. To make a difference for the greater good. It takes only one person's energy to join the infinite rippling of the Universe to create an effect, *popped into my head.* But I can't remember where I read that or if I made it up.

I also don't know how to tell Catherine I need to make a change in my life. She's reaping good profits from her investment in me, and now her reward will be to lose the profitable client she has carefully cultivated and created.

But then, Catherine is gone and I may be minutes away from dying. All my hopes and dreams are going to be sifted into a contribution of organs from my dead carcass. I can't believe this is real. I can't believe this is happening to me.

I know I've lived better than most people could ever dream and have been given all kinds of special gifts in the form of human experience. But there's so much more I can do with it. I need more time.

There's movement around my hospital bed. My breathing is still working on it's own. But what if this terror puts a stop to it?

I can see Catherine standing on the terrace of my new apartment after I had taken over the mortgage in my own name. We had been admiring the sparkling dome of the New York night. "Do you realize that each light represents millions of people who live here? Catherine mused. Usually bathed in sophisticated nonchalance, she turned to me charged with excitement. "I just negotiated a new deal for you that will make nearly every person associated with those lights know your face and name."

"That's a scary thought."

She ignored my comment. "I've never seen anyone catch on as quickly as you have. You prove my instincts are gold."

"You are gold," I said.

Catherine waved her hands dismissively. "For the first time in the history of VOGUE every country that publishes the magazine in any form of social media, will have the same cover for their December issue, the Christmas issue, the biggest of the year and the most read!" She paused to allow her tightly set mouth to quiver into the slightest lift of a smile then continued. "And that cover will be YOU! The magazine will have the story of your life and work and your rise to fame."

She looked at me and not seeing a reaction continued. "You will tell your story first person and you can write it yourself and get paid extra for that, or have it ghost written. Whichever you prefer. It will be translated into Spanish, French, Italian," she fluttered her hand, "Japanese, Swahili - whatever. It's VOGUE! Well," she paused, nearly exhausted from excitement. "What do you think?"

She smiled so broadly I could see most of her perfectly capped teeth. She was so happy.

I don't know what to do with my face. I don't want Catherine to see how I'm feeling since it would disappoint and hurt her. I know the agent isn't excited about the money since editorial photography paid minimum. Vogue editorials are opportunities for models and photographers to get exposure and stretch their creativity. When one reaches the echelons of fame that I have, along with the top photographers I'm lucky to work with, managing editors allow us lots of freedom which gives both the magazine and the creative people the opportunity to keep their content fresh and interesting.

"Jenny," Catherine went on, choosing not to react to my lopsided smile, "this is a remarkable opportunity. You can paint your future with your history."

"I don't have a history. I haven't made any real choices." I protested. "I've been lucky. The choices and business decisions are all yours."

"And what you did with them. Once you were in front of that camera you made the decisions whether you were guided or not. Your freedom is part of your incredible talent. You use your experiences rationally and positively and your choices are inspirational. They will affect many plus this opportunity is good for your career. We'll both make a lot of money from the ancillary benefits; The Story of Jenny Webster starring you," she spread her hands wide and took a breath. "Darling, the list is endless. You'll be immortalized."

"Catherine. it's never been my intention to be famous. It's just that I've always had this feeling that somehow I can help to make a difference, help people feel good about themselves. I'm not sure being a model or an actress is a way to accomplish that."

"Of course it is. Public exposure gives you power. People listen to the famous whatever their discipline. That's why it's called STAR POWER. And with it should come serious responsibility. Oprah understands that.

"You'll be imparting your own lessons, your inner wisdom. This can be your pay back, your thank you to the world. In fact, that's how I suggested they promote it."

I feel flushed and cold at the same time. A giggle works its way up that I manage to suppress. I truly admire this woman's drive and intuition – especially as she had obviously anticipated my reluctance. She totally knew how to put the right spin on it for me as well as the international Vogue editors

"I know what you're doing and I love you for it," I can't suppress a nervous laugh. "But it's embarrassing. It's so self serving."

"Of course it is!" shouted Catherine. "That's the idea. Take the fame and the money and use it in the best way you know how."

The memory of that time makes me feel better. More positive. Am I remembering it now because I'm meant to survive?

"It's a first hand lesson and it's yours to give," Catherine was saying to me.

"All I have are lucky genes," I argued. "You're the one who made my success happen."

"Your looks help, but what comes out through your body language is what touches peoples' hearts."

"Cheekbones and Angels, no conscious decisions. Everything just happens. I don't do a thing. You're the one who should be on the cover. I'm just lucky."

A shadow crosses Catherine's face and she looks at me intently. "I don't want to pressure you, so I won't go into what it took to sell the concept. I'm asking you to do it."

"I'll do it," I agreed. "But only for you." I continued haltingly. "These issues may be my last."

"Are you dying?" Catherine's lips twitched as she suppressed a smile.

"You know what I want to say and you're trying to make it difficult. I don't want to model any more."

Catherine stared at me coolly. "Yes?" she waited as she had a few years before when I had to make the decision to break my high school prom date to go to Paris to walk the Prêt a Porter.

"I'm looking for another direction in life," I tell her with as definitive a voice I have.

"Of course you are dear. You've been saying that since the first time we met." She sounded like an indulgent head mistress. "That's what the college degrees are about. I understand that. But take it one step at a time and make a living while you search for loftier pursuits. Create fantasy, but stay in reality."

I feel so trapped by people's expectations, people I owe so much and to whom I don't want to say no. I always want to make people happy. I won't tell anyone about the bouts of deep depression and confusion I've been having; the loneliness and feelings of distance, of being barred from some illusive place within myself where I can find peace and happiness, a place where I belong. If I confided this to anyone they'd think I was crazy. Maybe suicidal.

And now I can't speak to anyone. Tell them how I feel. Is this a lesson?

The energy of hope keeps ticking away like that miserable clock slicing off minutes of my life.

The painted eyes at the top of Swai Bodhinath come to mind. I remember the monks playing ten-foot long horns, the sky filling with legions of butterflies. Then a vaguely familiar thin man with cat shaped diamond eyes comes in close to me.

Chapter Twelve

Limousines line the streets for blocks around the French Embassy. Drivers collect in groups outside, collars up, caps pulled down, cigarette smoke mingling with the clouds of white air forming with their words.

The Embassy foyer, lined with brooding oil landscapes leads to a gallery where the reception is taking place. A string quartet competes with light chatter and clinking ice cubes as the beautifully dressed mingle among a setting of power and entitlement. Sound bites of politics, economy and gossip circle the room like sharks in a sea of gentility.

A staid white haired woman, her plainness offset by a dazzling show of emeralds examined me with unmasked curiosity. As she started toward me the French Ambassador stopped the dowager's path to take her hand and kiss it. I assumed he was the Ambassador because he was wearing a costume of a suit with a ribbon across the chest and had a Thirties Hollywood movie star mustache lining his lip. Is *this fantasy or reality* I wonder.

"I've been more faithful to my designers than I've been to any of my husbands," shrieked a voice as I approached a doppelganger of stick-thin women clad in tweed Chanel suits. Backing a quick retreat before they might notice me, I saw the Ambassador and dowager surrounded by fawning partygoers.

Smiling politely at those staring with surprised recognition, I manage to glide through the maze and get back to the drawing room where important looking people are exchanging potential words of transformational power they want to be public because they know simultaneously everything is being monitored, there are no secrets in this room. Every word and visual exchange is captured. The reception is an unannounced media event.

And thrilling. I love being in the midst of this power. I can feel it, smell it, it connects to my soul.

Even though some recognize me, I'm not the focus. At an event like this I'm no longer important, though I have to confess my stomach jitters a little at the thought of rejection. This is no time to get insecure, I remind myself. Doubt and fear clouds perception, a positive attitude brings good results.

Although the office had arranged this invitation so I could introduce Phillip Landfield to Tiffany Holland, it was also my debut with the Washington elite, a group with whom I had to break social barriers to be accepted as a player. Actually I would have preferred to run away right now. I'd feel better in a pasture with bulls.

Start focusing on the party and stop thinking about your feelings, I had to remind myself. So I searched for Phillip Landfield or anyone else who might be familiar.

Appearing to be self-confident, I thought I looked good, but this assemblage of glitter and power caused anxiety-causing doubt. Each time I recognized a face it was because I'd seen it on social media: Henry Kissinger, Ted Koppel, Diane Sawyer, Anderson Cooper, even Bill & Hillary Clinton. I felt uncomfortable and insecure because as I was used to capturing the spotlight with little effort this was a different kind of stage. I had dressed to fit in but maybe my costume worked too well. Beauty was appreciated in Washington, but the real commodity was power, changing shape as it traded and bullied, suppressed and flaunted maneuvers that affect the future of the planet.

Power is a tangible commodity in Washington. It can be sliced and served like the smoked salmon and caviar being passed.

"Please," screeched a sparkling tower of black sequins and silky blue streaked hair. Her flimsy equilibrium made it obvious her alcohol intake had surpassed her tolerance. "He uses so much hair spray he's responsible for the hole in the ozone." Shrill laughter shatter the black and white mosaic and shake my composure. Before any shards of doubt hit their mark, I flee to the comfort and sanctuary of the ladies' room, collapsing on a tufted velvet bench in front of a gilt-framed mirror to remind myself who I am.

Smoothing back my hair and re-doing the classic bun at the nape of my neck, I remind myself that being beautiful is a shield from which I can remain apart. But I also have to be accepted by the Washington elite so I can work with them. I hope I have chosen the right face.

When I started work at Bernstein and Kalman I used the vision of a face jumper that came from the Frank Herbert book, Dune. In it was a sect of women called the Bene Gesserit, High Priestess who could change their looks and control almost anyone with the use of their *voice*.

So like a high priestess of the Bene Gesserit I set out to morph into a Washingtonian. To be accepted I'll learn a new language, think and talk like a political player.

Tucking a few strands of hair back into my bun for a more severe look, I'm glad I had chosen the copper silk Dries Van Owen dress that shimmered a little. It's conservative but edgy enough to let me stand out - just a little. Plus it's a cocktail reception!

My image smiled back at me from the mirror as I thought about the little initiation ceremony I held for myself with roses and candles when I got ready for this party tonight. It was the beginning of a new way of life.

"Excuse me." The elderly woman with the emeralds settled herself on the bench beside me and patted her aristocratic, fine boned face. "It's terribly warm don't you think?" She smiled at me in the mirror.

I return the elegant matron's smile. Not by chance her fine Chanel dress is the color of her silver hair, it's cut and style so classic it looks brand new, though I bet it's an original the woman has owned for years.

The elderly woman, careful not to disturb the professionally applied makeup on her surgically corrected features, dabbed carefully.

"Forgive me for staring," I apologized, "you're so beautiful."

The woman smiles a practiced thanks. "As are you." She puts out her hand. "I'm Louise Armstrong and you must be Jenny Webster."

Louise Armstrong smiles and pats my hand when I react with surprise. "Everyone knows who you are, they've been talking about you for weeks once it became known you were coming to Washington to work for Bernstein and Kalman." She lifted her eyebrows, a mischievous grin. "Why did you? The power? I doubt it's the money. You can earn so much more at what you're doing."

"True." I fought to respond intelligently and not be rattled. This was the first of my Washington tests. "I guess I'm a political junkie."

Louise Armstrong smiles and nods with understanding.

"Money and power are good props to make things happen," I continue, thinking I should stop talking politics.

But Louise Armstrong nods her approval. "I like your honesty,"

Modestly I explain, "I've been blessed and I feel I should return my good fortune with something more constructive than modeling. Washington is a place where good things can happen. As a hub of world power it can affect everything."

"Ah," Louise Armstrong smiled and took me in. "Many people come here and say pretty much the same thing. And a woman with your looks and presence is a target for gossip. You're suspect. That's why I'm the first to acknowledge you. You should be safe from most gossip and slander working with those two master rogues. But first you must prove to be what you say you want to be. Washington has many appearances, but at the core, we do discover true essences. You must come to tea." Louise Armstrong rose from the bench and extended her hand.

"I would like that." I jumped up from the bench to take her hand, quelling the desire to curtsy.

"Does Wednesday at four sound good? I'll send a car for you." Louise Armstrong swept out the door without waiting for my answer.

Two red spots of color cover my cheekbones. The meeting is a good omen. The golden rule of any place of power is to know who everyone is and Louise Armstrong is an excellent connection. Plus I like her.

Stepping into the glare of the party noise, I search the atrium to see if Phillip Landfield has arrived. When I had first seen Phillip that afternoon at the Washington Athletic Club, he had been leaning against a marble pillar and something about the pose made me pause, hold my breath, then shake it off.

Something was up with me that morning when I felt insecure about what to wear. Settling on a feminine yet offbeat Comme de Garcon silk dress, it made me feel good about myself.

Fairly certain I had read everything there was to find on Phillip Landfield, I thought I understood his tastes. So I made an effort not to be like any of the sleek and preppy Town and Country type women usually photographed with him. I wanted him to have a fresh impression.

Though I wonder if I'm concerned about his impression of me because he's my first client or if there is something in those eyes that makes me excited?

Chapter Thirteen

At lunch I had told Phillip to meet me at the French Embassy at 6:00 P.M., but I wasn't sure he had been listening, or that I even verbalized the information. I had been so drawn in by his piercing gray/blue eyes I was mesmerized, he had taken me away, captured and swept me in. I was useing incredible control not to dither like a blushing schoolgirl.

Somehow, Phillip seemed to know I was coming and turned the moment I walked into the room. As I started toward him, he met me in a few strides and took the hand held out to shake his and kissed it, never once taking those compelling gray/blue eyes off mine. Tingles spread from his lips to my hand then straight to my heart.

"Mr. Landfield," I manage to say.

"Phillip," he interrupted, a smile on his perfectly beautiful face. "I'm Phillip, you're Jenny. We've already established that."

"Just testing."

We smiled together. He didn't let go of my hand. "I've gotten used to seeing you. Today, after lunch, I passed a news kiosk and saw your face and said hello.

You were familiar before we met, and now that I'm with you I know why."

"Kismet," I murmured as I tried to ignore his warm hand sending chills of excitement up my arm.

He cocked his head for explanation.

"Kismet." I repeated. "Fate, destiny, something that's supposed to happen. Like are you the one I've sensed in my dreams." I giggled to let him know it was a joke. He didn't smile, his eyes held mine, sending me a voiceless message. It makes me shiver. I hope he didn't see that. But I think he did.

Is it possible we were lovers in another lifetime? Are we just finding each other again like in Brian Weiss's book, *Only Love is Real?* I remember we ordered lunch because a waiter brought matching plates, but don't remember touching the pink prawns. The thought of the prawns made me shiver again. I know I had lots of sparkling water to wet my lips. He drank water too, sparkling, like mine. I don't think he touched his prawns either. He was like a mirror. It was weird - a fantasy that was real.

Leaving the restaurant that afternoon he touched my arm and volts of pleasure shot through me. I think it was then I told him the time for the cocktail party - or at least - those were the words that had been formulating in my head.

Next to him I felt a tugging that seemed to metamorphose into his body and soul. I want to feel his lips against mine, smell his skin, feel his heat, know his body like my own. Phillip Landfield has cast a spell over me. Did he know?

His smile said yes. "Well hello stranger." He took my hand and kissed it again, his fingers following his lips with a slight stroke. "Where have you been all my life?"

"Writing notes about you." I told him, not adding the notes were only for myself and no one else. Yet this was real time and I can't remember ever having such strong feelings for anyone like this before. I wanted him to hold me and hug me. *How could I feel this way after meeting someone for only a few hours? Plus he is a client, my first.*

A waiter came by offering glasses of champagne. I asked for water. I mustn't let Phillip hold my hand any longer. I must take my gaze off him and pay attention to what is happening at the party. I have to find Tiffany and introduce them.

But I don't move, caught in the hold of his warm and powerful hand, loving the sensations it was causing, the exotic, provocative thoughts that were growing and filling my mind.

It was as if I had stepped off the platform into another world where only Phillip remained. My emotions knew nothing except his touch.

103

Using the waiter as an excuse to pull away I sip the goblet of sparkling water gratefully and use the opportunity to search his face.

He laughs.

Like a laser, Bernie Kalman's steady and disapproving gaze broke through a trio of gossiping dignitaries and entered my circle of bliss like a slap of cold air. Like a guilty teenager caught necking, I quickly took Phillip by the arm and brought him over to Tiffany Holland who had just walked in. Introducing them I stepped back, an uncomfortable third wheel.

From Nirvana to the pits I searched for sanctuary when they started talking like familiar old friends and saw Louise Armstrong smiling and nodding at me. I smiled back then did a u-turn in the opposite direction toward the vaulted doors of the library.

Phillip's voice stopped me. "Jenny, what time are we due for that interview tonight?"

He mouthed seven and I held up seven fingers, trying to hide my astonishment at his lie. He turned back to Tiffany and poured out apologies and promises, then in less than a blink Phillip's fingers were tight on my elbow, leading me out of the party toward a red Ferrari parked at the curb.

Trying to stifle a nervous giggle my emotions gave way to a heady feeling as I glided out of the reception on a lie.

Settling into the low plush passenger seat of the high performance car, I sneak a look at the gorgeous head of its driver - a Greek God, a Roman Gladiator, a profile from which coins are carved. Good idea for publicity images I note in some working part of my brain. They can use that. I stopped myself. Will I have a job after tonight?

Phillip was unlike any man I had ever known. He was sensitive and strong and seemed to be someone I could trust. He's also very exciting.

Taking a deep breath I settle into the soft red leather seat of the Ferrari as my Knight in Shining Armor speeds us off to an unnamed destination.

Chapter Fourteen

Speed, breathless speed, race us to a destination Phillip has planned. Strong pulsing yearning I've never felt before is filling my body as we speed through the streets of Washington. Stopping in the circular driveway of a Georgian townhouse, a large mahogany door opens and a butler in a tailored blazer and tie steps out. I smile at him and in an uncharacteristic way, breeze through the marble foyer and up the wide central stairway with no hesitation. Phillip follows soundlessly, offering no direction, showing no surprise as he accepts my knowledge of a home I'd never seen before.

At the top of the landing I'm drawn to two magnificently carved doors and grab the brass lion heads in the center and pull them apart. A vast sitting room/bedroom with floor to ceiling bookcases, two leather club chairs framing a precious Khartoum rug is in front of a massive copper fireplace. It's perfection, like a movie set.

Sparks from the fireplace seem to be shooting golden arrows toward the massive four-poster bed or is it my imagination? I turn to Phillip and have the strongest impulse to take off my clothes and stand naked before him. I don't know where that came from. My imagination is taking me over.

All the fantasy I've used to be sexy and fetching for the cameras is rushing into me. For the first time in my life I can feel a power that resides in me. But the power is no longer an approximation, it's a hungry driving need to be with him, connect with him.

I kind of stripped once for the famous French photographer, Gilles Berlout, on assignment for French Vogue. I was excited to work with Gilles who came with a huge entourage including his staff and agent/manager, the sittings editor for the magazine and Westy, my agency's representative. The set looked like this room; burgundy cashmere throws covering leather club chairs and what looked like creamy silk sheets tucked in a huge chrome bed.

The studio had been cold, but it was cozy here. Perhaps heat from the fireplace or maybe its Phillip.

Weird, though somehow familiar, there is a primitive force charging through me that feels out of control. It's a new feeling but it's not unfamiliar. I recognize it from a time in my life but I don't know when or if it had really happened.

Perhaps it was prescience that I hadn't wanted lingerie lines to show, so I was wearing the flimsiest of thongs and nearly nude under my shimmering copper dress.

For the Berlout magazine layout they had painted my nearly nude body vibrant blue. Rimming my eyes with black kohl I looked like some kind of feline and the music made me want to stalk the camera.

The primitive rhythms of Mickey Hart's PLANET DRUMS took me over and I rolled and swayed, imagining myself an enraptured Macumba in ceremonial ecstasy. Reveling in the ecstasy of my naked flesh yet feeling covered with the blue paint, I fall to my knees and rub against the crumpled silk robe I'd worn to the set. I become a kitten playing in catnap, oblivious to the studio full of people and the constant strobe flash and Berlout's voice calling, "keep going, you're gorgeous, fantastic, touch yourself, I love it!"

One hand reaches downward, my head falls back, the other hand begins to reach for a breast, someone yells, "GREAT!"

"Oh God," the words startle me, but still my body has a life of its own.

My legs start to part and I hear a voice far away, "yes...yes..". Had it been Gilles, the magazine editor, the stylist, my own? Did it matter? I had been taken over by some energy, some fervor from which I can't stop.

"You're gorgeous," I hear. "Fabulous...." continues another.

I look to see who's talking and my legs close, my hips come down.

"You got it?" I ask, my voice sounds like a child's. I pull the robe tight around myself and stand up.

"We'll see," Gilles replied tightly, handing his camera to an assistant and walking away without looking at me. He was unhappy I stopped.

Shivering I find myself with Phillip, thankful to see him, grateful to be with him.

Sometimes my memories are more vivid then the present, and when I get into these flights to the past I forget which one is real - the memory or what seems like the present.

Yet alone with Phillip in the massive master bedroom of his Georgetown home, there is no photographer or stylist, no assistants or caterers to break the fantasy and secure the reality. In the studio no matter how far out I go, I can always count on being saved. But now I'm in charge of my own destiny. If I never saw Phillip again, if we never speak for some reason, I know I'm going to satisfy that strong need that has overtaken me. Phillip has been chosen. He is the one.

Slamming the door on all doubts, committing to my feelings, I feel a sense of strength, a place in my soul that is geared for passion, the place where no secrets are allowed.

Stepping back I disallow my logic and ignore the voices of caution clamoring in my head. I'm ready to offer myself, to grant Phillip full control of my body.

Standing in the center of the priceless Khartoum rug I'm going to lose my virginity tonight.

Phillip comes closer, locking my thoughts with his eyes, melting me, stimulating a feeling I can't identify. I merge into his gaze with absolute trembling desire and defect my sensible mind to the outer periphery of consciousness. My hormones take over, altering my chemical foundation, making me receptive to a sexual programming of a manipulating and compelling energy that comes in a casing called Phillip Landfield.

Drawing back the bed's velvet duvet to uncover creamy silk sheets waiting beneath it, I watch myself like a camera, looking in to his eyes as if he were a mirror.

Without permission he bares my breasts as tingles of electricity surge to my nipples and tighten as they leave their lacy cups and reach for his lips, waiting for them.

Eyes clouded over, I stop watching and become a thrilled recipient to the touch and feel of a man's hands and lips where no other has been.

Dizzy with emotion, faint with excitement, legs so weak I have to hold Phillip tightly, he pulls the zipper down the back of my dress and in what feels like a single movement takes it off and lowers me to the waiting bed.

Kneeling in front of me, he puts his hands on my thighs and slowly spreads them apart. The place between my legs throbs almost hurtfully as he sucks one nipple and gently squeezes the other, playing my body like a harp.

Tracing a path from my knees to my thighs with his tongue I vibrate and convulse with desire, watching with detached wonder as he slips off my damp panties and holds them to his face, turning them slowly and inhaling their scent with deep thirsty breaths.

I never dreamed anyone would do such a thing even though I had posed for world-famous photographers who specialized in weird sexy shots. As far as I was concerned it had all been make believe. People didn't do what Phillip was doing now.

I had never felt this way as I lay open and naked, exposed, a virginal offering on the alter of Phillip's bed, committing myself to be the source of his pleasure, ready to fill his needs without hesitation.

He lifts my legs and drapes them around his neck, bending to devour and drain the wetness creaming between them. The feeling sends me flying into a milky reality, euphoria closing my fist against my lips to keep me from the screams clamoring to vocalize my passion as Phillip sucks like a nursing infant from the fountain of my vagina.

I could never have imagined what these feelings of euphoria and eternity would be. Though I had faked it for the cameras, I had never been so exposed, never knew the extent of this feeling.

Drawing his soft head closer I pull my knees higher and spread my legs wider, his tongue going deeper as satisfaction mewes from his throat.

He moves me over him till I'm mounted on his face, riding him, thighs gripping his head, hips moving, barely breathing, every bit of myself totally involved. Turning me over he whimpers and moans like a primeval wriggling infant as he tries to swallow me into himself.

Encased in a timeless warp, intoxicated with ecstasy, I fly away from three-dimensional reality to other entities till his words bring me shattering back to physical three dimensional reality.

"You're a Virgin." He utters as he pulls away, leaving me breathing heavily, emotionally exhausted and panicked.

"I had no idea," he shakes his head. "You're so sexy, you seem so knowing." He kissed my hand and wiped a tear from my cheek. "I didn't mean to."

"I've waited my whole life for you," I hear myself saying, tears uncontrollably flowing as I pull myself close to him. "I want you. I want to feel you inside of me." I slow myself down with a deep breath, "Please." Tears continue to run down my cheeks.

He kisses my fingertips. "I didn't know," he said again. "You're so worldly. I've known many women, but..." he seems uncomfortable, "I've never known anyone like you. Your physical beauty is only the beginning. I want to know you completely, to know you by making love to you, becoming one with you."

He turns my hand and kisses my open palm. I try to hold on to him as he starts to get up. "I'll slip out of here and let you get dressed so I can take you home.

"No. Don't go... " I keep his hand in mine.

Reaching over he kisses my cheek and brushes away my tears with his lips. "You're so beautiful." He moves to my lips and kisses me. Almost grabbing his lips with my own I feel a strange turn happening in me. Opening my lips to his and matching the intensity we grow stronger, hungrier and demanding. Greedy and wanting more of something that is so physical, so over encompassing we open deeper and deeper into each other's soul.

"Please," I whisper, some force taking over that I don't recognize as my own. "I want you Phillip," the voice says to him.

Holding me closely he puts his legs on either side of me and holds me, head to toe as our bodies vibrate and melt into each other. Rocking in a timeless motion, my hips draw up with the force of primal passion, opening to him, creaming for him as his fingers guide his penis to the center of my wet quivering womanhood.

Gently he touches the small opening there, jolting me into a mix of fear and anxiety and absolute desire. My vaginal lips tingle so intensely they hurt from pure desire, demanding to be satisfied.

Surely and slowly, Phillip draws back slightly then pushes in harder.

A burning gush and I moan with pain so he stops and waits then pushes in stronger, not stopping or hesitating till he plunges through my hymen making me scream. I hold on to him, a protection from the passion and pain he's causing by propelling my senses to connect with the ripe woman lying dormant inside me. Filled with wonder by this remarkable transformation, I understand in that absolute moment of pure passion, what I had always been missing.

I had been painted and dressed to look like a woman, but it was a projection of an approximation, a concept rather than a fact or even an understanding. I can never be sexy for the cameras in the same way again. The reality of sex is so different than what I had thought it was. It's so much more intense, more profound then I had pretended.

Phillip ran his hands over my body, smoothing it like a sculptor, my curves soaking into his palms. Holding on to the bars of the headboard I arch my body, hips circling, begging him to keep touching me as I quiver from his touch.

Phillip watches with appreciative pleasure as I lick my lips and draw my hips higher, holding on to the copper bars tighter.

I love this feeling of pure emotional passion. It's being totally open, pure satisfaction. I wish it would go on forever. In giving up a physical part of my body I've learned more about myself. With a touch of a button I've discovered my true self.

Chapter Fifteen

Quivering with excitement, I enter Bernstein and Kalman's offices the next morning to join the group that produces sound bites and photo ops to create belief systems. The sheer technology and objective evaluation is thrilling and also a bit chilling. As a part of it I think I can use my consciousness and abilities to create a more positive world. This is my new career. I feel so different today. Stronger and powerful, a woman in love. What a great feeling.

I had felt a little like this when my Master's thesis was approved and I saw the title on the acceptance: MASS UNIT THINKING. In the opening was a quote from the futurist, Isaac Asimov, that I'll never forget *"If we all think alike, act alike and feel alike, then one catastrophe affects us all."*

What would Fritz, Phillip's houseman, think of that? I doubt he would get it. He went to the British trade school *Jeeves*, where young men are trained as servants for royalty, the titled and the super rich. His strict training appears to create a robotic focus on whatever he is told to do. Fritz would most likely accept the sound bites Bernstein and Kalman manufacture and hold them as absolute truths.

Fritz had either been conditioned or hard wired to accept a higher-up's beliefs. That's how he lives his life for Phillip.

But with all his superb training and discipline, Fritz couldn't conceal surprise at seeing me at the top of the stairs so early this morning. The consummate professional, he quickly covered his disapproval with a cement-like mask, a click of heels, and a sharp bow of attention.

"Madame." Fritz's strangled voice came tightly from his throat. "How would you like your eggs?"

"Hatched." I smiled.

Fritz didn't. Not a tinge of reaction showed on his expressionless face.

"No breakfast, thank you, I clarified. "Would you please call me a cab?" I continued the smile that earned both me and my ancillary entourage of agents, lawyers, business managers and taxes, hundreds of thousands of dollars.

But the power of smile had no effect on Fritz. The Gentleman's Gentleman looked past me as he checked the hour on the magnificent Eighteenth Century Grandfather Clock in the foyer.

I looked at it too. The little hand was on the gilded "7" and the big hand on the "12".

Fritz nearly clucked his tongue with disapproval when the chimes confirmed the hour. I waited patiently while he called a cab, his tone streaming with an attitude coating his trained vowels.

Was it because I spent the night with Phillip I wondered, the staccato sound of my foot nervously tapping, interrupting my thoughts to make me stop. Fritz was forgetting that he also was working early this Saturday morning. Actually he seemed to work twenty four hours, seven days a week, reachable and ready no matter the time. His job was a lifetime commitment with no time off for vacation or illness. I wonder if he has time to change into pajamas!

A rush of sadness for this soldier of the privileged momentarily brushes through my feelings. Fritz didn't have a life of his own. He may never experience the fullness of his own truth, set his own standards or be guided by personal beliefs. He was trained and committed to follow the rules.

But why was I obsessing on Fritz, I ask myself as I sit in the filthy cab on my way to the office. Am I angry for having to leave Phillip so I'm focusing on Fritz? Will I become Phillip's slave as well? A cold chill follows the thought.

I hadn't wanted to peel away from the musky sweat on the warm sheets to take a shower. I was reluctant to rinse the patina of Phillip's smoldering heat off my flesh.

But I'd made a commitment that work came first. Phillip was my client and I must do the best for him as well as Bernstein & Kalman.

An involuntary sigh came up making me feel regret then fear. Would I lose him? Or my job? My first time out and I break all the rules. I'm anxious about breaking the rules, but it's a new beginning, it's exciting. I've found something inside myself that has always been missing.

I'll have to choose between work and independence or love, Guess I'm reacting to all those self-help articles for women on social media. But if I decide to ignore my heart and feelings and choose a self-centered philosophy to empower myself, I'll be doing what I've already been doing, working to survive. But I've never felt this kind of love and it's not something I want to give up.

Travelling upward in the glass-enclosed elevator on the exterior of the BK Building, I marvel how Washington is laid out so neatly below. I love the dynamics of its engaging design and power. At this point in my life I have everything I could ever want or need; a challenging, glamorous job and the man of my dreams. Like the movies. I have it all.

"I love you," I whisper to Phillip as I float through the hall with the thought of him.

I have to stop this. My energy dances as as I think about what had been happening to me just a few hours ago. I can feel his skin, his fingers, his touch. Shivers rush through me. Everything is so vivid, Phillip's smell, that strange and wonderful essence that emblazoned itself on me is now my reality. Was it a dream?

"I'll always make you happy," he whispered, his fingers lightly brushing between my legs, making me tingle and cream where he touched.

"I'll give you everything," he promised, "more than you've ever wanted." His lips came closer and he kissed me gently which makes me melt, arching to his touch, rocking and creaming as he gently pushes himself into me. Drawing in deeper we merge in a rhapsody to the highest realms of ecstasy.

I've found the man I've always wanted, the feelings I never knew existed, all within the person and passion of Phillip Landfield. He's my totem of elation, my three-dimensional poster of rapture.

OMG! I'm standing in the foyer of BK's reception area, frozen with thoughts of Phillip. Thank god it's so early and no one else is around. Pushing myself away from the wall I remember the executives come in later on weekends to return calls and flip through their mail to make their presence obvious for their commitment judgements. BK is all about projecting image. For that, young assistants and secretaries come in on weekends as well. Ambitious ones would have preferred to stay 24/7 to make a name for themselves. Salaries and perks are quite generous once an executive rises to top management. During the climb however, all have to be satisfied with minimum wages supplemented with promises of potential and the prestige of working for Bernstein & Kalman for their CVs.

A buzz of adrenaline fills me as I walk down the hall. It's good to be here, I like it. I notice a beam of light casting a strange shadow a few feet away. A figure is taking shape. Icy ripples creep down my back. Unable to breathe my lungs freeze with fear as the shape becomes Phillip. He's wearing the pajamas that had been folded on the settee in his dressing room.

Am I going crazy? How can this be happening?

I move closer, reaching to touch him when suddenly a messenger whizzes by, rushing past and into Phillip's form, scattering it into millions of invisible fragments I can no longer see.

Had it been my imagination or some magical moment of split second reality?

When I have dreams I'm able to watch them with surreal detachment, like a third person within myself. Yet the vision of Phillip had been so real. It couldn't be a ghost, he isn't dead. Oh my God! What if something happened to him?

Imagination! Leave it. I hear in my head. *You've work to do.*

Then I see the words on my desk that had been written the day before. They were underlined in bold block letters so I wouldn't miss them. *The day before! Another century, another lifetime.* SATURDAY - FINALIZE ARRANGEMENTS FOR PHILLIP and TIFFANY DATE!

Phillip and Tiffany. I'd forgotten! Less than two hours since I forced myself to leave the arms of the man I was in love with, from the bed in which I had just lost my virginity, to go to work and make it possible for my lover to attend a premiere at the Kennedy Center with a beautiful accomplished actress. There will be lots of cameras then dinner at a paparazzi infested restaurant with more cameras to capture media. A perfect merger.

I should firm up the time and reservations.

But I can't. H*ow can I?* Forty-eight hours before I never even considered the possibility of anything like this. Though when I first saw Phillip's picture I did feel a thrill. His handsome, broody *p*icture excited me. His is the kind of sulky sensibility that I find exciting and challenging. All good media elements

I thought Tiffany Holland would be a good match for Phillip because she gets lots of media coverage, which would guarantee Phillip will get it as well.

The framed picture of myself on the cover of People Magazine made itself known to me. I can get Phillip media coverage too. Cameras still follow me, though not as much in D.C. as they do in New York and L.A.

I notice Bernie Kalman walking to his office. He hadn't stopped to say hello. Maybe he didn't see me.

I'll have to explain my hasty retreat from the party with Phillip. Will he want me to resign if I tell him that we had run off and made love till we collapsed at dawn?

Waves of regret start to come in. I hadn't thought I'd fall in love with Phillip. It won't look good but it's not anything I can control. Love is love.

I'll call Tiffany and cancel. But what if Phillip will be disappointed or angry I'd broken the date with Tiffany? What if he had been looking forward to being with her and I was there for the taking. I'd known about a famous dance impresario who never hired a female dancer till he slept with her. Was this my initiation?

Tiffany and Phillip's date tonight had been my own manufactured publicity stunt. If Phillip resists, Il have to encourage him to go. I should call him first.

Stalling I lift the piece of paper I'd been stabbing with a pen that has the list of key media journalists I was going to alert about their date tonight. Should I complete what I had committed to do?

Scribbling Landfield and Holland's names next to the journalists I thought their names looked good for headlines. I'll be good at my job, I tell myself, then scratch the names out.

Using the pen like a pendulum, I try to hypnotize myself to get my emotions out of the way.

One of my first jobs for a photographer other than Verruno was Sidney Greenspan, a well-known New York fashion photographer who took me aside after a few shots. "You're too anxious to please," he told me when the room cleared. "You're quick but too eager. The camera can see that. You're not thinking. You don't have to do anything but feel and react, then let your body follow what you're feeling. Watch the camera, tease it with your secrets. You'll have the world eating out of your hand. Your body is the vehicle of your thoughts."

It was the first time anyone had affirmed me the right to trust myself. And now everything within me is resisting the call to Phillip. I shouldn't care what he wants to do with Tiffany. But I want him to tell me to cancel Tiffany and be his date. What if he tells me to keep the date with the famous actress?

I look out the window at the Potomac River in the distance. If I were going with Phillip tonight I'd hire a yacht to cruise the Potomac. We'd dance between servings of dinner and champagne then retire to the stateroom where we'd spend the night holding each other as the boat rocked us.

I can almost feel myself cuddling naked with Phillip, his smooth chest against my bare breasts, his strong, muscular legs wrapped around mine and his powerful body heating me like a blanket when we finally slept.

Phillip is the warmth and comfort I've always wanted and never felt till now.

I force myself back to business mode and write; "LATER PLANS?" I'll keep the yacht idea to myself. But what if he takes Tiffany to his home? Every thought is making me upset. I can't go through with this. I've never felt this way before. I want to be with Phillip. If he doesn't want to cancel his date with Tiffany I won't be able to work for him. I'll go back to New York, maybe California.

I've got to tell Bernie Kalman how I'm feeling and ask to be taken off the assignment and offer my resignation. Quit after two weeks and one difficult moment. Am I going to risk my future for a man I'd spent less than a day with, or secure my job and dismiss what happened? Am I ready to serve Phillip up to a woman PEOPLE MAGAZINE title a "superstar"?

I'll go for broke, I decide. I'll have the tickets delivered to Phillip, make reservations for dinner and dancing, then call and ask him who he wants to go with.

I pick up the receiver and put it down. Indecision, pride, and fear of rejection rock me. I've never felt like this before.

Swinging back and forth in my large leather chair, I remember doing this when I sat in my father's chair in his office. It made me feel powerful, grown up. I rock harder. Will it help?

I wouldn't be here if Daddy hadn't died. I never would have gone to New York to work. I would have stayed home and done everything right – followed the pattern etched into my DNA and strived for no more than being *Prom Queen and a beautiful bride* to a darling and ambitious white collar husband. We would live in the suburbs and produce at least two genetic mixtures. I would have experienced the pain of childbirth and studied magazines at playgrounds to try to make myself feel beautifu. I would attend PTA meetings and dress up to entertain my husband's patients or clients, and keep going on a two dimensional existence without tapping into the depths of learning and experience.

The early death of my father was a mixed blessing. It made me self-reliant while I still had my youth and beauty so I could use them to become a success. Now, because of Phillip, I was thinking of giving it up, detonating my life plan of relevance.

The electronic sand clock is seeping. I have to make a decision between keeping my independence or devoting my life to a man I had known less than twenty - four hours. It's crazy. Yet it's a decision that can change my life. Is Phillip tied to my destiny? Is he the reason I came to Washington? Is he the carrier of some mystical force, or am I blowing this all out of proportion?

My hand still has his scent. I don't want to be at the office this beautiful Saturday morning and arrange a date for the man I just fell in love with. I want to be with him now.

Pushing back from the desk I stretch my back and look down the hall at Kalman's office. I have to tell the partners what happened. I'll say being with Phillip sexually was research and I learned more about him than I would have from media files or lunches. They won't believe me. It doesn't even sound true to myself.

I tap my fingers on the phone. How I wish I had someone to confide in. But there's no one. Any attempts at intimacy with mom always ended in anger. She doesn't seem to care or maybe she doesn't understand. Usually I come away from attempts to communicate with her feeling more rejected and lonely than before. Trying to deal with it intellectually, I've studied human behavior and fully accept that emotions are different then analytical suppositions.

I sweep over the elegant classic tradition of my office - a bit of Corbusier and Frank Lloyd Wright. The single white rose in the crystal vase still looks fresh even though the water has not been changed since yesterday.

Maybe I should take the rose out of the vase and run back to Phillip and put it on the pillow next to his head. I'd then quietly tiptoe to the bathtub and fill it with scented oil, pile my hair on top of my head and soak in the scented water till he found me. He'd lift me from the tub, wrap me in a towel and carry me back to the bed where once again he would take me to that dreamy realm where all is exciting and right with the world.

The phone is staring at me. Should I call him?

Bernie's voice on the intercom shatters the reverie, demanding I come to his office. Without a moment to analyze his voice for mood, and not feeling composed, I hurry to the corner of the building where the glass and steel domain is marked BERNIE KALMAN in fluorescent letters on the glass pane of his office door.

"Have a good time last night?" he asks as I walk in.

I knew by his tone that he either knows or suspects something. "Yes. I did." I feel the heat in my cheeks and know I'm blushing. "I slept with him. Would you like a run down because you won't get it. I'll support decisions I made. I totally get there is no sense in lying since there is no way I can hide an affair with Phillip Landfield in this town."

"That's right," Kalman nods. "You work fast - less than twenty-four hours."

"Well," I can't suppress a sigh. "I guess I'll go back to modeling."

"Are you crazy?" Bernie asks.

"It was educational," I hear myself say.

"I'll bet," replies Kalman, a smile twitching at the corner of his thin mouth. He hadn't expected this answer. He thought I'd lie.

He smiles. "What did you learn? We don't like skeletons in closets."

"None that I know of," The question makes me uncertain.

"You never know..." Kalman counters.

I shake my head. "I think there are certain things that a man won't do unless he really wants to be with a woman," I'm feeling less than confident.

"Really?" Kalman seems genuinely surprised.

"Bernie," I sit in one of the Corbusier chairs without being asked. "I've had to be sexy with so many male models I know the difference. I'm almost sure we won't have any compromising problems; no male lovers jumping out of the bushes demanding payment or they'll sell his story. I think Phillip would be honest about that if we had to deal with it."

Kalman's smile grows. "So, last night was research?"

I can't suppress a smile. "That's right, absolutely."

Was he buying my story? I sound immoral to myself.

"Are you really this tough or are you one of the best new liars in town?" Kalman growls.

His tone shakes my security. "I'm a liar. Do you want my resignation?" I try to keep the scared child out of my voice.

He looks at me sharply. "Absolutely not. You just started."

"I broke company rules. It wasn't research. I think I've fallen madly in love."

"Good, you're a gorgeous couple. You should marry him. Kills two birds with one stone. You may not be working here very long but not because you resign. In fact you make the perfect wife for Phillip Landfield. What do you think about that?" He didn't wait for her answer and put his finger on a speaker.

"Coffee?" he asks.

I can barely nod. He could be playing with me or setting me up. "Uh, Bernie," my head is swimming. Are my words slurred? "Please, I'd like to…"

He interrupts me, "We'll talk again. I'll have your coffee sent to your office. Cancel Tiffany Holland tonight. You go instead. Tell him she couldn't make it. Let's not push him. Let him think everything is his idea. We want you for him and we'll work to help you get him. No man knows another man like one of his own."

I don't know if I'm thrilled or upset.

"Good job. Well done. You're our new inside man."

"Gee, thanks." I was dizzy. I hadn't expected this.

The phone is ringing as I get back to my office. Before I have a chance to say hello, Phillip's sleepy voice rings out from the telephone, "Where are you? Why aren't you here with me?"

My heart skips and I grab the phone closer. "I haven't stopped thinking about you for one moment," I say before I realize I can even form a sentence.

"I miss you. Come back here," he orders. "Forget that silly job. You were hired so you would meet me and that's what happened. Now come home and live with me forever happily ever. You'll be my wife. That's your new job."

"Phillip…" I don't know what to say. I want this man more than anything, but something inside me is holding back. My gut is twisting. I haven't even been with him twenty-four hours.

"Jenny?" he asks.

"I'm overwhelmed," I'm stuttering.

"I proposed to you. Now do as I say."

I look at the research files on my computer that I have accumulated about the man on the phone, the one to whom I have just lost my virginity, the man who is now asking me to give up everything I had worked for, and yes, I wanted to be his wife.

"I'm speechless."

"Then don't say anything. Hang up the phone, I'll send Fritz for you or call a car, it will be faster. I want you here immediately and I don't want you to leave me again."

"I won't," I promise.

"Then hurry," he says. "We've just got started."

I am in a body no longer attached to my head. I notice the coffee and note on my desk. *GOOD WORK*. I clear my throat to call Tiffany to cancel the date.

Chapter Sixteen

A vision in lace, I watch out the window as the quirky fate of light paints a golden halo around the scene below me. It has an unearthly glow.

"Look at that," I beckon to Roger who had flown to Illinois as both a guest and a professional to make sure my makeup and hair were perfect throughout the week for what he labeled the ceremonial festivity of legal sex.

Pointing out the window to the hundreds of people milling about the velvet green lawns of the Landfield farm, I pull Roger over. "Look. It's not real. See the lighting? It's not for real. All those people are extras for a commercial, so I'm not nervous. I'm just a Princess Bride for a soap commercial."

"This is for REAL my precious." Roger is patronizing. "This is a reality hitting social media at earth splitting speed. Have you noticed the camera drones covering every inch of the grounds? The helicopters? You're Planet Earth's new Princess."

"For the moment. Anyway, why should a piece of paper say we're *legal* just because someone with a license reads some stuff and we say yes because it's expected."

"Sex." Roger answers definitely. "According to the laws of the land what you do in your bedroom will now be legal." He sprinkles gold and silver glitter on my hair then pauses to study my reflection in the mirror. "God I'm good. You are gorgeous."

We giggle together then simultaneously grow quiet.

I break the silence. "You know, ever since I got engaged, nearly every person I talk to thinks its ok to talk about sex."

Roger shrugged. "Wait till you're pregnant. Then everyone will want to touch your stomach." He mixes more sparkles into a pot of foundation. "They want you to share your magic. People like to be around magical people."

The thought sends a shiver through me and I look out the window again. "I've worn so many yards of tulle and lace we could sew them together and cover a corn field like the one the conceptual artist Christo did in Central Park."

"Good idea," murmurs Roger who seems to be barely listening as he examines my face for an imperfection. "Good publicity."

"I hope so!" peals Catherine Pearl as she bursts in with a diamond headband attached to a floor length veil of starched silk. Catherine is taking the role of surrogate Mother of the Bride quite seriously. She has pulled out all the stops and joined forces with Phillip's mother to make this wedding one of the most important of the year.

"Catherine, you forgot something," I tease.

"What!" Catherine looks sincerely flustered.

"To sell advertising space on the backs of the chairs."

"Don't be silly." Catherine says. "We're going to make millions with the media rights."

I can only shake my head. "Have you seen my mother?" I ask. She hadn't been involved in the wedding preparations and essentially waited for the invitation to tell her when and where she should wear the dress Catherine had sent her for the occasion. At first she had been annoyed when the dress was delivered, but when she tried on the cream silk Armani coat and dress she knew she looked terrific and felt as happy as she would allow herself.

"Catherine, what would I have ever done without you? You're the best friend a person could ever have. You've been more loyal then anyone ever has been in my life and even now, when I won't be making money for the agency, you have taken charge of the wedding plans. I couldn't be more thrilled and grateful as usual you shelter me from what could have been a problem. How can I ever repay you?"

Roger swooped in to blot a tear that threatened.

"You're proof that angels protect me," I continue.

Catherine reddened. "Don't be silly."

In reality, I never had a family once my father was gone. My mother wouldn't consider being with another man and often told me that without her husband she was only half alive and couldn't wait to reunite with him. This left me without a father and a mother. There was no one to take care of me.

However once I began my career as a model my mother seemed to enjoy seeing me on social and print media. When she was going through the supermarket checkout and I was on a magazine cover, she would proudly point out her daughter's picture to the clerk, a moment of social interaction.

My mother wouldn't come with me when I moved to New York and wouldn't call because she was concerned about the price of long distance calls. I tried to explain there was only one charge and it didn't matter if she made a single call or a hundred, but it was an unfamiliar concept she couldn't accept. So I called her every day to say hello and make sure she was okay.

I called her twice the day Phillip and I got engaged. I was bubbling ecstatically and told her I was marrying Prince Charming.

I didn't tell her about the celibacy vow Phillip had asked me to take till we were married. Phillip's precision and clarity had made my head spin when he laid out his plans for our life together.

Having earned a lot of money creating fantasies and romance for others, I was now having my life taken over and directed by a magician of a man who had come into my life to create new realities.

When I returned to Phillip's home the morning after we made love, Phillip was waiting on the street and opened the door of my car before it came to a full stop and swept me into his arms.

A powerful charge was coming from him, almost a physical penetration and a little suffocating.

You're trembling," Phillip held me tight. "It shows how deeply and totally we are committing to each other. We have a lifetime of love to build on this and we'll never take it for granted."

He was looking at me with what seemed like the most endearing smile I'd ever seen and when he leaned down to kiss the top of my head it felt like a benediction.

"Now we'll wait for our sexual energy to expand till we're burning. I want to know on our wedding day as I stand waiting for you to come down the aisle, that underneath your vision of chastity every part of you will be ablaze with desire and expectation, hot and glistening, wanting and needing me to fill you with seed. I want you hungrier than you've ever been for anyone or anything. I want to feel when you stand next to me at the alter and the veil is lifted from your face and you promise to love, honor and obey me, that your answer comes from your deepest and most profound truth, a truth enhanced by memories and expectations of our orgasmic pleasure."

I'm a butterfly caught in his web.

"When you make that vow to me in the presence of a minister of God, in front of our friends and families," he kept going, "I will know you have in some way ceased being Jenny Webster and that you are totally and forever Mrs. Phillip Landfield."

Bang! Resistance threw up an iron wall. Is he aware of what he's saying?

His deep blue eyes draw me in, his Patrician face smiling with love and devotion.

"Jenny Landfield," I hear myself say as I wonder if this is some kind of testing game. Mischievously I pull on his arm, "It's too long! make love one more time for practice! It will sustain us and give us more memories." I smile automatically with my impish smile, the one that wins so many hearts.

Phillip has turned stiff, resistant and serious. "I mean it Jenny, we have to make a commitment right now to love, honor and obey each other. Those kinds of values will make our marriage work. We will not submit to each other even though our bodies might be demanding something different. It's difficult but not impossible in the name of respect for each other's feelings. We must start immediately because if either one of us finds that we're unable to function this way, then perhaps it's best we discover it before we take vows, before we make our moral and legal commitment."

"Phillip..." unease tugs, but I don't want to acknowledge it.

I let him interrupt me. "Before you speak, please know that I give you the same commitment I expect from you. Equanimity within our gender differences."

I take a deep breath to calm myself. I want him more than I had ever wanted anything in my life. He would fulfill me just as my father had done for my mother. I was beginning to understand the totality of my mother's loss. I couldn't have known this depth of feeling till I loved someone the way I love Phillip. I'm ready to give up everything to love, honor and obey him. I don't want to lose him. So I nod my consent and agree to the commitment.

Turning away from the memory of that time I look at the reflection of the porcelain doll in the oval mirror staring back at me with eyes so sparkling and blue they could have been made of glass. I have to blink and look in different directions to prove to myself I'm still in the body I'm seeing in the mirror. A thinking person exists beneath the pale ivory skin, someone who can dampen those perfectly painted lips and feel the touch of her own fingers on her doll-like pink cheeks.

My Victorian inspired bridal gown had been designed by my dear friend and favorite designer, Rei Kawakubo, the Japanese designer who created the line, Comme des Garcons. She influenced the fashion world years ahead with her iconoclastic irreverence by layering transparent tops and dresses which is now a look both fashionable and acceptable.

The gown is made of fine antique French lace and the sheerest silk mesh. I had been a bit nervous about its transparency, though I loved the way it transposed the Victorian design into a contemporary, daring look that knew exactly how to move with my body.

Phillip's mother, Buffy, had given me a museum quality Cartier diamond brooch that sparkled brilliantly at my throat. The elegant matriarch told me it had been handed down through the family for six generations and it was mine to keep till I give it to my own daughter or daughter in law the morning of that girl's wedding. I was so overwhelmed I could only whisper my thanks.

I am becoming an entirely new image to myself as I look at my physical appearance through the single focus of my thinking. I had been a make believe bride many times, but I can't define this new feeling. Intellectually I accept that I am crossing a bridge to another dimension, but I don't feel elation. What is this nagging? Can it be fear? Am I dreading the loss of independence, my personal way of life? I will now be living with and making accommodations for another person.

Roger places the diamond headband low on my brow then arranges the delicate veil so it cascades perfectly to the floor as I watch the guests taking their seats on the flower bedecked chairs.

"Do you think our East Coast friends are enjoying the rustic charm of this little Illinois farm?" I ask my two dear and trusted friends.

"Rustic?" screeches Roger as Catherine laughs. "This is one of the plushest places I've ever seen in my life - and my dear, you know where I've been," he lifts his eyebrows.

"Did you see the Moo Moos?" Catherine asks with a laugh.

I cut off their chatter. "I haven't seen Phillip all day." Last night after the rehearsal dinner, we walked to the stables where I tried to tease him into following me into the hayloft. Phillip pulled away. "We can't spoil what is waiting for us.

Waiting to be with Phillip sexually has been torturous. When we were together Phillip hugged and kissed me in front of the cameras, then he'd cut me off emotionally, a move I know so well from hundreds of male models I worked with in romantic shots. But with Phillip I would try afterward to keep his kiss on my lips, block out the cameras, my adoration creating a romantic portrait for social media.

When I had told Bernstein and Kalman we were going to be married, they cheered.

"Phillip's marriage to an irresistible woman like you will give him an impetus among the public that he wouldn't have had otherwise. We couldn't be happier. Jenny, we're proud of you, it's a brilliant move."

"It's not *a move,*" I protested. "I believe in Phillip's potential and ability for high office as much as you do, maybe more. And I'm also head over heels in love with him. He's everything I ever wanted."

With the kind of timing that would have made Cecil B. de Mille proud, Lew Bernstein's secretary came in with a bottle of Cristal Champagne and three chilled glasses.

Kalman had been right. The speed and power with which Phillip became nationally known has been incredible. I realize I'm an integral part of that media explosion.

Throughout the media blitz, the biggest treats I have were the rare nights we had dinner alone. One night was at Phillip's cabin in the mountains where we had gone for a photo spread for VANITY FAIR, and the other was in my apartment at the Watergate. Both times I hadn't wanted to keep our celibacy vows, but Phillip seemed turned off sexually, preferring to discuss current and coming events, dialogue more appropriate for a spin doctor then a fiancée. But then, I had promised him celibacy and had to swallow my disappointment, telling myself I'm learning invaluable discipline for my new way of life as the wife of a politician.

Our celebrity grew till we became a phenomenon like a vaudeville act, dependent on each other. In our separate and individual ways we were still good media copy, but together we are bombshells - a portrait of wholesomeness, love and enviable beauty. Sheer fantasy.

Real time we hadn't kissed deeply or held each other intimately since our first time in Phillip's home. There didn't seem to be time since there was such a whirlwind of social events and travel, hitting every important party and every political opportunity, and then at night, I'd go back to the Watergate and an empty bed and Phillip would go home.

Few knew I was still working for Bernstein and Kalman and was the point person in Phillip's growing political campaign. One of the first things I did when I began to plan the wedding was to make Tiffany Holland a friend. I asked the beautiful actress to be a bridesmaid in the wedding and Tiffany laughingly agreed. "Phillip is so much better off with you than he would have been with me. You're sweet and innocent, just what he needs."

I wasn't sure how to interpret that. The truth was we rarely spent any private time together. Phillip had to be in Springfield Illinois chatting up and campaigning for constituents while I stayed in Washington planning Phillip's campaign as well as the wedding.

The Washington Townhouse was Fritz's domain and I stayed away from it. Fritz was in charge of all Phillip's physical needs and I appreciated Philip's dependency on his "gentleman's gentleman". Also I knew Fritz didn't approve of me, which made me uneasy. I wondered if after the wedding I could be happy with Fritz around. That would have to wait.

I've been giggling a lot lately and I think it's to cover my nerves and the enormity of this decision. I can't ignore or stifle my insecurity. Yet I know if I say anything negative about Fritz or our celibacy it will devolve into a fight. It had one night when I mentioned Fritz's seemingly hostile attitude toward me. When Phillip sided with Fritz's behavior and accused me of being jealous, I was shattered. Another time I playfully asked if Fritz would be coming on our honeymoon and a dark shadow seemed to pass over Phillip's face. He didn't answer.

With no idea where we were going on our honeymoon I kept asking so I'd know what to pack. But Phillip insisted he'd take care of my wardrobe. Everything was to be a surprise. Catherine, my agent, who usually knew everything, swore to me she didn't know either.

A knock at the door signaled the time had come for me to wait in the library till I heard the first few bars of the Bridal March. Then I'd begin my walk down the aisle.

Catherine kissed the air near my cheek, not wanting to ruin Roger's exquisite make-up. Roger had stopped fussing over me a few minutes before to check on the work of the other makeup and hair artists he had brought for the bridal party.

My mother told me the night before that she didn't want to see me before the wedding because she was afraid she would cry. I told her I understood, but I didn't. What is so terrible about crying? Tears are cleansing. But I never get into anything deep with my mother so as usual I kept quiet, wanting more than anything to avoid an argument, especially at this time.

Roger came back with his sponge and tissues firmly in hand. He gave me a thorough once over before allowing me to step away from him.

"You know Roger," I told him, "you are totally responsible for this."

He stepped back and blotted my makeup. "I know, and I feel terrible about it. You've given up a brilliant career to be a housewife. So what if you're First Lady. You're still a housewife. A wife is a wife is a wife, no matter what else she may be. He leaned in and whispered. "Wanna split before it's too late?"

I giggled and yes came out. Roger's humor held scalding truth. I had given up two careers and a potential one for a man who refused to be intimate with me for over six months. I'd never expected Phillip to hold to these celibacy vows so strictly.

A deep agonizing spiral of insecurity and despair began taking me over. "Oh Roger," I quietly wailed, tears springing to my carefully shadowed and lined eyes, reddening my ivory face and threatening to smudge the delicate colors Roger had blended so carefully. "You're right. I'm making a terrible mistake. Would you go out there and tell somebody, anybody to stop the music and make an announcement that I'm terribly sorry but I've made a terrible mistake. Tell the bridesmaids and ushers to forget their places at the top of the aisle. Get the waiters to serve the guests drinks while I run upstairs and get out of this stupid dress and sneak out."

"Oh no you don't," Roger said. "It's too late now. You're not getting out of this. I want everyone to see my gorgeous makeup and hair styling work. In fact," he cocked his head toward a man in a morning coat and a woman in a turquoise silk dress approaching them with a purposeful bustle. "Here come the wedding managers. They look like undertakers."

I start to giggle.

"Don't get hysterical," whispered Roger. It's time to walk down the aisle.

"Maybe it would be better for me to be lowered in a casket," I say as the heavy white silk veil is slipped over my face.

Chapter Seventeen

Counting to a slow wedding pace, I focus on the energy of the tempo as I glide through the white, translucent tube of my veil. Is this a harbinger of the life I'm walking toward? Will I be seeing everything through the tube of a housewife? I have no clear vision of what is outside this vacuum I'm moving through. I just want to get through it and into the air.

From the moment Roger shoved me out the door into this white conduit of flower bedecked aisle, I want to run in the opposite direction, away from the minister and the waiting groom, far from the expectant wedding guests, the ceremony and the caterers. Maybe I'm experiencing a genetic throwback to the millions of young women who were sold into wedlock through the centuries without choice, left only with their feelings and thoughts.

A tall figure in silk embroidered vestments I assume is the minister stops my march at the end of the aisle. His piercing eyes dart from me to a tall figure that stands in front of him. That must be Phillip, the groom. The figure turns and smiles. His dimples grab my heart and I tingle. He excites me. It's my Phillip.

Fighting to hold back tears, I clutch the frayed Bible mother had given me yesterday. I'd never seen it before. She said the bible had been her great, great Grandmother's who carried it on her wedding day - a day when she and her new husband had to flee across Russia to escape a murderous attack by Cossacks just moments after they received their marriage sacrament.

She said the story has been handed down for three generations and I find it hard to believe my mother chose the night before my wedding to tell me how the jubilance of her great great grandmother's wedding turned to abject horror. The Cossacks had stormed the small Russian Village church and pulled wedding guests from their pews. The young newlyweds escaped through the back of the church in the opposite direction of their relatives and friends, pausing a fraction of a second to look back upon all they loved; the ground running red with the blood of slaughter, the air thick with the high-pitched screams of those still clinging to life.

In their extravagant wedding costumes the young couple ran through the forest, slogging through rain and thick mud to flee the mindless destruction. Shimmying under barbed wire, attacked by insects crawling and flying, weighted from exhaustion and slowed by hunger, they had started as two separate people willing to commit to each other and emerged as a single unit, bound by the sacraments of marriage and the forge of loss and pain. Weeks after their marriage ceremony, clinging to each other like marathon dancers on the last rung of a death-defying dance, the young newlyweds crossed into Denmark to a new life of freedom.

I wondered whether that story of a century ago was true. Did my mother make it up, or is it too complicated for her to have done so? Or is there a lesson imparted that my great great grandmother had left, the promise of commitment in the face of anything that might happen with the man she loved.

Taking a deep breath to rid myself of the doubts that keep popping into my mind, I try to pick up on what the minister and Phillip are saying, but I can't hear the words, I can only hear the sounds. I'm like an interested bystander, my lips moving in soundless response to the imposing figures in front of me.

A nervous giggle threatens to escape, but it's jolted to a stop when hands sweep in front of me to lift the veil in front of my shrouded face.

Phillip doesn't react when he sees my face. No smile, no acknowledgement. Instead he takes my hand and pulls me against himself into some kind of a dancer's embrace.

I catch a glimpse of my mother, her face shiny with tears. Next to her is Catherine, *Ms. Ice in her Veins Super*

Deal Maker struggling to stem the tears rolling down her face.

Phillip is the portrait of flawless composure. But beneath that poise I feel a steaming undercurrent of jagged emotions. Perhaps it's nerves, I don't feel too serene myself.

Yet as Phillip bends close to me it's like electric, intense, a magnet drawing me to him, quivering out of control till I'm quieted in the comforting circle of his arms, his familiar breath, his luscious soft lips touching mine. I yield to him as we seal our vows. I am protected. I will always love him.

Supported by my groom we walk back through the brightened conduit, heat pouring from his hand into mine, bells and chimes, a cavalcade of applause, words of congratulation, choruses of happy medleys whispering against our cheeks as we emerge from the tunnel to squeezed hands, flying kisses, bombardments of good will and the music of Shamen's band that lifts the exuberance to a sexy, primal beat as we head for the reception.

Sounds of a wedding party greet us, loud and strong. I hear most of it, but a good part is separated from my emotional core so I can watch it as if it isn't real. It's a staged show like the others I've walked from the security of the runway.

My mother's tear stained face appears again and its back to personal. A gush of love covers me and I feel great love for her. Still I wish my father was here to walk me down the aisle. If he had been alive would I have married Phillip? Would I have had the chance to meet him? Is this event a step in a pre-ordained destiny?

Mother's wiry thin body wraps its arms around me in the stiff guise of a maternal embrace. I have to remind myself that this should be one of the happiest and most thrilling times in my life, yet there's some shivery cold foreboding that keeps creeping into me, darkening my thoughts as they permeate my mind that still can't understand it.

Bernstein and Kalman had decided it would be a marvelous opportunity to have this big wedding. It would provide great publicity for Phillip's political future as it would get major national coverage - INTERNATIONAL SUPERMODEL MARRIES *MIDWEST CROWN PRINCE* - *a*n opportunity for glamour and good old fashion romance.

At our last meeting in Washington before we all left for the wedding, Bernstein and Kalman told us they decided that it would be best if we waited at least 8 months before I stopped taking birth control pills. If the election results are positive, then I can stop using birth control and allow our genetic mixes to combine and make a baby. The pregnancy would create marvelous human interest for a national campaign trail.

I couldn't believe they were actually saying this to me. I wanted to have a baby, maybe more, but not as a political side show. It was something I had put away to think about in the future. The distant future.

I had thought that once I was immersed in the pomp and tradition of the wedding ceremony, I'd be buzzed with feelings of selflessness and devotion. I pledged myself to Phillip, to give up the person known as Jenny Webster and become Mrs. Phillip Landfield. Having children is an expected condition of marrying a man like Phillip and I'm anxious to experience the total commitment of being pregnant it would require. Creating a new entity, a new being through the merging of two souls would be exciting.

But first I'm excited about the election campaign. I can't do that if I'm pregnant. I plan to wait at least a year or two. I'm only twenty-two years old.

I sneak a peek at Phillip. Did circumstances sell me to him? He looks gorgeous in his custom Tom Ford tuxedo. I remember the afternoon Ford came to Phillip's home for a personal fitting and how hurt I felt when they ignored me completely.

Thinking of ways to lift my sinking heart I thought of his kisses, the burning sensations he left on my lips. But a heavy thumping started drumming inside me, dark clouds coloring the bright wedding decorations. I'd never considered the fact I was willingly participating in a centuries old ceremony to formalize a primitive necessity to generate the species and populate the planet. Marriage was a celebration of genetic guarantees that would instill the need for survival of the species.

"My dear," whispered Roger, the last person in the receiving line, "you need a touch-up." He whisked me off to a small room where he sprayed my face with chilled rose water from a Lalique crystal spray bottle, making me feel so much better. I needed that splash of cold water on my face.

Carefully blotting excess moisture, Roger applied a light dusting of color "to enhance my bridal countenance." He didn't speak again. This kind of interlude was routine for us. We had done it many times on so many locations it was automatic.

"Darling," Phillip burst in, trailing an invisible cape of party sounds and smells. "I've been looking all over for you. You've been away from me too long!"

I stopped Roger's hand from painting my lip. Phillip was so dramatic it was almost comical. "We just popped in for a second to repair damage from all the kisses."

He interrupted my next words and kissed me deeply.

My heart pounded. He was so exciting.

Roger fiddled with his brushes, watching in the mirror as he waited to finish his work once we stopped whatever we were doing.

I giggled as Phillip nibbled my ear then grabbed his head and kissed him deeply, moving as close as possible with the voluminous yards of French lace in my way. Then Phillip pulled away and left. Crushed I turned to see disappointment, rejection and surprise on my face in the mirror.

Roger watched from his mirrored vantage point as his beautiful bride crumbled, betrayed with rejection, slumping with the weight of the new husband walking away at a heightened time.

Roger grabbed a large sable brush and exhaled loudly, a soundless dialogue between us. We knew what the other was thinking. There was no denying what Roger had seen. We once decided we were two old souls from many past lifetimes, fellow travelers who had come together now to give each other support and love.

"Is this going to work?" I asked Roger, not able to stop my lips from quivering. "What if he doesn't love me? What if he only married me for the press coverage? It has nothing to do with me!"

Roger screwed up his face. "Don't be ridiculous — with your ugly puss!"

We broke into giggles, dissipating the tension.

"Phillip prizes you." Roger took her hand adoringly, "Trust me. I know these things."

I had to smile. "How?"

Roger ignored that. "Phillip is being responsible," he continued. "Bridegroom or not, his first obligation for the next few hours is to be a host to the guests. Now that you're married, you're his adjunct, his helpmate. You're to nurture him at home and sell him in public. Most of all your duty is to love him and give him the warmth and energy he'll badly need when he comes home from campaigning or a cabinet meeting."

I took the lipstick Roger held and filled in my own lips, careful not to exceed the line that Roger had drawn with great precision. "Sounds like servitude. "How did a modern, independent woman like me fall into a trap like this?"

"Shall I tell you?" Roger asks, pursing his lips instead of smiling.

"No."

Roger spoke anyway. "You fell in love. Your feelings hooked you and you forgot your own ambition and traded it for his. You'll do anything for Phillip. He's your drug. He created an addiction that no matter what you do, he spun a world which has put your intellect and your instincts into competition with your desires and needs."

"That's ridiculous!" I protest, feeling a tug of fear it might be true.

Roger snorted huffily. "I realize this is a lousy time to say this, but you're going to have an emotional roller coaster ride. Give him the nurturing and the caring but be sure and take care of yourself. If it doesn't work you can always get out."

"Right. This is a lousy time for advice like that. You could have saved yourself a wedding present."

"I didn't buy one yet."

"Good. Don't. I probably won't make it through the honeymoon. Do I look ok?"

"You're gorgeous, the quintessential bride. You'll honor your commitment. I know you will," he said as he lightly pushed me through the door for the second time today.

Chapter Eighteen

Boy, how could I have doubts, I ask myself as I look in the mirror of the dressing room on Landfield's A380 Airbus. We've been married 6 hours and I'm even more in love. My image smiles back at me. I send it a kiss.

Changing into the white silk lounging pajamas Rick Owens had made for me, I couldn't help regretting leaving behind the trousseau I had collected. I had put it together with the thought I wanted nothing from the past in this celebration of my new life.

The 2,000 square foot mirrored dressing room in the house Phillip's parents had given us as a wedding present sanctioned my indulgence to shop for new clothes. Programmed with computerized revolving racks, the closet delivers any combination of clothing and accessory from a database with stored past choices and potential new ones. Having lived as a young girl who had to be satisfied with her mother's castoff clothing, beautiful new clothes is still a thrill.

While we wait in the lounge area of the private terminal for our bags to be loaded, Phillip suggests the three black canvas suitcases I brought would not be needed and points to a large 6-foot custom built wardrobe trunk being rolled up the ramp into the sleek jet under the sign JUST MARRIED flying from the tail,

"I've chosen the things I'd like you to wear," he took my hand and nuzzled it, kissing my fingers and palm lightly as he gazed deeply and intensely into my eyes.

Billions of neurons and synapses clicked in my brain as it flooded with resentment and fear, struggling to keep away the warning signs of dread starting to rise in me. He is taking control of the way I look, and I'm afraid to confront him with my feelings because I don't want to hurt him.

Returning to the seat I take another sip of the pink Dom Perignon the pilot had given us and gaze at the beautiful man I can now call my husband. Tingling to think of him as the man who will protect me and my mother, I'm grateful we're finally safe. We're loved and protected. Now I can take care of Mom without a worry, and I have a man who loves me as much as I love him.

The engines rev and I lean toward Phillip to kiss him, but he takes my hand and lifts it to his lips and kisses my fingertips. Still holding my hand he settles back into his seat, closes his eyes and drops off to sleep.

Feeling a bit drowsy from the champagne and excitement I decide to do the same. Startled when after what felt like minutes my eyes open to see the sky has turned gray with the color of dawn. Dark mountain shapes loom beyond us, growing higher as the plane approaches its descent.

"You slept well." Phillip comes back to his seat and sits down. "You were sleeping so soundly I decided not to wake you for dinner or breakfast. We don't have time to get you anything now because we're about to land, so you're going to have to wait to sample the Landfield version of airplane cuisine on our way home. For now we're approaching never never land."

"I can't believe I slept like that," I straightened the back of my lounge with a rush.

"You had a big day my blushing bride, and we're about to embark on a bigger one. It's good you got the rest. You'll need it."

"Where are we?" I asked, leaning over him and looking out. Phillip had refused to tell me the destination of our honeymoon before we took off.

"Ah - will we ever know - shall we ever find out?" Phillip teased, twirling an imaginary villain's mustache, his dimples cutting deeply into the hollow of his cheeks.

His eyes didn't match his tone. A little shiver of fear rushed through me and I scolded myself for turning the positive into a negative. Why was I reading dark thoughts into my fairy tale? My Prince was leading me to an adventure the first day of our fairy tale life. Remain positive*!*

Shaking and bucking, the plane descended into turbulent air streams. Phillip took my hand and held it. "We're flying into a mountain valley. That's why it's rough. Be calm, this is where it all begins."

I don't see any villages or towns and no lights with the exception of the lightened landing strip. I can't imagine where we are. The mountains are deep green, terraced and cultivated like many parts of Asia,

"Are we in Nepal?" My heart is quickening.

Phillip reaches over and pulls the shade down. "The surprise continues. I don't want you to have a clue where you are. As soon as we're down and before we disembark, go to the dressing room and freshen yourself. We have a bit of a ride. There's something in the closet for you to wear with a note."

When the plane taxies to a stop, I'm stiff as I get up from the lounge chair. The cabin feels errily quiet, dark though the interior lights are blazing. It must be my eyes.

A luscious triple ply cream-colored cashmere sweat suit hangs in the closet with a note, *don't wear anything under this. Let this heat your body.* When I emerge from the restroom a Steward is waiting, holding a large alpaca lined coat.

I hope you don't mind the coat." Phillip comes up behind the Steward. "It's a bit ethnic but I like it and thought that because of the cold temperature, indigenous clothes are best for the environment."

"It's great. I love it. It's very Gucci," I strike a pose.

He watches in a strange piercing way, but maybe I'm interpreting excitement as apprehension.

Phillip takes me and holds me soothingly. I melt and give myself up to him totally and gratefully.

"Where are we?" I ask, my voice muffled against his strong muscled chest.

"We are in the Universe." His voice is intense. "You are a true Goddess and I don't want anything to stand in your way. I want you to be open and powerful with everything you do. Nothing shall impede your growth and development."

Love bubbled as he acknowledged my potential.

"I will never make you regret your faith in me. Never," I told him. "My gifts are for you. I love you. What is mine is yours."

Phillip kisses the top of my head.

Chapter Nineteen

As we enter the carpeted salon off the tarmac a tall, thin man waits, his head bowed low. "This is Virendra", Phillip shouts back to me as he jumps into Virendra's arms. Laughing and whooping, slapping each other on the back like long lost brothers, Phillip seems to notice me again and motions me over to the imposing man whose eyes are so dark I feel unstable when he looks at me. The intensity of his gaze makes me dizzy. It's as if those black marble eyes are lasers looking into me, piercing my inner being and touching my soul. He's wearing a traditional collarless Indian tunic with full pants gathered at the ankles. I get the impression he'd be more comfortable in a three-piece Brioni suit. The mixed messages make me uneasy.

Though I've spent some time with Phillip and his family, I've never seen him behave so exuberantly and spontaneously. He and Virendra have a freedom between them, an infectious affection that makes me smile. But my head is separating from my body, sending me a message. I want to think everything is all right, but my body is tense, something is bothering me.

Then comes the first blast. Instinctively I thought it was coming, but when it did, it nearly knocked me over, literally.

"Virendra is going to join us," Phillip declared joyfully. "He'll be our guide on the honeymoon and more. Anything you want."

Phillip and Virendra stand together, arms around each other, a single entity with two heads.

For better or worse. The vows from the day before ring in my head. Just a few minutes ago I vowed to Phillip I'd do anything for him. But not this. It's not what I envisioned.

Maybe I can convince myself this shared honeymoon is a compliment. I'll put on my happy smile and make my eyes twinkle. But my heart says I'm watching a disaster. My own.

"And you, most beautiful woman," Virendra was saying with a large tense smile, his arms stretched out to fold me into his. "I have seen you many times and now because of Phillip, I have the pleasure of holding one of the most beautiful women in the world in my arms. Welcome to our humble country."

"Thank you," I keep my inner bubble machine sending out smiles of happiness and radiance. "What country is this?"

"God's and Goddess' country," answers Virendra without pause. "It shall uncover the secrets your husband has planned."

"Secrets?" I don't want to show my annoyance and remind myself to stay adorable. "A mystery tour?"

"Perfect! We'll call it that," he said. "The mystery tour."

I turn away. I have to think clearly. The honeymoon is supposed to be the beginning of our life together. We were supposed to be one, not three. Why would Phillip want to share this with someone else? Someone I knew nothing about till now. Am I being jealous? Possessive? Trust is the foundation of love.

Virendra is staring. Can he read my mind? He's staring with a warm smile and eyes sparkling. Is he using my technique or am I being paranoid, my overactive imagination?

Stop this, I warn myself. But the feelings won't stop. Its nerves. Last minute jitters and jet lag. I'm physically shaken and it's affecting my feelings.

Virendra led us toward a low bench piled with cushions and motioned us to sit. I settled on the oriental carpet using the bench and pillows for support. Virendra nodded with approval. "You understand how to use our seating arrangements."

"I've spent a bit of time in Asia, where I assume we are now," I answer, hoping he will acquiesce.

"Many travelers spend time in exotic lands," Virendra cast his eyes down, pouring politeness on to his words, "but they see little. They don't look at the culture or the customs. They see exotic souvenirs and snap shots, stamps in their passports. They take the currency because it's pretty and not worth cashing in and changing. You are not one of those people Jenny. You're different. You watch and absorb. You fit everywhere. I knew that before I met you and you confirmed it for me just now. I welcome you with my open heart. I think you will find additional happiness here. This is a very special land for those who are coming together as one."

Eww, I feel a little guilty for the way I reacted to him. He's trying to put together the ultimate honeymoon for his very dear friend and I'm reacting with suspicions that are coming from nowhere.

I'm tired, I console myself. My nerves are frayed by all that has happened. I want to make Philip happy.

"It will take a few minutes for the vehicles to be loaded. May I offer you spiced tea?" Without waiting for an answer Virendra snaps his fingers and a young boy in a richly embroidered vest brings a large silver tea tray. With the tone and attitude of someone accustomed to giving orders, Virendra orders the boy to pour three cups.

My skin is prickly beneath the thick cashmere sweat suit. I wish I had left my silk pajamas on, but Phillip's note said not to wear anything under the sweat suit and I ignored my instinct to layer the cashmere. The note was strange. Why would Phillip want me to do that?

"You must be exhausted. We'll get you started on your journey as quickly as possible," Virendra was saying. "It is auspicious that you should arrive on the first day of the festival of good luck and fortune. We have brought holy men to anoint you for this journey."

As if on cue two slight dark skinned men approach. Their hands and faces are covered with white ash and they wear the orange robes of Buddhists priests. One holds a small pot of red paint. Squatting in front of us they chant as they paint a circle of red in the middle of our foreheads.

"You are not to wash that off," said Virendra. You must allow it to wear off naturally, otherwise you'll break the spell.

"How funny. I fly half way around the world to find another makeup man. By the way, don't we have to go through passport and custom control?"

"It's taken care of," Virendra said.

Phillip has been silent the entire time but has a strange smile that is kind of weirding me out. I love this man who is my husband. I've got to get rid of these fears and doubts in my brain. Why are these horrible thoughts coming in now that it's too late?

The tea is sticky sweet, a peppery liquid cane sugar and I love it. A perfect pick me up. I peek at Phillip over the cup. He looks like it's affecting him too. Virendra is staring at me and when I notice, he smiles. I smile back, using every trick I know to make it look genuine.

Why didn't I know of Virendra's existence till we landed in this strange place that could be anywhere. I'm the third person out. A stranger in a strange land. I don't belong on my own honeymoon.

If I disappear would anyone know I was gone? The thought sends unsettling chills through my body. I close my eyes and take a deep breath, willing myself to feel love.

"Are you cold?" Phillip takes me into his arms. "You're trembling." He looks at Virendra who walks away.

Phillip is making me feel warm again. Shivers and fear are melting into the warmth of his arms, the heat of his body. I'm so lucky. *Yet* I'm so anxious.

A thought rolls through my mind. Is the roller coaster ride Roger warned of getting ready for the downward rush?

Chapter Twenty

The thick smell of animal is like a second layer enveloping me as I bounce in a covered wagon drawn by oxen. Though a bit rough, the animal skins that must have been killed brutally, still offer coziness and warmth.

It's too dark for me to see anything. This could actually be funny and I wish I could find the humor of a bride alone on her wedding night being bounced around in an ox cart. But it's not. It's pitiful.

I have got to get away from here. I won't be married to anyone who could do this to me. Does he think this is some kind of prank, a joke? I'm scared to death and I don't know if I can handle this alone.

Phillip is in another wagon. When I told him I didn't want to be separated, that I'm afraid to be alone, Phillip said I was safe and not to worry and everything will be beautiful when we're properly alone. He delivered this with a steely demeanor that made me scared. I'd never seen that level of power and cold detachment in him. I don't know what to do. I can't demand to go to a hotel or take the plane back to the U.S. I don't know where I am. I don't have a choice. I'm totally dependent on Tim and that friend who came from nowhere

A dark pit is opening in my stomach and I'm being drawn into its black hole. Look for the light, I demand of myself.

In the airport Phillip treated me with sensitive understanding. I held on to that warm demeanor, believing it, letting it make me feel secure. But when he reverted to that cold brittle behavior of power and superiority, I knew there was no getting to him. I've experienced it before. He shuts totally off till sometime later a switch appears to go back on in his head and he becomes another person. Blameless and unaware of where he has been and what he has done, doesn't interest him. He cares nothing of residual fall out. He just doesn't care

I had blamed the behavior as a byproduct of the tension surrounding the upcoming marriage and his senatorial race.

But this was the first night of our honeymoon and I'm alone in some wagon in the dark and he did this to me. No empathy. Steely detachment, truly uncaring. I wish I could stop crying.

Bernstein and Kalman wanted this wedding. It generated great press and saturated social media. It worked. Phillip won his party's senatorial candidacy from

Illinois and his campaign would start in earnest after the honeymoon.

The wagon jostled. Why didn't I wait till the newness of the romance wore off and I could see him more objectively? What was the rush! I'm so angry with myself. I'd been so swept up with the romantic image and the excitement of my ambition for Phillip. I lived his fantasy because I didn't want to lose him. I agreed to the wedding to keep him. He said he loved fantasy and I was the ultimate. I thought he was being romantic.

Cuddling under the nest of blankets I hold the top one tight, trying to get comfort from it. This is the second night of my marriage and I have not been intimate with my new husband since the first night we met. We barely kiss unless it's for cameras. Our wedding night was on a plane passed out from excitement and champagne, and now I'm loaded in a wagon in the middle of nowhere.

I try to pull the blankets tighter, thinking about that freshly made bed with the silk sheets and Phillip's hard yet soft naked body tangled around me.

I stroke my stomach and pull down the top of the cashmere sweats, my hands reaching for the throbbing place between my legs. These are Phillip's hands, I tell myself as I put them between my legs and find the pulsing and swelling spot that is tingling and burning as wetness coats my inner thighs. Each breath brings a throb so intense it almost hurts.

I push my hips higher, plunging my fingers into my wet self. I'm so hungry for him.

The wagon stops, Phillip climbs in.

I leave my hand between my legs and lower my hips.

"I heard you moaning. I want to make sure you're all right."

"I'm not." My voice sounds loud. "I'm pretending we're making love and you're inside me and we're becoming one."

"Yes, my darling," he smoothed my hair back from my forehead. "In time."

My fingers inched deeper beneath the cover of the blankets. I want to tell him to take me away from here, I don't like this fantasy. But I'm afraid to say anything. I don't know what he'll do. I don't trust him yet I want him. What is wrong with me?

"I look forward to being with you, to come to me wearing nothing." He strokes my arm.

"I've removed my body hair in preparation for you," I tell him instead of my fears.

"Next time I'll pour hot wax between your legs and wait till it hardens so I can rip it off of you. Then I'll lick your burning skin till you're so hot you won't be able to stop screaming, wanting me more then you want me now. You want me now, true?"

171

"Of course I do." I turn over and pull my knees to my chest. Phillip reaches under the covers and continues to stroke me. My body shudders with another explosion.

"Come to me," I roll over. "I want you more than I've ever wanted anything. Please Phillip," I beg. "You're my husband. I want you."

"Hush." He strokes my face gently with the back of his hand. "You must wait my Goddess. When we consummate our marriage it will be with the most exquisite precision. You shall become the Goddess of the temple. We'll be ready in a few days."

"A few days. This is our honeymoon. Why wait?"

"To replace your learned behavior and genetic limitations so you will soar. You will experience the rite of sensual being. When we reach it together there will be such a high degree of frequency we will be carried to incredible heights. I knew what you were doing before we entered the wagon. I'm so proud of you."

"What do you mean "we" and how do you know?" I feel myself backing away emotionally. Anger is taking over. He's a stranger now. "Do you have a camera in here?"

"It's pitch dark. Not possible." He strokes my back. "A woman should love her body. She should cream herself till she is brought to climax to be an open vessel for her man at all times. I will use you whenever I want. You will always be ready so I can fill you at will."

He has to be kidding. I can't laugh. What if he means it!

Phillip puts his hands under my sweatshirt and rolls me over on my stomach. He pulls my back up till my knees are bent.

I cradle my head with my sticky fingers as my body and feelings take on a dynamic all their own. I'm now the observer and the recipient of my senses.

"Let go," Phillip whispers into my ear, his warm breath making me tingle. "Give in to this, open and be my chalice"

I watch from somewhere in the back of my head as some primal force raises my hips. I can't see anything. Cold air is coming in, the blankets are lifted from below and strong fingers part my legs.

A head comes between my thighs, so close I can feel its breath, a tongue licking then entering me so deeply it has an energy lifting and buffeting me till I'm out of control. I want it to stop. I can't go on. I hear myself screamble.

Chapter Twenty-One

Light. I can see outside the wagon. It doesn't look real. We're going through a dense forest of giant rhododendrons and magnolias covering the hillsides with rainbows of color. Wild orchids hang from the trees surrounded by the sounds of exotic birds and animals I can't identify. But I can't identify much this morning. I feel numb, worn out.

The wagon stops and Virendra and Phillip part the curtains. "From this point we have to walk."

They help me from the wagon. My legs are wobbly and when Virendra's hand touches mine, a jolt of electricity passes through me. I don't know if it came from his hand or if he had some small buzzer concealed in it. But I definitely felt an electric jolt and held tightly to Phillip.

Silent porters looking like Elves with close-cropped hair and slanted black eyes transfer the goods from the wagons to their backs.

Leaving the wagons and oxen behind, we follow the line of small elves trekking up a narrow path that winds like a ribbon around a sheer rock face. Looking down I get dizzy when I can't see the bottom of a drop that appears to go on forever.

Coming to a bridge made of wood and iron chains swinging freely across a chasm, I'm terrified. This can be my path to oblivion. I'm going to die. I'll panic if I look down. How can I get across this? I'll freeze if I panic, but I can't go forward. I'm going to die.

Virendra took my arm and starts to lead me. "Phillip will be behind you for support."

He's not fooling around. I want to object but if I pull back I could throw them all off balance and we'll all fall into the abyss. He knows that, *he's* willing to take the risk.

I have to follow. I'll try to use what I learned in yoga, to focus on breath to bring calm. Survive, I'm going to survive.

Holding my breath and barely feeling my body, only Virendra's massive shoulders and Phillip's hands on mine, I hold my breath and don't exhale till I feel we're on solid ground.

Dizzy from the terror, I collapse to the flat earth. I've never felt such fear in my life and feel empty after having to put all my faith for survival in the hands of Virendra.

It's easy to forget fear now as I drink in the beauty of the mountain range that is so magnificent it takes my mind away from the terror I just experienced. In a crazy way I even appreciate that chasm guarding so many from coming here. Breathtaking and forbidding it seems impenetrable, but I had done it. Hooray for me!

In the distance there's a large white structure that looks like it's growing out of the mountain. A commanding man made presence in the midst of amazing natural beauty.

Virendra takes my arm, his hand strong and intense, commands attention. "That's our destination," he points in the direction of the building. "It's carved from the side of the mountain and perches on the ledge of a 3000-foot cliff. They started building it in 1626."

I'm transfixed by the beauty and obvious technical mastery.

"If you look carefully," Virendra's hand swept over the vista. "Some of the walls glow translucently when lit by the setting sun. You'll see them better when we get closer."

"Magnificent." I'm breathless, overcome by emotion and exertion and the beauty. "I never dreamed anything this extraordinary existed."

I turned from Virendra and hugged Phillip's arm. "We're in Shangri-La! I kissed his cheek. "You've brought me to Paradise."

"Yes my darling," he smiled warmly. "I've brought you to Paradise. And we're just starting."

"No one who visits this place writes or talks about it," warned Virendra. "Many have made the attempt but none succeeded. When they try, it's never finished."

"What do you mean?" Foreboding crushed my excitement.

Virendra didn't seem to hear the question. "The building was commissioned by a Maharaja who died years before it was completed," he continued. "It had been a monastery for centuries and through the years it's been enlarged till it now contains many temples." He pointed to the golden symbols on the shingled roof that reflected the holy shrines below.

Phillip took me by the arm and escorted me up a flight of steep wooden steps with heavy chains that led to a pulley system that had been designed as a safeguard in times of turmoil hundreds of years before.

"Listen," said Virendra.

I could hear the low vibrating resonance of a single conch blowing across the mountains, filling them with sound. The conch stopped and was immediately covered by the wind and muffled sound of monks chanting somewhere in the distance.

A woman in a white sari banded in gold, opened the large bronze doors and bowed to us. We entered a vast rotunda tiled to the top of a vaulted ceiling with a mosaic of a Mandela, a mystical pattern that is said to bring harmony with the universe.

A darling Golden Languor monkey the size of a kitten, came bounding gleefully across the floor and yanked at the hem of the woman's sari. Gracefully the woman bent her knees, a signal of permission for the monkey to scamper up her side to her shoulder and perch there. The monkey pulled its lips back into a very human looking smile and kept his head turned toward us as the woman led us down a long hallway to a large carved door.

Behind the door was an enormous room with a polished stone floor covered with an array of warmly colored oriental rugs. The stucco white walls held richly embroidered wall hangings and the sitting room and sleeping area are divided by a large screen inlaid with mother of pearl. On one side of the room there is an oval pool, it's water bubbling and smelling as if it had come from a natural hot spring.

"This is your domain," said Phillip. "I shall not enter it nor shall any other man unless invited. We have female servants to care for you. We don't want you to do anything for yourself. You might find that difficult but I ask you to try because that is what I'd like you to find here, the ability to allow others to serve you and take care of you. I don't think you know how to do that and I want you to learn how.

I felt like I was sinking. "Do I get to see your quarters?" I try to stay as neutral as possible. Keep the panic off my face, out of my voice. "I assumed we were going to share the same room."

Phillip took my face and gazed in my eyes. "You can see anything, the other men's' quarters if you'd like. All the men are here for you if you'd like them."

My heart dropped down to my toes as his words crashed into me, flinging me into wary comprehension. "What is that supposed to mean?" I manage to say without screaming.

"I just want you to know I'm not jealous, darling."

"Well, I am." I'm trying to stay calm as possible.

"I would anticipate you would only want me on our honeymoon," Phillip was saying, his voice serious, his eyes cold. If he cared about my feelings, he wasn't showing it. He was distant, as if he wasn't there.

"If you'd like to try multiples," he was saying "and you see someone you like, by all means go with him or her. You will grow to understand that I accept anything and everything. I expect the same consideration from you."

"You don't have it. This is something we should have discussed long before the wedding, not now." My voice sounds far away from myself, maybe because everything I had believed about Phillip was wrong. I never should have married him even though there had been signs. But I didn't know it till this moment. "If you loved me you'd want me only for yourself," I heard myself saying in an exercise of futility. "That's how I feel about you and I thought you felt the same way about me. It's my mistake. Is your celibacy vow a sham?"

"It was maintaining our purity till the consummation of this marriage. It was gathering the energy for this transformation of love into pure ecstasy. I love you Jenny and know you have great pools of loving energy that can be shared on many levels. That's why I was attracted to you. That's why I married you. Not to have sex so much as to take our singular energies, merge and expand them into a universal expression of unity."

He held my gaze. I couldn't believe what he was saying.

"We'll have sex like we did before and it will be wonderful. But things change, sometimes during a honeymoon, and we should be prepared for it." He touched my face and continued. "Life is change. Energy is motion. It's the simple law of physics. Accept it. Physical law is our human reality. Beliefs, feelings and truths change from one day to the next. You know that. We live with change."

"Not the kinds of changes you're talking about. I've never been with another man. You know that." I can't control myself. I have no restraint. "You were my first, then your celibacy vow." I'm crying so hard I can barely talk.

Phillip pulls away.

"I want to go home,"

Patiently Phillip spoke in a soft voice. "I want you to open your mind to me as you opened your body. You don't have to be fearful. I'll be your support, your main source of reference. This honeymoon shall wed us forever."

"This is not a honeymoon. It's some kind of frightening caper. I thought I loved you, but I won't be part of this."

How many people learn they married a stranger I think to myself. Are they all as frightened and lonely as I feel right now?

There were times when I was modeling that I had to suspend my belief system for the sake of a picture. I can do that. But this isn't a situation in which I can just get up and leave if the fantasy gets too real. This fantasy is real. Frighteningly real. I'm surrounded in wilderness with no place to go.

"I'm not ready for what you're asking. I had signed on as your wife, a helpmate and a companion. But I'm not a selfless non-thinking shell of a puppet. I expected to lose a little freedom and independence but not my soul, not my right of self-determination. I was hoping to having a new sense of security, the merging of our two energies evolving as one. This is not anything I can accept."

Phillip watched me impassively evaluating. Then quietly said, "you have no choice."

The words I had told myself hit with new intensity when it came from Phillip. It made me weak. I have to escape. He had promised *a great adventure*, but I had anticipated something totally different, a romantic fantasy like those we create for the cameras. A fantasy to make the public want the same for themselves. But now I'm supposed to step into his script and live it. "No choice." I'll have to pretend to go along till I find a way to escape. I'm a prisoner. A kidnap victim.

"Fine," I cast my head to the side and put on my sweetest and most ingratiating smile. "Are we to have dinner together or am I to dine alone?"

"Whichever you prefer," he answered.

"I prefer to be with you." I keep my tone light. "This is the first full night of our marriage." I keep the smile on my lips hoping I look sincere and not fearful. Nothing excites a predator more than fear.

"Good," he said and heads for the door, pausing a moment to turn back and blow a kiss before he leaves.

Chapter Twenty-Two

Phillip is at his most charming as we nibble on tidbits of Asian appetizers with no sign of Virendra. Cheeks warm and smiles bubbling, I'm surprised I'm actually having a good time.

Though I do keep watching out of the corner of my eye for Virendra. Like a moving blanket of toxicity he changes Phillip the minute he's with him. I want to keep this time away from Virendra as long as possible.

I listen to Phillip talking about his love of pageantry and drama with a tinge of heaviness. Now anything he says has no meaning. He's beaten me down so much emotionally I don't care about anything he's saying. I'll just keep myself positive till I escape from here.

"I want to use drama to create larger than life metaphors to express singular and simplistic feelings," he was saying.

"Why are you with me?" I ask, not out of curiosity but to make him think I'm listening.

"I wouldn't have noticed you if you weren't spectacular. You're not only a great beauty, you're intelligent and brave, a cutting edge version of an

Amazonian warrior. You're the perfect symbol of what I've wanted. I knew it the moment I saw you."

To hide I put a warm smile on my face and tilt my head in a pose of interest. Not long ago I had hoped he was in love with the real me, the inner being, the true self who had loved Phillip with a passion born from purity. But Phillip was talking about externals - how I looked, what I did, my good luck – all surface.

"Darling?" Phillip asked, "Did you hear me?"

"I'm sorry it's difficult to concentrate when one is being described as a trophy."

"Don't be silly. I didn't do that." His annoyance was contained but not hidden. "I said I've admired you and wanted to be a part of your life ever since I saw you. It's you I'm talking about, your inner beauty, not your looks. Do you think I'm that shallow?"

Taking a deep breath to speak, "I'm sorry. I didn't mean that."

He kissed my hand then snapped his fingers and a young servant brought in a bottle of port and poured it into crystal cut glasses.

"This was bottled the year you were born, a year to which I'm grateful." He lifted the glass to me in a toast then sipped.

I followed suit, feeling the sweet pungent wine circulating warmly through me.

"The wedding at my farm was only one aspect of our life and marriage in the Western way" he's explaining. "But now, I want to bring our union to a consecrated level in which we will be joined at the highest echelons. Other dimensions."

Encircling my shoulders he guides me toward the small balcony overlooking the mountains. "Our bodies are our temples. Our hearts the door to those temples," he pauses and sweeps his hand across the majestic view from the balcony. "Our sex organs are the holiest of holy, our tongues the wafer, our juices the wine, our lips the sacrament and our moans the liturgy. Waves of ecstasy are baptism and we sweat with light. We will swim in endless timeless seas of joy and dance in the heart of space. Our magnetic attraction is the ultimate purity. We shall attain nirvana as we combine our energies."

I don't know what to say. Is he for real? I don't know if I should laugh or be intrigued. I had read ideas such as his, but Phillip spoke with a belief that seems to come from another dimension.

"Virendra," the name shot through me like an arrow, deflating any lofty muse I was having.

"Virendra is here," Phillip continued, "because he is a conduit between the esoteric spiritual levels and those of us who aspire to be there. You and I deal in the physical aspect of life. For the most part, that's the market place. Virendra lives above that. He decides who will be exposed to the great secrets and meanings of life. We are in a very sacred place and there are very few uninitiated allowed to come here for this experience. This is Virendra's wedding gift, our initiation."

I thought I had loved this man with all my heart. Even now, I wish I could trust him. I had given him my vow. But I know his words are lies. I've been set up. I'm a hostage.

"We are privileged to be exposed to those who know the secrets of life and the reason for existence," he was saying. "Some say Jesus spent time in the Himalayas and was opened to the truths of the universe here."

He had said here. We are in the Himalayas.

"I have met people who can take me closer to what I seek," he was saying. "I've chosen you to join me with this consecration to take us to the highest levels of consciousness, the blending of male and female energy. We shall become one in the total sense of the word."

With a soft kiss against my cheek, he leaves the room and I turn toward the opened wardrobe trunk from the plane. On inspection I find it contains costumes for different characters and situations. Two Asian women stand on either side of the trunk and curtsy in an obviously well-rehearsed way when I come in. Holding my breath so I don't laugh I turn the impulse into a smile. I quickly learn neither women speak English, however they are proficient with sign language and giggles.

Keeping Phillip's wishes in mind, I allow them to guide me to the full bath and take off my clothes. I'm used to letting people undress me during fashion shows, but these women had no knowledge of English and lingered over the color and tone of my skin which is obviously different from anything they'd known. Apparently, they had never seen a woman this tall, thin and light skinned either. Guiding me carefully they lead me to a steaming tub with the slight sulfur smell of a natural hot spring. Just warm enough, I luxuriate in the soft water then fall asleep after a few sips of perfumed tea.

No idea how long I napped, I have to acclimate myself when the women get me up. I follow them to a low cushioned pallet where they lay me down on my stomach and spread heated Jasmine oil over my body, massaging it in tenderly as I lay passive, my vagina quivering a little as they lightly caressed the inside of my upper legs.

I nearly doze off again as the two rub the moons of my buttocks with the heels of their hands then the small of my back. Turning me over, a soft scented cloth is placed over my eyes and they gently massage my breasts. One of them brushes my nipples with swift light caresses from what I think is a feather while the other soothes my stomach with warm, slow circular strokes.

As they lift my knees and spread them apart, my thighs open at their touch. Deeply and tenderly they massage my calves, behind my knees, between my legs, dabbing at my vagina with a cloth when it grows damp.

A finger strokes me between my legs as I lay in surrender. The other woman's fingers tighten around my nipples as the other's finger enters me. Throbbing and reacting on its own, my womanhood sucks the finger and draws it in deeper.

Turning me on my side, fingers coated with Jasmine oil, the two put their fingers into me front and back, arousing me in a strange new way. I had never allowed a woman to touch me sexually and never had the kinds of sensations I was having. It's soft and deep and very intense. Shuddering violently then again gently, I instantly understand why men like women making love to them. Women are inexplicitly different than men.

"You're glowing" Phillip remarked when I join him for dinner totally naked beneath a nearly transparent white silk gown. The two women have done my make-up, making my eyes darker and more pronounced then I would have. I thought it looked a bit hard but Phillip told me I looked ravishing.

During dinner I tell Phillip about the incredible massage, leaving out the intimate details and suggesting that perhaps some time we could receive a massage from the two women together. He grunts and pushes himself up and away from me. My heart jolts. I want my conversation to turn him on, make him desire me, but he bends over and kisses me lightly on the forehead, a butterfly kiss I had called it as a child. Whispering good night he leaves me with a hole in my feelings. Sinking with hurt then anger I try to force those feelings away. There is no way I can resolve anything by fighting a losing game. I'm trapped. I can't get out. I've got to stay passive, be watchful and careful. I have to blend the different parts of my psyche into one to stay balanced and strong. But tears are running unguarded down my face. I look at the other side. I'm nothing but a slave on an invisible chain. Snagged by a hook of hope.

Chapter Twenty-Three

Relaxing into the unacceptable, the next four days almost made this feel like the honeymoon it was supposed to be. Day treks following oceans of snow, walls of multi-colored flowers and a kaleidoscope of nature's visuals made the difficulties of the reality almost possible for me to endure.

As part of the daily ritual Virendra would disappear after the morning trek and I wouldn't see him till the next morning on a new expedition.

In the evenings my mineral bath and herbal tea would be waiting. Massaged afterward by the two handmaidens who brought me into a zone of pure feeling.

At dinner I wore translucent silk gowns in various shades of blue, silver, and gold. My hair would be soft and curled and I finally got the two handmaidens to tone down my makeup and make it more natural.

I pray I can please Phillip so I can go home. He has to release me from this tension I feel. No matter how sensuous and comfortable the surroundings, I know they are fake. There is a sinister element here and I don't want them to know I feel vulnerable. There are sharks in these waters, circling me on two feet.

Once again Phillip is so charming at dinner and so great to look at, I doubt my own feelings. I find myself wanting him, hoping somehow he would become the man I thought I had married. And it ended the same as it has every night. Phillip leaves without touching me. I feel rejected and empty. This is all so hollow. I can't give in to it because of fear. I've got to live it all consciously and survive. Play the game till I can get out.

He barely seems to notice I'm naked beneath the translucent silk. I had been excited by the girls and I know I carry a sensual energy that should affect him. I was sexually ready for him, and he knew it.

"The Initiation will be this evening," he said quietly. "You are to be prepared." He leaves the room without a touch, without a kiss or a glance behind.

The two handmaidens remove my silk robe and spread a soft fluffy layer of cream over my entire body that smells heavenly. Playfully they concentrate on the places between my legs and around my breasts where they know I like being touched. I almost forget Phillip's denial of me, the terrible way it made me feel. Using brushes and sponges they overlay my naked body with fine gold leaf, careful to leave small hidden patches of uncovered skin so my body can breathe.

Two thin chains lay over my bare shoulders that hold draped layers of transparent silk with intertwining threads of gold, silver and platinum. It floats like a whisper over my gold leafed body. My feet are bare, with the exception of a light cover of gold nail polish on my toes, matching the gold paint on my fingernails.

Two other handmaidens in nearly transparent white saris set a table with gold plates bearing fresh fruits and cheeses. So many pillows had been piled around the low tables I wonder if we are having guests, though who could the guests be with the exception of Virendra.

Turning away I study my image in the mirror. The makeup is bizarre, dramatically theatrical; a sweep of gold eye shadow painted in a rectangular bar across my lids and two lines of gold tracing my cheekbones. Somehow the design on my body and face created a surreal look. I liked it. Roger would be in heaven if he saw me with nearly every inch of my flesh covered in gold. I spun around and created a metallic aura. Totally cool.

A gong sounded and a woman came in and bowed, "Master Virendra," she whispered.

I stiffened. My body might be painted, but I'm still completely nude. I don't want Virendra to see me, but I don't know what to do. I try gathering up the silk wrap but it's as transparent as a cobweb. I can't think of a way out of this situation.

Virendra came to these rooms without an invitation. He broke the rules. But then, he made them. Makes him think he's different than others.

He comes closer. I hold my breath to hide my shaking anger. I don't want him to see that. I've been in situations similar to this before, a higher up with the client or the client itself thought they had the rights to my body as well. But the gates came down with that kind and stayed down. I had protection. No one who wasn't essential had been allowed on the set and I never took off my robe till the lighting was set.

But this was neither a film set nor a photography studio. There is no one to protect me. The two handmaidens receive orders from Virendra.

Virendra stopped when he saw me and studied me critically, a museum curator checking his new acquisition. "You're a living sculpture, a magnificent warrior," he said, his voice more throaty than usual.

Vulnerable and helpless I throw modesty to the winds and use an offensive position as I stand and face him.

Bowing my head and taking a long deep breath, I cross my arms at the elbows, cover my breasts, bend my knees and curtsy deeply like all the pictures I had seen of Egyptian princesses.

Virendra puts his hand lightly on my elbow and leads me to a pile of cushions against the wall. "Sit here so we can talk." His tone is friendly but detached, not reacting to my nakedness at all.

"Phillip is more nervous than you are," he smiles. "You know you're quite beautiful, breathtaking. Quite remarkable." He said it simply. He seemed to mean it. I hated him for that.

I don't respond.

Virendra snaps his fingers. A young woman in her twenties appears. She wears a gold and white sari and her hair is pulled straight back in a single ankle length braid. Sitting down she curls next to me like a puppy.

"Security for you," explained Virendra. "You can keep her next to you all the time or you can dismiss her. It's up to you. We thought you might like someone who so graphically exhibits the internal Jenny who fears she might lose herself tonight. This girl is your comfort zone."

Fear totally takes over. Virendra has brought someone who should not be subjected to this kind of environment. "This is disgusting. It's not acceptable. I will try to get through whatever has been planned for me, but not with anyone else, especially a young girl."

"You don't make the rules."

"I'm able to go through this on my own."

Virendra bowed. "She will stay with you while we further prepare you and escort you to the next room. She will leave then if you still desire it. But remember, at any time before she leaves, you are able to change your mind. This young woman will be of help. Remember that."

Nodding automatically I wonder what he had just said. What kind of *further preparation* will I have? Goose bumps are braking out. Another young girl with huge eyes and a melting smile appears holding a small gold tray with two crystal goblets.

Virendra picks up the goblets and hands one to me. "A toast to my dear Phillip's bride,"

I detect a sweet smell and take a small sip. It tastes like roses and vanilla and is delicious. Instantly I feel an inner glow and I'm smiling, feeling good. "Thank you."

Virendra smiles and stands up and holds out his hand. "I haven't yet given you my wedding gift." He holds out his hand and the second girl places a small velvet box into it which he opens and holds out to me. Inside are two perfect pear shaped canary diamonds.

"They're beautiful." I lift them from the box and start to bring one of them to my ear.

"Let us help you" said Virendra, gesturing to the two young girls who take the diamond pins from me and hand them back to Virendra. They then take hold of both my hands and hold on to me, lightly but firmly. However I don't try to pull away. I want to see what is going to happen.

"You shall be catapulted beyond your wildest dreams into a universe of fire and ice - the greatest extremes, a world that goes far beyond what you have experienced so far. This is the beginning of your choices tonight. Think carefully and choose wisely."

This sounds over the top.

We continue down the hall, the two young women holding my hands on either side, then stop at a small antechamber. In the center a stream of white light comes directly through the high ceiling, bisecting the fountain.

"You may say a prayer to whomever you want. Use this time to center yourself," Virendra is saying. "You shall be going through a change of awareness and you want to keep yourself in control. Pray for self-discipline and know your higher self shall be the ruler for what you experience. You will gain power with this."

Those words are scary. I don't know what to do. Can Phillip save me? I need him.

"Good," said Virendra seeming again to read my mind as he hands me a crystal goblet with the sweet vanilla mixture that made me feel good. It works again.

Large bronze doors open and I'm led by the young woman into a vast white marble chamber with no other color than my golden body and Phillip who sits on a large marble throne, his body also covered in gold. A gold loincloth is suspended from his waist by a chain that barely covers his penis like an ancient Egyptian Pharaoh. We're in the Twenty First Century and travel by plane to this remote part of the world to go through some primitive rite with contemporary knowledge and attitudes. This is nuts.

Yet there is something in the atmosphere that makes me kneel when I approach Phillip and put my forehead to the ground.

It's part of the pageant, I try to convince myself as I hear Virendra, "you may rise."

His voice shatters my thoughts, making me acutely aware I'm naked and totally exposed.

Phillip holds up his right hand and nods as the two young girls step to either side of me and hold my arms away from my body. Covered only with gold paint, I feel vulnerable in the center of this large marble room as white hooded figures file in and line the sides of the hall. I can't tell if they're men or women. Their shapes are hidden by the hooded robes.

Trying to steady myself as the two young girls pull my arms in opposite directions, I have to plant my legs apart and stand silent, praying I won't crumble and faint which is what I feel like doing.

I'll live out this fantasy, my life depends on it. I'll be strong. If this is what he wants he'll get it. I won't crumble. Mommy needs me. I want to go home.

Phillip steps from his throne and walks slowly toward me. "We shall adorn you my Goddess and make you even more beautiful than you are at this moment. Do not resist anything that is going to happen tonight." He comes closer.

He still makes me tingle. I'm like putty in his hands.

"This has all been pre-ordained,"

He's soothing and oh so compelling.

"Your only choice this evening is your perception. If you go towards the pain you will not feel discomfort, you will embrace it's rapture."

Searching for the love and security I hope to feel from him, I get only cold distance. He is not connected to me.

"Pain is cleansing and purifying." He's reciting like a robot. "The ultimate gift of love is pain," he is saying. "It shall take you to heights and new worlds of sensuality. You can prove yourself the Goddess you are or sink into your weaker strains."

Weaker strains. What is he talking about? Did he mean my mother? In retrospect she has taken better care of herself than I have. I wish I had respected her more. I'm sorry mommy…

"We don't want you to experience pain on the physical or mental level," said Virendra coming close, wiping away a tear that was running down my face. "Our counsel is don't react with your conditioned responses. You are poised on the threshold of accelerated space and you'll be moving through a different variation of time.

Everything you do during this time will affect you for decades."

I want to say something more profound than bull shit, but what can I say?

"You shall not utter a sound unless given permission," Virendra interrupted my thoughts. "You must understand and accept this, or this will be hard. It's your choice to choose pain and victimization or transcendence and ecstasy. Your choice," he repeated. "Choose wisely. It's a decision to grow." He stepped away.

Without taking his gaze from me Phillip puts out his hand and receives one of the Canary diamonds that had been embedded in what looked like a short stickpin. He lightly ran one finger around my nipples watching the traitors tighten and strain toward him like an eager puppy wanting a pet. Putting two fingers around one of them, he brings the pointed end of the diamond pin and pushes it in slowly and deliberately.

I gasp, the shock. I shudder with pain. The two young girls hold me tightly as Phillip pushes the second pin into my other nipple. Dropping to my knees, I try to deal with the waves of pain doubling and undulating through every part of me. Phillip's face shows no emotion other than a beautiful mask with large blue/gray eyes. He could be a robot, he shows no feelings.

"Good," he says. "You cry with surprise. Now you know you can capture your own discipline. No more surprises. You have held up well and the affect is dazzling. Would you care to look?"

I struggle to contain the cry that is ripping inside me. Another young woman brings a mirror and holds it so I can see the two yellow diamonds glistening brilliantly with intensity and blending with the gold of my painted naked breasts. Two droplets of blood run from the pins. Virendra touches the blood with two fingers and brings them to his mouth to suck.

Trying to ignore Virendra, I look into the mirror at the two glowing diamonds embedded in my painted breasts. The image is startling, taking my body to a stage of perfection. And although I resent their insistence on submission, the survival instinct is peeling away another layer of innocence and showing me how to use that new image, to use that power.

"We knew you would like it," said Phillip, "but we aren't finished."

The two young women imprison me with their soft grasp as Virendra opens another small velvet box. "The second part of your wedding gift," he gives it to Phillip. Inside is a small round hoop that looks like an earring.

Phillip holds it to the light. "The platinum is so delicate it's almost surgical. Don't worry. We've taken the best sanitary and medical precautions as well as having this item blessed."

Holding my breath but unable to keep the tears streaming down my gold cheeks, I know what that ring is for and I don't want him to come near me with it. But fear of Virendra is keeping me silent.

The two handmaidens smile with gentle understanding. One holds a moistened cloth and dabs at my nipples causing them to sting.

The women's presence gives me some kind of permission and I allow myself to cry with the pain. The women cluck motherly sounds and blot my tears. It still hurts.

The crystal goblet is held to my lips and without thinking I drink from it. Warmth washes over me and makes me comfortable as the two women ease me down to the ground and place a cushion under my buttocks. Like they had for the last four nights, they take my thighs in their hands and spread my legs wider, but this time they are opening me in front of Phillip and Virendra. Their familiarity and gentle touch don't comfort me through the dread and embarrassment rushing through me. They give me another sip of the sweet brew and I find myself opening wider, pushing my hips higher. Drugged and moaning, a handmaiden dabs at my vagina with a stinging liquid that is probably alcohol.

The two women continue to hold my thighs open as Phillip approaches and hands the ring to Virendra who kneels between my legs.

Searing pain screams through me as Virendra pierces my clitoris with the thin gold hoop. But I can't make a sound as Phillip has put his stiffened penis in my mouth while Virendra licks and sucks me; links in a chain, joined as a circle.

"Ecstasy," mutters Phillip huskily. "Your choice, your perception. We will take you where you wish."

Phillip pulls himself out of me and goes back to the throne where a young man sitting on the step below gets on his hands and knees and attaches his mouth to Phillip's penis. Virendra holds the ring he has inserted in me between his fingers and licks the area like some primitive animal.

It hurts," I whisper, hoping for comfort. There is silence. "It's sadistic."

"Pain is beauty," replies Virendra as the women help me to my feet. "Your conditioning makes you think it's bad and to be avoided. Yet when you turn to it and let it encompass you it is ecstasy, intensity, it takes you through stifling comfort zones. It's the ultimate freedom from bondage. For that reason you will continue to wear the ring the entire time you're here." He nods toward the two women. "They will clean you and get you ready. You seem to be fine."

Get me ready? I look at Phillip on his throne, his head thrown back, his eyes closed as the young man whips his head up and down Phillip's large pulsing penis. As I turn to leave, walking gingerly with this foreign metal object between my legs, I hear the cries of the man I thought I had loved as he ejaculates. I'm sickened, weighted with despair.

He had swept me off my feet. I had thought I was safe with him. And now he has created a forbidden reality, forced me over the threshold of acceptability to the vestibules of hell.

I'm torn by my revulsion and the taste of Phillip still with me. Angrily I turn to Virendra. "I'll be ready."

He bows and watches me leave, then turns to Phillip.

Chapter Twenty-Four

The women sponge off the gold makeup as I sip a cup of the rose, vanilla mixture. The mirror says I'm still beautiful, but there is sadness on that face, a portrait of lost innocence.

Regret snakes through my feelings as I try to condone my passive behavior. I have to get away but I'm reacting instead of thinking. I'm so scared I have to find a place in myself where I can deal with this fear. There is no right or wrong suddenly comes to me. Without evil there is no comparison. Without evil we would not know good.

I shake my head in denial. How can I see this as a lesson? Through pain there is love?

"*That's bull shit,*" yells some voice in my thoughts. *Love is not born of pain.*

What if there's no choice, I hear myself asking.

See it through, I hear again. *When there is no way out you have to go deeper into yourself, away from the pain.*

But where do I go? I continue the conversation in my head. I'll die in the mountains if I can get out of this fortress or whatever it is. They'll kill me if I don't go through with the initiation. No one will know what happened. They'll say I was lost in an accident in the mountains. What will mom do without me? I have to survive. I have to make them think I'm one of them or we'll both be dead.

The women blended iridescent pink powder and smoothed it on my cheeks, eyelids and lips. My hair is slicked back behind my ears and the canary diamond pins remain in my breasts. The women attach a three foot gold chain to the ring in my clitoris and give the other end to a young, naked girl standing quietly to the side.

Virendra's voice enters the room. A hand on my shoulder signals it's time to go. Fear grabs me. Virendra may have powers beyond my understanding, but I still understand the difference between right and wrong. It's all I have. This is wrong.

When I told Phillip I give him every part of myself, I had no idea what I was offering him. He wanted my soul. And sometimes I think he's taken it. I have to look in mirrors to remind myself who I am.

With a tilt of her head the young woman motions me to follow both her and Virendra. Led by the chain I dare not pull back or resist. Taking a deep breath I concentrate on staying in step.

Entering the marble chamber the young man who had swallowed Phillip's semen is sitting on the throne. Anger grabs me but I can't let that control me, I have to stay neutral.

Catching a glimpse of the white robed figures I'm gently pushed down to my knees and made to rest my head on my arms. They elevate my mid section with a tall narrow pillow. Settling myself comfortably, the young woman suddenly mounts me and sits on my back. She's light and not uncomfortable. And I'm very scared.

An oiled, perfumed finger starts to rub between my buttocks. I barely notice the young woman as the finger works its way to a place that is pulsing almost to the point of hurting as it swells and wets itself with my cream. Quivering swollen lips vibrate throughout me as the finger gently touches the spot where the handmaidens had already excited me. It circles slowly. Tremors spread. The young woman reaches down and squeezes my nipples.

My handmaidens must have reported my reactions back to Virendra or Phillip after they had tried various techniques to discover what excited me night after night.

But now the finger fondling didn't feel like either of them. This was stronger, more aggressive. It was a man's. Could it be Phillip? Is it Virendra?

The young woman shifts restlessly, knocking her knees against my body. Wiggling to shift her weight she jerks the gold chain. I scream most by pain but also absolute terror. I'd forgotten the power this young woman has in her hands.

Someone puts their hands on my buttocks and hot breath precedes lips then a tongue. The young woman reaches over again and grasps my nipples, squeezing and pinching them whenever I shuddered. The tongue goes away and is immediately followed by another, then a succession of tongues licking and sucking and putting their fingers into me as the nude young woman lays on top of my bare back, playing with my nipples.

I want to be brave, but this is off the charts. If I give myself up to it what will I become? If I pull back I could die. They'll kill me. Should I believe the promises they made, the chance for freedom? I'm so disgusted and so scared. How can I continue? I'm losing myself. Fearing the pain. Sensations circle. I can no longer touch the way I feel. I watch them as they leap from my body and dance into infinity.

From somewhere in the cosmos I can see myself being ridden by a naked young woman with amber skin. White robed figures queue up to take their turn with me.

"Stop," I hear and, like in a dream, I float in a cross-legged position to land opposite Phillip. His eyes are closed in meditation, his palms turned up on the edges of his knees.

I touch him cautiously and he grabs my wrist, pulling me to him with a roughness I had not experienced before. He kisses me forcefully but I don't melt into him as I usually do. Instead I stiffen and pull away.

He takes my shoulders, "you thrill me!" Touching my cheeks, my lips, my forehead with the back of his hand. "You're more exquisite then I have ever known. You are a Goddess. You understand. You let yourself be used. What a girl, what a woman!"

I try to get up but the young woman tugged on the chain and I sit back again, an obedient prisoner to avoid further pain.

"Leave her alone Sirena," Phillip snaps at the girl. "Unfasten her chain and disappear." He turns and makes a sweeping gesture toward the white robed people who immediately file out an inner door.

As Sirena unhooks the chain from the ring I draw her close and kiss her. Phillip watches, his eyes brim. Is it love or self congratulations?

He takes my hands and looks into my eyes. "When you make others happy," his voice is husky, "you make me doubly so. We are all one and we must share ourselves. You have been given great gifts of beauty and it is beholden upon you to share yourself with others. That is what you did tonight. You stayed moist and received your takers. You were marvelous, brilliant, outstanding for a first timer."

He reaches over and kisses my lips, his lips are tightly closed. He pulls back. "We have perfect balance which means everything. I'm so proud of you darling, I wish you didn't have to rest. But don't fear, we'll continue."

"Continue?" My body shivers and my head roars.

Phillip pulls me against his chest and strokes my left breast, running his finger around the canary diamond, pushing it in a little bit. Which hurt. "I know how much you enjoy receiving oral sex so for your next gift I shall have Virendra do it for you. He loves it and is better at it than I. It was he who was with you in the wagon. You didn't know because you enjoyed it so much. I watched so I know."

I close my eyes. I don't ever want to see him again. He's disgusting. Everything I felt for him is wiped out in a flash. Everything I believe in, everything I trust, has been blown away. I've tried to keep my pledge to transmute negatives into positives, but he pushed me too far. I can't forgive this. I won't. Betraying my most open intimacy is beyond anything acceptable. How could I have married him?

"You've chosen the wrong woman. This marriage isn't going to work. I want to go home."

"I have chosen exactly the right woman my darling." He takes me by the shoulders and puts on his tender face. "Don't you think I appreciate your absolute loyalty? Don't you know I can feel that you're upset and I can understand it from your conditioned point of view?"

"Conditioned." I stop. I'm too exhausted to argue.

"Yes my love. As much as you wish to deny it, you're different. You're more beautiful than others, you've been blessed with a good mind and strong intellect, and you're also extremely lucky. Look at your life - it's charmed, don't you agree?"

Not any more Prince Charming, I hear in my head.

"You've been taught to think in only one way. What we want to do here is expand your inner vision, show you new aspects of your God given gifts and the great opportunity to give thanks for them and use them. You don't have to think like the others, you're not one of them." He kisses my hand then looks at something behind me, then back to me with a quick half smile.

"I know one of the reasons you wanted to marry me is to help me politically. I appreciate that. There is selflessness in you which is one of your great assets. But you must also understand that everything you have been taught about intimacy and sex is from a singular, simplistic perception. It doesn't apply to people like us. We're different. We have different values and rules."

"Oh Phillip forget it. We're not different and I loved you. You're my husband. I wanted to be with you and no one else. I waited all my life for you. I never dreamed of being shared or knowing my husband is with someone else. But now that's smashed. Everything is ruined."

"Ruined?" He laughs. "You're enhanced silly girl. You're better than you ever were." His mood suddenly changes, anger crosses his face. "There won't be porters or Guides for two weeks. They were told to come back when this idyllic honeymoon is over. They left the day we arrived. You have no choice. The best thing to do is to remain open to all that happens."

It was confirmed. There is no safe guard. My world has been blown apart.

Then, in one split second Phillip turns gentle again, taking my hand up to his lips and kissing the palm. Holding my arm in his hands his kiss moves slowly and gently to my shoulder, then the hollow of my throat.

Physical feelings start to take control. Relief floods in with them. I'm peripherally aware I'm not thinking and only reacting. I want to think again but it's not working.

I feel the weight of loss dissipating as his touch makes me feel whole, luxurious, transcendent. I'm relaxing into his hands, like clay as I submerge myself into a zone of all feeling. Everything is soft and tingling.

Phillip carries me back to my rooms. Candles and incense have been lit. We lay in each other's arms feeling each other's heart ticking, our breath caressing the other's lips, tickling our ear lobes and cheeks. We hold each other closely and stroke each other softly, whispering the other one's name. Passion is left at the doorstep as we reinstate tenderness.

"I'm starving," Phillip abruptly pushes himself up and away from me, his little boy charm lighting his face. It ignites my heart and erases the moment of anger and rejection I had felt only micro seconds away. "Shall we eat?" he asks.

"Yes, but I have to dress. I'll only be naked for you."

"What a pity," said Phillip. "You're so magnificent. I wish I could share you with everyone."

I look at him, unbelieving what he said just now.

Reacting he adds, "but I won't."

"Thank you." I pull myself away and go to the dressing area where the two women wait for me. He thinks I don't hear him say, *"till tomorrow,"* before he hits the floor hard with his hand and leaves to probably find Virendra.

Chapter Twenty-Five

For the first time since arriving I insist on choosing my own clothes.

I can't help giggling at Phillip's choices. He is a sophisticate with elegant taste, but fashion is not something he understands. He thinks in cliché, a mix of sophisticated and elegant with a touch of cookie cutter copies of old movie stars. He's conservative in his perception of what he thinks makes women sexy. Sexy is my talent.

The silver sequined slip dress will form a halo as I move. It's the one item I would have chosen for myself.

I wish I could explain to the two handmaidens who look so anxious watching me go against the rules, that everyone should have the right to choose the way they want to look and most important, to think for them self. If they're not allowed to have their own physical reality, they can create that reality in their heads. No one can take another's thoughts away.

Or can they? I hear flash in my brain. I've got to stop trying to communicate beliefs to women with social consciousness so opposite my own. When they're ready they will know.

The one thing I managed to bring with me is my makeup. Using a lighter foundation then the handmaidens and smudging my eye liner instead of a thick straight black line I was liking what I saw in the mirror and feeling better about myself. I'm no longer the heroine in the palace tower, I'm a modern warrior in a sexy power dress. The two handmaidens giggle with pleasure at what I've become. I try to open the door. It's locked. I gesture to the women to open it, but they put up their hands in the universal sign of helplessness.

Waiting for someone to free me from this room, I pace in my silver armor, refusing offers of the vanilla and rose drink. It changes reality. I've got to stay alert. Think clearly. Be aware till this nightmare is over.

Anger continues to build a new layer of emotional armor inside. This won't happen again. Never again will I wait helplessly for someone to release me from behind a locked door.

On cue – or is he reading my mind, Virendra comes into the room.

I say nothing and look through him. Virendra is like a crocodile, capable of destroying without a thought.

I can never tell Phillip what I'm thinking. He and Virendra appear to be different, but its only in image. They're made from the same core.

Unknowingly I had committed not only to Phillip but to Virendra as well. The vow to love, honor and obey had fallen to "obey" both of them. Will I ever get home? These men are capable of unimaginable things. They'll kill me if I betray them.

Virendra watches me, a taunting smile on his lips.

"Why are you smiling?"

"Because you are stunning beyond words." He bows, seeming to enjoy my consternation at his words. "You're breathtaking," he continues.

I wish I'd never met Phillip. I made a spiritual pact with a devil. Two devils!

Virendra takes my hand. I pull it away.

"You're not going to play it that way." His eyes are cold, his voice menacing.

"I'm not playing."

"Good evening," interrupts Phillip walking through the door. Clicking his heels together he bows formally. "I understand you have decided to take over your handmaiden's duties and dress yourself." He tilted his head, amused. "I'm pleased with your appearance. That would have been exactly my choice."

"You were pleased by my choices before we were married. The romantic damsel image was getting tired."

An amused smile cut into his face, but I could see now how fake it is, how practiced and professional. Why didn't I see through his boyish charm, the easy look of innocence? If only he was ugly, so hideous I would be repelled. How could a man so beautiful be so terrible? And why? Something bad must have happened to him. But I must stay tuned. Keep objective.

Yet neediness and insecurity are starting to rear their hideous heads in this high stakes game. Death is an answer. Then I won't have to go through this. My destiny, my choice.

As I walk toward the window I stop myself and grasp the edges. If I jump it will be quick and easy and I could die within the folds of the mountains I love.

But my mother will be alone. She needs me. I'm her life, she has nothing else. If something happened, how would she survive another death in her circle of life? If I don't escape I may never see her again.

"Would you like to take a walk before dinner?" Phillip ask in his charming mode. "We have a surprise for you."

Any outsider who saw him now and knew what I was thinking would call me paranoid. Phillip had a remarkable ability to make people feel comfortable. Even now he is being successful with my feelings even though in my heart and somewhere on the thin periphery of objectivity, I know I can't trust him. When you lose trust in a person you can never love them the same way again.

"All right." Wrapping myself up in a large cashmere shawl and exchanging my silver sandals for sheep skin boots, I join the two men even though anxiety is clutching my heart. Are they going to kill me?

We're going to have to cross that single swaying bridge again. Virendra and Phillip will be on either side of me. Oh my god. I'm so dizzy I have to stop. They're going to kill me.

"It's all right darling," a tinge of tension in Phillip's voice. "You're safe. Just keep going."

I let them lead me, trusting that I will live to reach the other side. Reaching firm ground I look back, my breath catching at the incredible sight of the monastery carved into the side of the mountain, making me feel empowered that I survived the bridge across the chasm. It may be a sign I am meant to live.

Traversing a small gully we hike up a sloping path till we reach a precipice overlooking a canyon lit by the full moon.

Millions of stars twinkle against the velvet black sky with no bleed of light from any civilization nearby. Suddenly something swoops from a mountain peak, then another that lands close to them.

"Those are the monks," said Virendra, hushed. "They fly on full moon nights."

Spellbound, I watch dark objects fly through the air, their robes like billowing sails. "Incredible,"

217

I wonder if these monks who defy gravity and perform with the grace of seasoned circus performers, could be the robed figures in the room.

Virendra looks at me, smiles and shakes his head no.

Again he's reading my thoughts.

I feel despair sinking deeper and deeper into me. Paralyzing me so I can't defend myself. Not only does this man know me in the most intimate way, he also has the ability to enter and read my mind. Am I going insane or am I caught in some ominous space from which there is no escape?

Phillip hugs me. "Remarkable, isn't it?" he gestures toward the darkening chasm.

"It's terrifying," I look at Virendra rather than the monks flying through the air.

"What's wrong with you?" raw impatience sharpens his voice. "Are you going to see everything from the dark side? This is our honeymoon."

"Do monks die doing this?"

"Doom and gloom." Phillip said sharply. "The positive becomes negative. That's not good."

"What do you expect? Prisoners usually feel that way."

I move away and climb a large boulder and sit down, drawing my knees up close to my chest and wrapping my arms around them.

Phillip starts to follow but Virendra pulls him back. They walk away, their arms around each other.

He's probably telling him what I'm thinking. I scan the heavens for another glimpse of the flying monks, but the Earth has moved and they probably can no longer fly because the moon doesn't cast the kind of light they need.

If only I could use this shawl as a sail and jump off the mountain and fly away from the man I had thought was my love.

Married less than a week I have gone through the most depraved moments of my life. I want my life back. Do I have a way out?

The two men walk toward me in their unholy alliance.

I back toward the edge of the boulder. Should I submit to them or kill myself? Submission or death?

Chapter Twenty-Six

I chose to join them for dinner and couldn't stop giggling. It was probably the wine, but the stories Virendra and Phillip were telling about prep school were extremely funny.

Just a few hours ago I thought about throwing myself off a cliff, and now I'm having a good time. Glad I didn't die. I'm going to survive this. I have so much to live for. "I need a refill."

"You're beyond your usual limit," Phillip smiled as he poured more licorice brandy into my glass.

"That's right. I am beyond my usual limit. This is all beyond my usual limit. And this is a beyond the usual limits celebration. It's about having our lives together, not usual limits."

Virendra stared at me. Frightened I look away. *Remember light takes out the dark,* that voice in my head said.

Be care*ful what you think,* warned the disconnected voice. *Virendra could be listening.*

Seemingly clueless Phillip has reverted to the man I had fallen in love with. Charming, enticing, playful and funny we could have had such a wonderful time if

Virendra hadn't catapulted me from wonder to debasement.

I can't turn off my repulsion of this exotic man and his influence over Phillip. The influence is so iron clad I know Virendra could take me against my will without Phillip's interference. He is the core of evil. Perhaps Phillip is less his ally and deeply afraid of him?

A servant brings in a large silver tray with a bowl of soft vanilla ice cream. Next to it is a chafing dish filled with bubbling hot fudge. Hot fudge is my favorite though I rarely have it. But tonight is special.

"Let me serve you," Phillip's eyes are shining. Maybe he's come back to me, the man I loved. My Prince. My love.

Taking the spoon he fills a large dish with ice cream and a heaping portion of hot fudge. "I want to feed you. I want to give you treats and good feelings." He scooped up a huge helping of ice cream and hot fudge in the large silver-serving spoon and brings it to my mouth. Some dribbles as I swallow the huge helping and he licks it off.

Taking the spoon from Phillip, I spoon up an even larger serving and feed it to him, spilling it and doing as he did to me.

Feeding each other playfully, we smooth the ice cream over our bodies and lick it off. The licks are turning hot, pulsing two energies into one as our bodies feel like they're melting into a single soft moving entity.

We don't notice Virendra leave or the candles burn down.

"Take me," I whisper in his ear. "I want you inside me. I want you to fill and empty into me." Wrapping my naked legs around Phillip I rub my body against his. "It can always be like this. This rapture. This forever."

Helping me rise from the floor Phillip drapes my naked figure with a linen tablecloth. Then, hand in hand like two young children we leave the dining hall and go to my rooms where the mineral bath has been circled with scented Jasmine candles.

Removing the linen tablecloth, the two handmaidens sponge my sticky body with soap then, rinse me with clear warm water from oak buckets as Phillip, being washed as well by his man-servant, watches. Submerging completely in the mineral pool, I emerge to Phillip holding the towel and carefully drying me.

"This week has been difficult for me as well," he whispers, as he picks me up and carries me to my bed, placing me carefully upon the pillows.

He kneels. "May I join you?"

"Of course." I settle back on the soft silk pillows as Phillip begins to trace a path from my neck to the tops of my thighs with his lips. "Please," I wet two fingers and circle my nipples. My knees open to display the glistening place between my thighs where so much could happen.

Phillip watches with growing excitement as my nipples harden, I wet my lips and my hips quiver.

Holding his gaze I whisper over and over again, "I want you, I need you," I feel myself growing wet as my hips start to follow some inner rhythm pulsating and shuddering in a primitive beat for his body to connect with mine.

My hips lift high and wait, begging him to enter me. Instead he kneels and covers my shaved labials with his mouth.

Stretching toward him he takes me and turns me over, running his hands over me, exploring every part of me as I quiver with unresolved passion. Putting his hands under me he raises me up and I automatically, without thinking, spread my legs wider.

Trained to detach from personal feelings, the actress/model in me watches the proceedings. I'm the observer, surprised I can behave with such unbridled abandon. Phillip is insatiable as he gnaws and sucks and licks me into orgasmic spirals of pleasure.

"We're going to put you in the GUINESS BOOK OF RECORDS if you have any more orgasms," he says, turning me over and holding the hands I had automatically placed over my head.

"Please." I pleaded, my hips straining up to him.

"Are you sure?" he asked.

"Very."

223

He pushes into me, withdraws then slams, pounding as I lift my legs over his head. Pausing for a freezing instant, a shout accompanies a mutual explosion as we lock together in rapture, soaring to a universe where only the two of us exist. In absolute concert we float back to the cloud of our bed and drift to sleep, arms wrapped around each other.

In total darkness a dark shape approaches the bed.

Chapter Twenty-Seven

Waking up to daylight streaming through the slats of the ancient windows, Phillip still sleeps, holding me. Was I dreaming Virendra climbed into our bed last night? There's a spicy essence like turmeric on my pillow.

Did Phillip hold me as Virendra entered me? I think I tried to scream but Phillip's mouth covered mine and I was so dizzy, so completely into a new and mysterious sensual state, I'm not sure it happened. It's so fuzzy I may have lost consciousness.

It's tender between my legs. Phillip and I had been very passionate. But what if Virendra had been there?

I pulled away from Phillip's hold and joined the handmaidens for my bath. As they soaped and massaged me I tried to ask if I was alone with Phillip last night. They responded with shrugs, either not knowing or not wanting to understand what I was asking.

But so what. After everything that's happened if Virendra joined us there was nothing I could have done. My life is no longer my own, my body no longer belongs to me. Others have taken control. I can only watch and try to remember so some day I can give testimony to this horror I'm in. I've got to use my discipline and training to keep separate from this terrible reality

Tying a white gauze robe loosely over my naked body, I climb back in bed with Phillip who sits behind a large breakfast tray of fresh fruit, yogurt, thick chunks of bread, black tea and honey. I kiss his proffered cheek and begin to eat voraciously.

Phillip watched, amused. "I've never seen you eat like this."

"I had an exhausting night." I dipped a chunk of bread into a bowl of honey and licked the bread suggestively. "I need my strength, maybe a few extra pounds. Or maybe a lot of extra pounds so I can guard myself with my flesh."

I searched through the fruit in a basket till I found the right fig, carefully cutting its purple skin into three parts and exposing the juicy pink center. "The two of you can be quite exhausting." I put my mouth over the fig and sucked the center.

Phillip's eyes widen but he doesn't say anything. Quietly and elegantly he puts his teacup down. A smile flutters at his lips for a brief moment, then he's serious again. "Darling, did you think Virendra was with us?"

I nod and try to keep my face free of expression as I stir milk into my tea. I want to read his feelings.

"We made love, darling. Did you want Virendra to join us?

His question surprised me. It was shocking. "Of course not." I stammered.

"We have been alone." His voice is soft and gentle. "You know darling," he picked up the tray and put it aside, "there have never been others. I was teasing you when I said that Virendra was in the wagon with you. Perhaps I shouldn't have done that." He took my hand and kissed it.

"Then why did you?" A strange prickly feeling moved up and down my back. I had seen him oozing sincere so many times for the cameras, I know this behavior is fake.

"I want to see how you would react to the idea of a different partner. I can't tell you how glorious and stunning it is to watch a beautiful girl like you being fucked, whether you're doing it yourself or not."

I can't say a word. I don't know what to say. I just can't believe this is happening. Will his lies and betrayals ever stop?

"Did you think there were others giving you oral sex in the marble chamber?" he was asking me.

My voice is choked. "I know there were. I saw them."

"Did you see anyone's face?"

"No, of course not. They were hooded."

"You *think* there were others," he continued, "because you really want to have them. It's your fantasy."

"Absolutely not."

I'm reacting. My emotions are taking over and I'm getting defensive. I need to ground myself, keep objective.

"That's what the test is for, to see if you would believe it. We created your fantasy for you. We set the stage and put in the suggestions and you filled it with your imagination. You had contact lenses inserted while you were in a deep sleep that created a virtual reality program for you. You only saw what we had programmed you to see. What you were feeling was coming from me."

"If this is true, how could you do such a thing? Why in the world would you do this?"

He continued. "That's why you had the dream about Virendra last night. I expected this reaction, it's exactly as I thought it would be and I couldn't be happier. You are absolutely marvelous, my love. I knew you would want to give yourself to others, otherwise you wouldn't dream it. We will have a wonderful life together, I know it!" He kissed my cheek and smiled, looking strangely young and innocent.

I stared at him in disbelief. He's crazy. Could he possibly think I would do anything like that?

He kissed my face but I didn't respond. I stayed quiet and composed as he got out of bed, naked and hard, rubbing his erect penis. He stood for a moment looking at me. His excitement had vanished and he had put on his most somber expression. "You'll understand this much better once you're completely into it," he said. "Right now you have to deny it. It's your conditioning. You think you should not enjoy any of this. But we've talked about that and I have no doubt you'll grasp it."

I can't speak. He's lying. There had been other people touching and entering me. I remember the feeling. Despair is creeping into me. Doubts are darting in and out. Maybe he's telling the truth. There were no others. I made it up as he said I was.

"Dress in trekking clothes," he told me on his way out. "Have the women pack a case for a few days. Make sure they pack the long ivory dress in the wardrobe with its accessories. I think we're all getting a bit of cabin fever and need to go on a little excursion. I'm certain you'll enjoy this."

"With Virendra?" I try to remain calm.

Phillip smiles, a strange kind of knowing smile. "He's gone ahead to make arrangements."

Ignoring me completely he kisses the air goodbye and turns to leave, covering his naked body with a robe over his shoulders, his penis still erect.

How I wish I could call him back and try to change his reality. But he doesn't want me. I haven't felt really connected to him since our first night together He has someone else. Virendra.

I want to hate him, to feel disgust, yet I still want to please him. Is it because he was my first, or am I playing with the devil? Where is my mind?

Virendra is making the arrangements. I'm facing the unknown.

Chapter Twenty-Eight

The chimes of the Monks calling the birds to get their morning breadcrumbs did their best to soothe me. It was such a peaceful environment, but my physical soreness dissected the calm with its stinging reminder of the sexual extravagances of Virendra and Phillip.

Phillip had called this "a small excursion," but the amount of baggage and people made it look more like a pageant. Since I met Phillip, everything has become an extension of the norm.

Once again I fault myself for ignoring my instincts to postpone the marriage even though I was practically trampled with warning signs along the way. Instead I kept riding the merry go round of my self-imposed fairy tale, existing in a foggy half-life of single focus on Phillip; his loving helpmate and pin up doll who dressed for him and filled his expectations, ignoring the smudged clarity of my doubts. I had accepted the unacceptable.

A handmaiden came over and wrapped a cashmere shawl around my shoulders. I was grateful, I hadn't realized how cold it had become. Like the avalanche...

Oh my god. The avalanche! I don't want to think about that. I want to stay where I am now. There is something to learn here. I don't want to go back to that body in the hospital. It's too frightening. I could die. What if I lose what I know now if I die? Can I change the way I experienced my honeymoon? Can I make the image positive in my heart?

The picture perfect sky with it's pastel of powder blue and indigo vapors becomes a trail to traverse from earth to heaven. If I look carefully, maybe I can see Angels and perhaps God watching our caravan.

Phillip came up behind and hugged me. I turned and kissed him. I think my eyes are shining. "We have an audience," I tell him, tilting my head with a smile and looking past him.

"Really?" He looks over his shoulder intrigued, then back. "Who is it?"

"God. The Angels. If you look closely you can see them." I gesture toward the sky but he doesn't look where I'm pointing. Instead he stares at me a beat then takes me by the arm. "I love your imagination." He starts up the path, urging me along. "Let's hurry. We're to meet a great and revered teacher."

We come to a simple garden made mostly of stone and a few well-placed shrubs. Long and narrow, the focus appears to be on a pyramid shaped alter so simple it could have been a natural formation, but it wasn't.

"I'd like to stop here a moment." I'm drawn to a stone bench from which I can appreciate the sculpture. A sense of peace encompasses me. My short life has been exhausting till now. I've lived with the constant struggle to be perfect in order to survive. And now, surrounded by the gray/purple of the mammoth mountains, the sharp thin air fills me with vibrancy and truth. I can sit back and watch life float around me.

A shiver goes through me. A reminder to pay attention and not let my mind play games. Almost every time I cancel a feeling because of reason, I learn later that my instincts were right. But why don't I learn the lesson to listen when things don't feel right?

Phillip is a mistake. I had fallen in love with an image rather than the reality. I ignored the clues and was mesmerized by the glamour.

Stop it! My mind is rattling, shaking my trust. My intellect and feelings are sparring and struggling, each one looking for dominance, forgetting that joined, they work better as one.

Perhaps, there is no right or wrong. It's how we choose to see what happens, it's our perception. Are we a victim or victor? Oppressed by an experience or educated? Do mistakes bend us or are we uplifted in the light of new awareness?

There should be triumphs in the course of experience, stepping stones for self-knowledge. We need to recognize clues in the game of life that will help us read our genetically implanted road maps to Nirvana or Heaven, whatever one calls it.

I look at Phillip. For the first time in a long time his eyes meet mine. It's times like these I believe we're meant to be together.

He puts his hand on my knee and its then I realize I've been sitting with my legs drawn up, each foot placed over the knee of the opposite leg in what Yogis call *the Lotus pose*. Its not an easy position to get into, and I have no memory of doing it. But I'm definitely sitting this way.

Phillip's eyes stayed fixed on mine. I had hoped he would be the brother I never had, my best friend, my confidant. I believed he offered protection, strength and love. As my teacher I respected him and as a lover he promised new and mysterious feelings that made me crave him. I had hoped we'd never be apart. But now I can't trust him and without trust, there is no love.

We continue to gaze at each other till a slight, middle-aged man in the maroon robes of a monk stops at the bench and bows, his bald head gleaming. Virendra comes up and stands next to him, his head bowed as well. All my good feelings leave when I see Verendra. Every bit of me tightens with anxiety, maybe fear. Virendra, introduces the monk as Sonom.

My uncontrollable anger at Virendra is escalating by the second. I can't bear his hold on Phillip. He has too much power. He has easily driven a wedge through our relationship and destroyed my trust in the man to whom I had pledged my life. He is Svengali, Rasputin.

Knowledge is power and for that I will not be one of his victims. Fighting with objectivity and light I'll win.

"Sonom will escort us to the teacher," Virendra interrupted my plans.

We walk through two more gardens before reaching a white washed brick building. The clean bright white of the painted bricks and the maroon tiles of the roofs perfectly match the robes of the priests I had seen. In the distance I hear the tinkle and chimes of bells, joyful sounds that penetrate my anxiety and help to calm and transform my fear.

Quickening with anticipation we walk through the dark cold halls and enter a small room where an older man in the maroon robes of a monks sits signing papers. Like Virendra, he looks as if he would be more comfortable in a three-piece suit.

With a friendly easy smile and an agility that belies the wrinkles on his face, he swings around the desk and holds out his hands, taking one of mine in both of his as he gazes at me, his eyes boring intensely into mine. He's reading me. I know this man has come into my mind and can see what is there now and what was there in the past.

I don't understand what is happening. I return from the past and replay what I believe is the present. Each event seems to have solidity. But which is the present? Am I going nuts or am I immersed in a new kind of reality? A parallel universe.

My mother used to accuse me of falling into the grips of an overactive imagination. But a new and insistent self has taught me to step outside all I know and join a new aspect of perception, an objective reality. I had it as a child and had forgotten I knew how to do that till now. When once again I'm in a stressful position that I can't get out of,

"Yes," the man said finally, his gray eyes withdrawing from my brain and going back into his lined, twinkling face.

Could this man be other than mortal, or am I just going off the deep end?

He motions me to sit in the simple wood chair in front of his desk. The office is sparse with the exception of a bouquet of mountain flowers and leather bound books. "So my dear Initiate, you have learned many things here."

"*Initiate?* Perhaps you can tell me what that means and what things have I learned?"

The man smiled. "You wish to remember and see more clearly?"

A twinge of fear flutters through me. Remember he's the teacher, he's supposed to understand the truths of the universe and bring disciples to understanding. "I'm not sure," I admitted for the first time to myself.

"We are very happy to have you here," he said. "We open our doors as well as our hearts to bring you through this journey. You are here for experience. Convention is not allowed nor judgment upon others, unless of course, another is made to suffer. That is not acceptable. We strive for perfection and we do not compromise. The experience is the teacher."

I listened expectantly. Perhaps Phillip is telling the truth and Virendra is not the villain I think he is. Pangs of guilt and remorse try to creep into my feelings, but something inside me brushes them away.

"You shall be the only judge of your behavior," he was saying to me. "We are here to serve you. That is all."

"Serve me in what way?" There is tension in my voice.

"Ritual," he answered firmly. "Ritual implies understanding," he explained. "Understanding the order of events best suited for the fulfillment of a goal."

"To what activity is your ritual designed? And what is the goal?" I already knew the answer.

"The particular ritual for which you have been brought on your wedding trip is the joining of your spirit, your entity with your mate's. That is a part of the verbal vow you have made is it not?" he asked.

Warily I nod.

"Ritual love making elevates the mundane to the spiritual. It empowers the sexual act with a meaning that lasts beyond life itself."

"The ritual act is transcendental," he continues, "a bridge between the known to the unknown. Sexual ritual can open the soul to the deep experience of ecstasy. Ritual lovemaking is the quickest and most direct way to liberation within a lifetime. We have dedicated ourselves to the liberation of our souls and therefore have chosen as one of the ways, the practice of sexual energy."

I heard his words and knew I wasn't dreaming. I was definitely in a cold drafty temple somewhere in the mountains, probably the Himalayas. If I yelled and screamed for help, who would hear me?

There are people dressed as priests, but how can I be sure if they're authentic or not? I'm not sure of anything. I don't know if this is my imagination, a dream or reality.

"Accounts of sexual rites and rituals exist in all ancient religious traditions," the man was saying. "Paganism was born out of sexual ritual and recognition of the power and joy inherent in the sexual act."

So, this is it. I'm to be subjected to more, probably worse sexual scenarios than those in the sanctuary. "Paganism" is a red flag. I can try to resist but what good will that do? I'm all alone and I'm beginning to feel sick. I don't want to submit to the will of others, to please them, to go beyond my personal and private boundaries to fulfill someone else's. Will I ever be in charge? I'm so afraid of the future. I've seen myself in the hospital and I'm not sure if it happened already or if I'm deep into my past life and living it again.

None of this is right. Dread is making its presence felt and this time I'll listen. It had tried to warn me once and it's doing it again. I must save myself. I'm so afraid of losing my freedom. But if I don't submit I'll be dead.

Some of the models I worked with had told me stories about young women seduced with promises of lucrative modeling assignments who were then sold into white slavery. Is that what is happening? Is Phillip the pimp for some high-class slavery ring?

I can't stop crying, I feel so weak, so devastated I can barely see as the two handmaidens lead me to a simple monk's cell that is to be my room.

I sit on the low cot and focus on the beam of light coming through a long narrow slit in the wall. I don't notice the two women leave.

From a source deep in my consciousness I am drawn to the beam and ask it to fill my body. A quivering, rumbling, something like an internal combustion machine enters every particle, atom and cell, catapulting my body into a rotating orbit that dissolves it and lets me slide through the slit of the window into the brilliant mountain air. I've done this before but I don't know when nor do I remember how. But I do know I am safe as I soar above the mountaintops, searching for the bells filling the air.

Like a bird I sweep toward a donkey train, it's lead donkey is festooned with bells. The tinkling and ringing actually lift me through the layers of air and I swoop over a town of multicolored prayer flags waving from the tops of the temples. I wave back. I'm having a ball. The little voice in my head is cautioning me not to get lost with the joy I'm having and to remember the monastery.

Can I go back to NY now? Can I do that? It's natural to talk to the voice. It's the only friend I have. I don't doubt its part of me. It's more real than my skin, another part of me no one sees but me. It's in my head.

Someone's pulling my hair. I'm in a chair as the two silent handmaidens paint my face and comb my hair straight. There is no sign I've been away. The handmaidens say nothing.

How did I get from outside the Monastery to this room? Did I never go away? Did I dream I was flying? My imagination?

Yet I know in my heart it had been true. I'd done that before. I know how to leave my body but I have to be careful, doubt and fear can prevent it from happening again.

What are they going to do to me? Am I to be a shadow puppet for Phillip's social and political display?

Will they kill me if I don't bend to their demands? If they believe I'm sincere I'll survive.

There are no mirrors or shiny surfaces to see myself so I have no idea what I look like. Only that they painted me with a light dusting of sterling silver powder ground from silver sheets. The powder was held together with a lilac scented cream. They left my hair loose and unadorned, the way I like it. Then wrapped a floor length white cashmere shawl around me before we set off through a labyrinth of winding passages constructed of cold gray stone.

Leading me into an austere room made of the same stone, it's filled with people wearing hooded gray cloaks.

This could be a movie set, but real or not it feels eerie. I don't see cameras but they can be concealed.

Why would Phillip bring me all the way here just to reach a sexual climax? A giggle is threatening. Am I wrong not to believe him? Are my fears shading his desire to unite with me?

I'm told to sit on the stone bench in the center of the room. I comply and close my eyes, focusing on my breathing to quiet my nerves. When I feet quiet I open my eyes to see Phillip kneeling in front of me, wearing nothing but a light beige cashmere cape. A rush of excitement comes over me and I start to say his name, but he quiets me with a light hush and lifts my hand to his lips.

"My darling, he practically whispers. "You have the attributes I most desire and would like to make a part of me. I believe that if we follow the strict rules of sexual ardor, I will merge with you in a blending of energies that shall produce a single entity – we will become one."

Part of me is excited by what he says, but a larger part doesn't believe a word and I'm scared. Very scared. I don't try to see the faces inside the hoods of the monks or search for a camera. Once again Phillip has engulfed me in a reaction of relief and love. I connect with him. He makes me feel better. He joins with every part of me and I feel whole with his energy blending with mine.

Seeming to sense that, Phillip puts up his hand to stop me.

"I'll lead you."

He settles himself on the floor against a large gray cushion. "The fluids you secrete when you become aroused are very precious," he says. "They are not to be taken for granted nor should they be wasted. This creamy fluid is nectar for the Gods from their Goddesses. If I drink your nectar or take it into myself with my penis inside you, it prolongs my health, my life and my virility. It shall bond me to you because by drinking your nectar, you become part of me. When we are joined our senses become more sensitive than the separate ones we have.

I say nothing. It's hard to keep from laughing. We're out of light giggle country and verging on uncontrollable hysteria.

"This initial part of the service is important to me," he was saying. "I teased you about the wagon and I hope you will forgive me. Let me take you now with all the love I hold in my heart and the hope in my soul that we shall become one."

How I want to believe him. My body opened to him long before permission came from my mind. But the script he read is so disconnected from his heart. He had not meant anything he had so obviously memorized. And worse, we have an audience. Yet I'm moist between my legs.

Images of the erotic engravings of sex acts in the entrance of the temple whirled into my head. Was I to be a temple whore like the ones I had read about in ancient Egypt? Supposed holy men used temple goddess's bodies to transport themselves to higher consciousness.

Recoiling at the thought I steadied myself as the two handmaidens help me up and Phillip's boys help him to his feet. As the women remove the cashmere blanket wrapped around me, Phillip's eyes widen with pleasure at my silvered vision. The two young men come and sit on either side of his feet and begin to run their small hands up his legs to his inner thighs. As his penis quivers they caress it in a loving gentle way.

At the same time one handmaiden gently rubs my nipples while playfully the other woman kisses the tip of my nose, my breasts then nuzzles playfully between my legs.

Phillip is getting excited.

The handmaidens spread my legs wide then dab my sex with a damp perfumed cloth.

Phillip's penis twitches and swells as I open my legs where the place between my thighs is glistening.

A handmaiden produces a small tub of honey and with a delicate ivory spoon fills my vagina with the golden creamy substance. She offers the last spoonful to me and I lick off half and motion they take the rest to Phillip.

He nods his approval and licks the spoon with relish then comes to me, his penis swollen and throbbing. The handmaidens and young men withdraw to the sides of the room.

I sit on the hard bench, legs spread, hands gripping the edge, open, waiting, glistening with vibrant energy. Tilting my head back, lips parted, breathing deep and slow, I offer myself to Phillip who takes my nipples in his fingers and squeezes them so hard I nearly crumble from the pain. Continuing to squeeze my nipples, he holds me with his eyes while an all encompassing pain grabs me and makes me melt into its angles, turning the sharpness into pleasure, a pleasure of such an exquisite nature I can hardly believe it's happening. Pain is the other side of pleasure. I can see why people choose death instead of enduring it. But to melt it with objective clarity is the key to freedom and I choose to use that.

Phillip replaces his fingers with his tongue and lips, lightly licking and kissing my nipples, soothing and loving them, making my body relax with relief as his hands move to my navel then travel to my inner thighs, then hold them as his mouth follows to that warm dark place.

Turning me over he drapes me over the bench, his fingers caressing me softy, spreading my knees as he laps the honey that had been spooned inside me.

Watching on an inner split screen - participant and observer – with feelings in my body having sensations of which I never dreamed. I had never done anything like this, let alone in front of other people. But Phillip excites me, makes me want him so much I can only think of satisfying him, pleasing him, making him happy.

He draws back. "I worship you." He holds his hand out to me to join him on the carpet.

I lay there, knees raised, thighs spread, arms over my head as I arch and wait for him. He places his mouth between my legs and begins to gently nibble. My moaning sparks titters and movement among the cluster of robed figures but I block feelings about it.

Phillip pushes back the hood of my clitoris and keeps it there as he fixes his lips against it and sucks.

I shudder in orgasm, writhing, wanting, begging him to enter and fill me.

He pulls back, his face smeared, exuding a primal energy I had not seen before as I roll with desire, wanting him so much. In one movement he turns me over and lifts my knees to a crouch then slides in beneath me, pulling me down till I'm sitting on his mouth as he plays with my nipples and drinks from me.

I held on to his hair, his legs, not knowing what to do with myself as again and again and again he brings me to the outer limits of total pleasure. Lowering my back against his knees I face him as he continues to drink from what he calls my fountain of nectar.

Chapter Twenty-Nine

If I've felt shrouded since the day I walked down the aisle, the days since we made love in the temple opened up and became the opposite.

Phillip has the power to lift me out of my body and give me a happiness I've never had before. I'm drunk with it. Ecstatic.

During the days we trek through the countryside, hiking through jungle environments to ice covered rock and snow. Traversing in a single day spectacular examples of Earth's treasures, we're also on a marathon sexual odyssey, exploring every position in every location whether inside a temple or outside in snow. Breathing thin oxygen we climb rocks and clutch each other in passion, thoughts altered and visions magnified. In our minds we create a single beam of light.

One overnight trek after a late afternoon shower I returned from meditating on a promontory overlooking a lush green valley. Everything had been so sparkling and fresh I envisioned myself in the center of an emerald. But as I enter the tent my elation deflates when I see the strange look on Phillip's face. Following his gaze I discover I'd been sitting in the midst of slimy black Leeches that covered the bottom half of my yellow rain pancho.

Lighting a cigarette Phillip approaches me, grinning. "I'll burn them off like Humphrey Bogart did to Katherine Hepburn in *The African Queen*."

"Oh no, you won't. These are *real* Leeches." I start to turn away but Phillip's two men come into the tent and hold me while Phillip strips off my clothing and attaches the burning end of the cigarette on to the leeches that had made it to my skin. Every time the heat of the burning cigarette comes close to me I try to get away but I can't. Squeezing my eyes shut I hear the sizzle of the leech's death. Each time I pray it's the last.

Phillip then wraps me in a rough wool blanket and takes me to another tent where he grabs me with such brutality I'm stunned. Without kissing me he roughly throws me to the ground, straddles me, unzips his fly and puts himself into me, never touching me with anything other than his penis.

But as brutal and devastated as I feel, the moment he enters me a familiar peace comes over me. I love this man and despite the brutality, I allow him to become a source of sanctuary.

I didn't recoil when Virendra came to our bed the morning after the trek. He sat on the side of the bed and took my hand and kissed it. "You were very brave."

"I was terrified. If I hadn't been fantasizing I was Katherine Hepburn in the AFRICAN QUEEN, I don't think I would have been still enough for Phillip to do that."

"Next time rub salt on the leeches. It gets them off immediately," he advised, smiling.

"Now you tell us! Thanks!" I actually found myself genuinely smiling back at him.

"Forgive me." He lightly stroked my hand. Phillip moved closer, his warm breath blanketing his soft kiss on my bare shoulder.

Shivering I grab the bed sheet closer, drawing it to my neck and scooting down into a fetal position. Phillip kisses me lightly on the forehead.

Virendra gently rubs my neck and shoulders and together the two men relax me into a dreamy half sleep. Sensually I'm aware Virendra's hands had moved further from my shoulders to the tops of my breasts and down to my nipples. His strong fingers are strange as he circles and rubs me, touching me in front of my husband who lay naked besides me, watching.

As Virendra massages my abdomen and thighs then backs of my knees, I push myself closer to Phillip, gasping as Virendra's hand comes around to my groin. I hold Phillip tightly as Virendra moves down between my legs and begins to suck my clitoris, exploding me into a level of feeling I have never had before.

Phillip enters me from the front, kissing me passionately, shutting off my scream as Virandra enters me from behind. Moaning and sobbing the three of us rock in tandem, limbs and emotions melting, merging into one.

Strange energy rushes through me as the two friends vibrate inside me, holding each other as they hold me between them and ejaculating simultaneously inside of me. Tightening I draw their semen up, pushing it up like the snake of Kundalini shooting past my chakras.

Withdrawing, the two men hold me as a strange man comes in followed by one of my handmaidens, a large Boa Constrictor coiled around her arm. Any power I had envisioned the Kundalini had given me quickly evaporated. I wanted to run away from this man, the handmaiden, the snake and the bed that Virendra and Phillip had left.

Nodding to me the man introduces himself, "I'm Satir".

I love animals and have good rapport with most of them, but snakes, lizards and rodents are in another universe for me. Once I had done a famous poster lying nude on a bare white floor, a python stretched from my mouth to my toes. The shot was particularly powerful because it showed the two tongues touching. But the tongues hadn't touched for real, the snake was done in the computer. I wasn't nude either but had on a sheer body suit and the snake was added after the shot was taken, in the lab. Still the image affected me in an uncomfortable way. So now I'm being confronted with a reenactment of that shot for real. How did they know?

"We are bringing you the snake to prove your openness and trust in all things," said Satir. "This symbol of evil in the Garden of Eden is also part of the life force. And as part of that creation you and the snake shall become one. You are both created from that which gives life," said the teacher.

"Oh no. I won't."

"Yes," said Virendra in the low dulcet tones I was starting to respond to.

The man they called the great teacher came in to watch. Phillip stood quietly to the side.

Uncoiling the snake from her arm, the handmaiden placed it on the floor next to me, signaling to the snake to keep its head high. I freeze. I'm afraid to breathe.

The handmaiden walks away and the snake starts moving up my leg. It's cold and heavy. There is no warmth in this terrifying being.

"Breath normally and stay still," Virendra whispers as the snake explores my waist and rib cage.

I pray everything is going to be all right. I'm going to survive this. It's not really happening. It's my imagination.

But it's not. Something is wrong. It's too quiet, too posed. Something else is happening but I'm too scared to

251

move, to look around. Maybe this is staged, I want it to feel unreal. It's the worst test of my life. If I tense or gave in to fear, the snake will kill me. I don't want to die this way. It would be horrible.

Is this a test to leave darkness behind and experience only the positive as Phillip said I needed to do? But this test is beyond acceptable. It's put my life on balance. I'm so *scared*. But if I show it, I'll be dead.

Or am I dead already? Am I lying on a slab reliving a life I chose when I buried my personal code of ethics to save my life? Have I crossed the line and entered a consciousness in order to join with this stranger I married?

Wild, crazy, outrageously inventive, Phillip is able to stimulate me to heights so extraordinary I never would have known existed without him. I never dreamed I could step this far out to please someone, but can I look at myself again? Will I have the chance?

The snake slid between my breasts, it's head on a parallel with my mouth, it's cold heavy weight on my chest. I don't know if this snake is tame or wild or if you can train a snake. It's a huge, alien, cold primitive. and I think, unfeeling, mind. If I don't breathe naturally it will react and strike and kill me. At this point its striking point is my face. I could be blinded, maimed or killed. But then, if I'm supposed to die, then I'll die.

Almost, on cue, the snake begins to slither downward, pausing with its tongue on my nipple for a cold, chilling, terrifying moment, then continues down between my legs.

The handmaidens grab my ankles and keep me steady while the snake explores me, poking it's head into and up inside of me. I shut my eyes tight. *Please god. Help me.* It was then the snake exits and slides back to its original position, curled like a rope at my foot.

Only when the handmaiden takes the snake away does the room come back into focus and I see I have an audience. Not caring I fall to my knees, forehead on the floor, thank you Lord for this deliverance, I pray. Looking up I see I'm alone with Phillip.

"I'm so proud of you," he said like he had so many times before, his gorgeous smile lighting up his handsome face. His smile is what made me fall in love with him. The smile that had made me happy.

It no longer did. I see him clearly. His face is a mask. He's not proud of me. He's glad I got through one of the worst experiences of my life. Testing me in front of a group of nameless strangers, putting me through a paralyzing terror he says makes him proud.

Fury rushes through my body. Everything is suddenly clear. Phillip is using me for his agenda. I had held the right kind of emotional and material props for him, promising a life of submission and performance. I was his property and he'd keep me happy as long as I performed for him and his guests.

As he takes me in his arms a shiver of fear turns to sobs. I'm saying goodbye to the man I loved, the joy I had with him. He lost my trust and I'll never trust him again.

If I tell him how I feel he might do something terrible, even kill me. I'm not like his circle and they know it. There can never be mutual trust. Yet even with all of this, I still feel something I can only identify as love for what I believed is hidden somewhere in his soul.

Soaking in a hot scented bath after we return I can't stop thinking about what had just happened. Had it all been to prove that nothing outside the self ever lasts, that physical joy is fleeting, just a quick blink in life? If one acts without heed to the future, will the ramifications destroy that person? Or does it matter?

It may be pre-ordained, said that voice in my head.

Scrubbing myself as clean as possible and feeling a bit better, I dress in the thick white cashmere pant and sweater and the sheepskin coat Phillip had given me the first day we landed. Hugging it close, hoping to re-create the positive feelings I had when I first received it. It didn't work.

"I'm taking a walk," I announce to the two women who race to get their jackets. They would never allow me to leave by myself, they even escort me from one room to the other.

I had not yet explored the temple. I was sure there were some very interesting things to see. Phillip had said because of the sanctity and priceless worth of the treasures there were rules all visitors must follow. I don't believe him.

Access to the temple is not a big issue and Phillip could have made light of my curiosity, but he didn't. He chose to lie. A choice he has continued from the first time we met.

Admittedly, I was fascinated with the perversity of the sexual play and its strange sensations. But the absolute terror of that snake widened the sliver of consciousness and shed reality on the prospect of unconditional love. It wasn't possible. My gates had closed.

Opening the huge wooden door of the temple I walk out, the handmaidens scurrying behind me before it slams shut.

Chapter Thirty

I hadn't thought much about crossing international borders once my career took off. Flying around in jumbo private jets to exotic places meant little more to me than deciding what clothes to bring. Glamour was my norm.

So it was with a bit of surprise when the plane came in over Manhattan, I got tears in my eyes as I looked down on the vibrant island holding so many people and their manifestations.

I wondered what would happen if some super entity ripped away the bridges and tunnels leading to Manhattan, loosen the underpinnings and detach the entire island so it could float out to sea as a non-functioning city, a floating urban museum, a world park for people to visit and stay no longer than a few months. The floating city would depend on the currents of the ocean to take it to various locations and climates which would add a bonus for mystery and excitement.

Leaning over I kissed the cold glass window that framed the city I loved so much and had done so much for me. I wish I could wrap it up and keep it in my pocket so I could have Manhattan anytime.

I can hardly wait to get to Phillip's Fifth Avenue apartment so I can arrange to see Catherine and my mother. I think I'll walk to their apartments on those streets I can call home.

I want to get in touch with these familiar feelings, regain the sense of who I was and how I might have changed. Have I lost myself? How can my past life integrate with the new person I've become? What's left of who I thought I was before this silent and secret transformation? Will others know? How will they feel about me?

Strangely I think the honeymoon/initiation has made me ready for Washington, a place where public exposure means a single misplaced word could end a lifetime career. I've learned that it's a place where privacy is so precarious one of the most important ingredients one needs to survive is self-discipline. Life in Washington's public sphere is like walking on a razor's edge, knowing hungry beasts of prey wait on either side for you to slip and fall. In order to walk that edge one has to be inured to pain.

Minutes after we had taken off from Asia, we received a crackling cell phone call from Courtney Jenkins who breathlessly announced we were to be the guests of honor at a party she was putting together to honor our return. Speeding north on the Connecticut turnpike to her Darien Connecticut estate she explained that

Bernstein and Kalman had arranged the party to greet us before we went back to Washington. She rattled off a guest list that included some of the top people in the financial, corporate and communications world.

"Talk about radar..." Phillip said when he finally put the phone away. "We're Courtney's centerpiece," he said ruefully.

"Shall we pop out of a cake together?" I suggested.

"Marvelous." Phillip hugged me. "Lets arrange it!"

Days later, we came through the foyer instead of a cake. My presence seemed to cut a swath through the throngs of social heavyweights at the welcome home party, later described in Vogue as "a magnetic presence as bright as a neon sign."

I did feel great in the short silver sequined slip of a Chanel dress with it's transparent cut outs that played peek-a-boo with my bare flesh. My hair swung like a silken pendulum across my bare shoulders and I felt as if I filled the space with self possession. Most important I felt secure. When I had left for our honeymoon I was a virginal icon. Now I think I returnas a powerful, Estrogen - soaked woman. At least, I hope so.

The choreography of the party seems to underline that thought. Women who previously shunned me and had leaked rumors to their favorite press, now flocked to greet us as we entered, enveloping me with a flock of invitations to lunch and various charity events.

I know only too well that the invitations are being offered because I'm married to a man who is considered a prime candidate for President of the United States. With my fame as a super model I'm a centerpiece for bragging and political marketing. How silly and trivial it all is. And how dangerous because it's effective.

The New York and Washington cabal that had been running most of the politics and big business in America are now accepting outsiders such as Phillip as long as he has the money and camera friendly looks for the public. I was the bonus arm candy. Together we are a package vote getter thanks to public recognition and extra exposure for Philip.

Despite my intense feelings of regret and guilt, I accept and understand I'm a key player in Phillip's political career. I'm the bow on the wrapping of his public image. Also the political circus will keep my focus away from my feelings and make me accept what had been.

Excuses aside, the truth is deep down inside myself I am still in love with Phillip and trying to understand why he did this to me. I know we have something special. I believe the connection we have is good. I have to believe that.

I look at my image in the mirror. I am no longer the young woman I had known. She's replaced with a mask, an empty palette to be painted then activated solely for

Phillip's satisfaction and pleasure. What do I think I can accomplish? I just don't know what to do. Who will believe me if I tell anyone what happened? They won't believe it. It's too impossible and besides, what proof do I have besides my words? I'm not sure I believe it myself – yet I know it happened. There is no turning away.

Thankfully Virendra didn't come to New York with us and maybe without him we can start a real life together and I can file all this horror away. I still feel excited when I see Phillip, though at times I have to remind myself to keep my emotional distance. He's fun and interesting and maybe that will expand and wipe out the resentment inside me. Maybe.

I'm not surprised we're separated at dinner. But I'm shocked the former Governor of New York, Smith Wellington, now Chairman of the Board of Leeko, a huge international communication's company, sits to my right and immediately puts his hand on top of my knee in a proprietary way. Almost immediately he begins to move his hand up toward my thigh then slide it up through my panties, ignoring my attempts to push it away.

I'm trying to discreetly get Phillip's attention away from the intense conversation he's having at the other end of the table, but everyone seems to be involved in conversations except for the elderly gentleman sitting opposite me, watching carefully through the slits of his hooded eyes. He winks when I realize this owlish man is

Timothy Slayton, a senior statesman and former President of the World Bank. His high visible profile is from his global financial consultancy to countries such as China and the U.K.

Smiling slyly and nodding, Slayton lets me know he is well aware Smith Wellington is ignoring my attempt to push his hand away as discreetly as I can.

Wellington starts to dance his fingers inside my lace panty. Slayton's stony face allows a grimace of a smile at what must have been my look of disbelief when Wellington pulled his hand from between my legs and licked his fingers to wet them with his saliva. With no discretion whatsoever, he then puts his hand back under the table and sticks his lubricated fingers into me. Crossing my legs tightly I try to push my chair back and get away with an excuse, but Wellington won't let go and Phillip remains engrossed in his conversation across the table, so far away.

For a split second I thought Phillip had glanced at me along with a few other people, all looking my way at once in unison. But maybe only Slayton seemed to be aware, grinning broadly as former Governor Wellington plunged his fingers back and forth inside me.

Picking up a fork with the thought of plunging it into the top of his other hand, I close my eyes and hold my breath. I can't pull away without creating a scene. If I did, I'd be ruined and bring Phillip down with me. La Crème de la Crème of international money and power are seated around this table and if I said anything about one of their own members finger fucking me, they'd destroy us. I don't want to sabotage myself or allow this man to keep his fingers in me. I've got to keep myself from melting down and slapping him.

Courtney Jenkins proposes a toast to the newlyweds and suddenly everyone is standing and looking at me. Former Governor Wellington pulls his hand away so I'm able to stand, my professional smile a bit wobbly but in place while people say kind things about us. Phillip walks over to me and hold me around the waist as he brings a champagne glass up to my lips.

I don't remember anything after that. Just that everything had grown cloudy and my head began to swim. I feel myself slipping down and remember grabbing for a chair.

But now, as I can see more clearly, the chair is gone and so is the table. I'm alone in a spotlight, the hem of my silver sequined slip of a dress is pulled up around my waist. The top is pulled down from my breasts making the dress into a sequined belt. I try to move but I'm restrained by the ankles and wrists with thick gold chains that spread my limbs apart.

The dinner guests begin to file into the spotlight and come close to me. The first woman, a sharp nosed matronly woman whose features are familiar but who I can't place, slaps me in the face. I'm shocked. Before I have a chance to compose myself, another follows and tosses a glass of champagne on my bare breasts. Trying to pull away, reeling in disbelief at this nightmare, one of the more distinguished men who also looked familiar, wiped my tears and the champagne away. As he did that another man kneeled and licked my thighs till he was told his time was up, then a younger man came and began to suck on a nipple and cry and call me "mommy".

Phillip appeared in a black sequined cape over his naked body, stroking his swollen and erect penis as he approached me.

I watch him approach with a sense of relief because he is at least familiar. Everything is still a little hazy and I tell myself I may be dreaming. Maybe I ingested something like the anthropology student from Harvard who had gone to Haiti to study Voodoo. He was given a drug that turned him into a zombie before being buried alive. Was a similar fate waiting for me? Had I become a Zombie?

Two footmen picked me up and laid me on a long refectory table covered with rose petals and two large candelabras on either end.

"The audience for the re-enactment of our honeymoon," Phillip whispered.

Like rote I felt impelled to lift my arms and rest them over my head producing a collective "ah" from the assembled guests clustered around the table.

If this wasn't a dream and I had been slipped some kind of drug, there was nothing I could do but try to stay calm. I can't fight these restraints. I'm totally at their disposal and hopefully their mercy. I wish I could curl up and go to sleep then wake up and find this is only a dream.

I had heard little snatches about parties like this, powerful game players engaging in kinky sex. I never dreamed I'd be involved with them. Not till I lost my virginity to Phillip.

The implication of sex had been a great part of my work when sizzling for the cameras in someone else's clothes or stroking a product for the buying market. Is this my punishment for being an accessory to creating a sexual climate?

Phillip climbed on top of me and drew my hips up off the table, bending my knees and inserting his penis into me. In what seemed to be a ceremonial exhibition, he plunged carefully and slowly, while behind me some unknown woman stroked my breasts.

As I grow excited with Phillip inside me, the cream I had been withholding welled up and pulsed around him. Another pair of hands stroked my forehead and cheekbones, keeping my eyes closed as the sex began to elevate me. Dizzy from whatever I had been given and lulled by the rhythm of Phillip's slow and steady plunging, I begin to swim in an ocean of primordial sweetness, regressing to the time when I floated comfortably before birth.

Barely aware I was sucking something I open my eyes and see Virendra withdrawing his penis from me then extending his hand to help me off the table. I don't want him to touch me, but I want to get off this stage and away from these people.

Virendra and Phillip come on either side of me as I use all my camera training to keep my mask intact while they usher me through the gushing guests offering their congratulations for my impeccable performance.

Once I had my dress back on with some semblance of structure, Virendra and Phillip lead me out to the car where I collapse. *I have to get out,* is a mantra in my head. It's all I can think of. I'm against a mass of sexually driven energy. I'm in over my head.

Sitting between Phillip and Virendra in the Silver Cloud limousine, each man with a hand on top of my thighs, I try to make sense of what is happening. How did I get into this? Is this how I'm going to spend the rest of my life? Please God, make this a dream.

As the doorman escorts me out of the limousine at the Fifth Avenue Co-op, my stiletto heel catches in a crack in the pavement and I turn my ankle. The shock of pain doesn't wake me. I'm not dreaming. I'm painfully here and now and going through all these experiences in three dimensional time and space. This is my *reality*.

How I wish I had someone to talk to. If I told Catherine the hard nosed agent would most likely get angry and unwittingly make me feel it was my fault.

I don't know how to say that I should have gotten out, but I couldn't. I had no choice. Perhaps it's Stockholm syndrome. But compliance or subservience, whatever it's called, is the only road out of this hell.

Betrayal, loss of choice, public humiliation has taken its toll. I don't think I could have done anything other than what I did. I was the portrait of submission, trapped by an emotion that wanted and needed to bond and belong. I had to prove I'd do anything for Phillip. Now I hate him for what he has done to me.

I can't confide in Bernstein or Kalman. Everything I say will be treated as currency. And they may be involved with everything that has happened to me from the moment I first met them. Maybe before.

Roger could have set up this job with Bernstein and Kalman to be recruited for Phillip. It was good casting

Roger. I've been calling him and he hasn't answered. It wasn't like him. His phone is like another appendage.

Dread starts to come up following by panic grabbing me again. Why would they orchestrate the marriage and now the public sex? I don't understand. What is the purpose? If the marriage had worked it could have been a dream come true. I loved Phillip. Now I resent him, maybe detest him. But when he comes near me, I feel that excited tingling. Am I crazy?

Smiling automatically at the doorman, I nod at the elevator man but stop my forward movement once inside the apartment, pausing in the round foyer, like a bug caught in a web. Phillip turned to me. "Join us for a drink in the library."

Prickles run through my body as I back away and murmur "exhausted" and go briskly to my room.

Never wanting to see my dress again, I throw it off and leave it on the floor. Something I've never done before. Gratefully I slip into the soft silk sheets of my oversize bed, gather my knees into a fetal position and try to make myself calm. I've been raped and I can do nothing about it. He owns me. I'm his commodity. If I try to leave or report the truth of any of this they will kill me and my mother.

Chapter Thirty-One

Walking up New York City's 57th Street on my way to lunch with Catherine, I catch a glimpse of an older, tired and drawn version of myself in a store window and stop. The woman wears the same outfit I have on but the mirrored image is not what I thought I had dressed and painted. Not what I created. The woman in the store window is thick and looks unhappy.

Shaking my head in denial I tell the unrelenting likeness that she isn't me. But it shakes it's head back, mimicking my motions, even my walk as it moves with me to the other side of the reflective window. I could always make myself sparkle, but this image is resisting me. It looks strained. Her movements are forced.

Don't be sad, I tell the image. You're getting tons of attention and live in luxury with two powerful men.

That's when the tears came and the image started crying. It's the window's distorted glass, I tell myself. But the eyes of the image don't believe me.

Going into the store to the cosmetics counter, I buy duplicates of all the testers I use. Going back out to 57th street, I feel a bit better. It's a familiar street that I had walked up and down for ages when I was a young model making rounds.

When I first moved to New York I walked everywhere. But today, just walking from Sixty Second to Fifty Seventh Street was tiring. I feel heavy too, even though since coming back I've been swimming daily in the enclosed endless pool on the patio and had even gotten in a few rounds of tennis. The month of my honeymoon I trekked in thin air and had lots of exercise.

Sure I did - non-stop sex. The image in the window shows it has taken its toll. I want to ignore the loss of innocence, but it's so apparent, it has a permanence that can't be eradicated or covered. The true wide-eyed innocence is hardened. All will know.

I don't want Catherine to see it. But I can't change our date, Nikko, the gregarious host of the Russian Tea Room has seen me and is rushing though the door to escort me into the famed Restaurant.

Bringing me to one of the private booths in the back, I thank Nikko for have a platter of black caviar and blinis waiting for me.

Grateful I spoon a heaping mound of the caviar on to a Blini, a thin Russian version of a French crepe and add a dollop of sour cream. About to mollify my sadness with this bandage of salty luxury Catherine is approaching the booth.

"Caviar and you! What a way to lift my spirits," totally forgetting I had dreaded letting Catherine see me like this.

"Hello my love," Catherine slid into the other side of the booth. "How's the newly wed?"

Tears threaten as I embraced Catherine's familiar, comforting essence. I took a deep breath. I don't know what to say.

"You always look good. but you don't," she said, pulling back into her agent's role. "If you piled all that makeup on as a mask it isn't working. You can't cover what's wrong, it's streaming from your pores."

"Well thanks for the compliment. You actually look good and I'm happy to see you." Tears welled on the verge of spilling out.

Catherine becomes human again and her face creases with concern. "What's going on?"

I start to talk but stop and call a waiter over to order a Stolichnaya straight up.

Catherine draws back and arches her brows, then flicks her eyes for an instant to her watch. "We'll have two Badroit waters with a twist of lime," she orders.

"I really needed to see you." I tried to keep the tremble out of my words,

Nodding. "I wanted to see you too." She patted my hand lovingly. How different her hands feel, how warm and familiar and not demanding.

I pull my hand away as the waiter brings the drinks. The physical and loving contact from Catherine's hand has shaken me. It was so opposite Phillip and Virendra's demanding touches on their roller coaster rides through the realms of the senses.

I lift my glass for a toast. "To my dear wonderful friend." I take a quick swig of the Vodka and grimace as I wait for a thrust to the never land of sub consciousness. It doesn't come so I take another swig.

"Should you be drinking like that when you're pregnant?" Catherine asks.

I nearly choke. "What?"

"I don't think you're supposed to be drinking alcohol if you're pregnant. It can cause birth defects."

"But ..." I don't know what to say. My head is racing. I've been ignoring the queasiness I've been feeling and the tenderness in my breasts. But that could be from some of the rough stuff I've gone through and maybe I have jet lag.

"Alcohol is bad for a fetus," Catherine repeated.

"You think I'm pregnant?" I shook my head, incredulous.

"Your skin is milkier than I've seen it - chalky to be exact." Catherine was smiling. "And you look like something is draining your energy. Am I right so far?"

"Well, yes." I was stammering.

Catherine squinted, "You always had a great body - right?" she asked rhetorically, "but with boobs like those I could have gotten you a $20 million-dollar contract for your first film. My God, you could be the next Marilyn Monroe. You're either pregnant or they're silicone."

I don't laugh. "What a horrible premonition. "You're right. Of course you are."

Catherine didn't pick up my tone, she was off on the yellow brick road of preconceptions. "Well Mamacita, are you going to tell Mother Confessor the truth? When is the heir to the Landfield fortune going to be born?"

"Maybe never. But I think you're right. This may sound strange because it's only a few weeks at the most, but I can feel it." I put down the vodka and picked up the Badroit and toasted Catherine. "You're always right. I wish I could drown my sorrows, blot everything out, and do all the wonderful things other people do as they ruin themselves."

"Great ambition," Catherine calmed down from her baby fantasy and looked at me more carefully. "But you don't need booze or drugs to do that my dear. Life has many other choices to ruin oneself."

I take a deep breath. I can't tell Catherine everything, maybe just a small piece of the truth. "I've been having an affair." For some reason it just blurted out. I waited for her reaction.

"On your honeymoon?" Catherine's mouth twitched a bit with surprise. "I wouldn't have expected that." Her eyes seemed to drink me in.

I could feel myself blushing. "Phillip isn't very sexual," I thought I'd say just to end it. I can't lie to Catherine, but can I tell her the truth?

The waiter brought another order of caviar which Catherine immediately began to spoon on to the blini. Folding it carefully she offered the bulging pancake to me but I shook my head no.

"Don't worry," said Catherine, "these eggs aren't fertile."

"You're terrible!" I whooped at the top of my voice in the fashionably crowded restaurant, starting both of us laughing, the laughter growing raucous as I poked around the pile of tiny black eggs.

"So you don't know who the father is," Catherine finally said, nearly back in control.

"No idea. And that isn't the problem. Phillip more than knows." My laughter is replaced by the heaviness pressing on my chest.

"It's easy to know who the father is. Have a genetic test. A doctor will tell you what you want to know."

"Perhaps I should bring his heart in as well so they can see if he's human before we test to see if he's a father," I said.

"That bad?" Catherine wrinkled her brow again, eyes narrowing.

Tears spilled down my cheeks.

"I'm so sorry," Catherine's voice broke, her eyes reddening and filling as well. "You looked so perfect together - it was," she paused, searching for a word, "perfect," she finally decided. "A fairy tale."

"A nightmare. I scoop the edge of a blini onto the caviar.

"Normally I would have suggested you wait a few years before you got married," Catherine built a mountain of caviar for herself. "Your career was so hot it would have gone through the roof. It still could, you know." Catherine carefully brought the caviar stuffed blini to her mouth. "But for all extensive purposes," she paused with the blini, butter dripping in mid air, "Phillip Landfield appeared to be the catch of the decade. But I forget how those perfect *catches* can be," she shook her head ironically. "Like a virus. I should have warned you instead of buying the Cinderella story. Did he hit you?" she asked, taking a huge bite from the rolled up blini and quickly wiping her mouth and chin.

I shook my head and looked down, playing with the caviar knife at the side of my plate. "No," I finally answered.

"Look, let's call your doctor and get you a D & C," She took her cellular phone out of it's Hermes pouch.

"An abortion," I correct her.

"Call it what you like. I'm just trying to make it easier for you," she said earnestly.

"I'm sorry but I have mixed feelings about abortion, especially now. I'm married. I mean, I could condone it if the baby was deformed or if it's a hardship or rape but..."

"Stop the sound bites," Catherine interrupted. "I know them. And I also know how much your politics have changed since you married a political wannabe. But the reality is you have a life to live. You may have made a mistake in the choice of your mate, I don't know if you're sure about that yet. But no matter what kind of potential you have, money, security, fame, the reality is that your life is screwed up, you're screwed up and it isn't fair to bring a child into a mess like that. Maybe if you want to have the baby then give it up for adoption - that's an option."

"Oh sure." I banged the bone knife down causing a woman at the next table to give me a disapproving glare. "I'm sorry," I apologized both to the woman and Catherine. "Please don't get tough, I can't handle it. You're the only one I trust."

"I'm sorry Jenny, I don't mean to upset you, but I want to get your attention. Everything I said is true. I care about you, and I know how good you are, you have everything going for you and I don't want you to screw up your life."

"I have already," Tears were now splashing down my face, and uncontrollable sobs were quickly following.

Catherine got the waiter, signed the check and steered me out the door.

Winding our way through the horses and carriages waiting patiently at the curb for parkland carriage rides, I manage to get control of myself as we cross the street and enter Central Park. "It's a world of changing colors this glorious Autumn afternoon," marveled Catherine as she tried to lighten me up. "When the weather, light and even the fragrance is so perfect it's hard to think of New York having problems. If any of the French Impressionists had lived in New York at a time like this, they would have immortalized this city instead of Paris." She gave me a hug as we continued through the park, stopping at the cement moat around the Penguins and sitting down. It was there I confessed to all that had happened since I met Phillip. I told her everything.

When I finished, Catherine couldn't speak. "Well," she finally managed to say, "you certainly don't fool around. You got tested in the toughest markets: survival, betrayal, submission. I'm not sure I know anyone else who could have survived all that. If it means anything Jenny, I want you to know I'm enormously proud of you and admire you very much.

"How could you? I gave in to them. I didn't resist."

Catherine comforted me and I thought I saw a glint of a camera, but I wasn't sure.

Catherine must have felt something too because she reacted the same time I did. The successful businesswoman has learned to listen and act on her instincts and it appears she has a feeling we're being followed.

Putting her arm around my shoulders she whispers to come and soon we're flagging down a cab to plunge us into the flood of cars swarming to get out of Manhattan on a Friday. A filthy rendition of a cab slowed a bit and Catherine yanked the door open and jumped in oblivious to the driver's protest when she told him to take us to Canal Street, Little Italy.

The cab driver scowled, whining, "There's too much traffic to Canal street. It's Friday rush hour lady."

Catherine ignored him, her mouth a silent line. "Please watch the road," she softly but firmly replied.

Getting the picture he drove, keeping up a monologue about his fucking bad luck.

"I want traffic so the ride will take a long time," she whispered. "This is a dangerous situation you've gotten us into and we have to be extremely careful getting out of it."

"Catherine, you're not involved. These people are kinky, not dangerous. I made a mistake. It's over now."

Catherine shook her head motioning her to keep her voice down. "You can't stop anything. These are not innocent, innocuous people," she whispered feverishly. "You're the innocent! There's a good reason Phillip is doing these sex parties with this guy with the V name from wherever. The kinds of people you mentioned play for keeps. They have not worked all their lives for their money and power without protecting it. Actually, they want more, need more to fill that big hole in their lives where they lost morality. So to enhance their lives, they've gone to you. They want the biggest and the best of everything and if you try to pull away from their world, you become a threat to them and maybe their place in history."

Catherine paused, took a deep breath then continued. "If their kinky behavior gets out, their future is ruined. No one is going to name an airport or a federal building for an accused sexual pervert."

The words Phillip had said about security and the people with too much to lose came thundering back to me. "Oh my God."

"We are going to have to be very careful," Catherine repeated, "If they find out I know I'm as good as dead."

"NO!" I grabbed Catherine's arm. I felt like my life had just fallen apart. "Oh my God!" I hugged Catherine closely. "What have I done"!

Catherine was calm. "Nothing. You've done nothing. Life is on tape. you're a component, a small player in one of many life dramas. Whatever happens is supposed to happen. What matters is our perception of the experience. We can be victims or we can be students and learn from it."

I look at Catherine. This woman whom I love and trust more than anyone is feeding me a Pollyanna Rose-colored scenario that isn't possible. I'm so out of control. This woman who has done more for me than anyone else in my life has been put in life threatening danger because of me.

Catherine tells the driver to stop in front of a small Italian restaurant just before Canal Street. The driver is overjoyed not to go any further, and to show his gratitude does a screeching u-turn to make sure we notice he's not going further into the graveyard of rush hour.

The restaurant is fairly empty before the dinner rush so we had our choice of any table. Catherine chose a back table where we could watch the door. The waiter smiled, used to those kinds of choices.

"You need to find a way to distance yourself from Phillip and make him think it's his idea," Catherine was saying. "He has to feel he's tired of you and doesn't want you. It has to be his decision," she repeated. "His decision to end the marriage. I don't know how you are going to do that, but it has to work. Here." She pressed a note into my hand and closed her fist around it. "Read it later," I stuffed it in my pocket.

After a long dinner we went to two art movies in Greenwich Village to pass the time. Afraid to say too much we were both fearful, afraid we were being watched.

At 3:00 A.M. after a final drink at a small tavern near First Street and Sixth Avenue, we tearfully kiss goodbye. I had begged Catherine to come to Washington with me but she refused, so we decided through a rudimentary code that I would go to Newark airport and fly back to Washington and Catherine would go to Grand Central Station to get the train to Connecticut.

With dark and heavy feelings we left each other on the street that evening, each with the unspoken feeling we would never see each other again.

I later learned there had been a tracking device in the beautiful gold Hermes watch Phillip had given me.

Chapter Thirty-Two

Catherine took the first cab but leaned over and told the driver to wait till I got into the next one. Then I saw her cab turn in the opposite direction she should have been going and wondered if she was going to The New York Times.

My last glimpse of her she was settling back, resting her head on the headrest, then picking it up and laying it back down as if she was fighting to stay awake. Or at least that's what I imagined I saw. Later I learned that a hermetically sealed glass shield of bullet proof glass was between the driver and passenger that cut off all air between the two sections of the cab. Once lethal ammonia gas was expelled in the back seat of the car, the driver had enough time to dispose of both the car and body and escape. When found it looked as if Catherine had a heart attack. But I didn't learn that till much later.

Phillip was waiting in the drawing room when I got back to Washington early the next morning. Though I hadn't called or connected with him, he'd known I was coming.

Without one word, he took me in his arms and kissed me gently on the forehead, then cradled me closely as he led me to the bedroom where he tenderly undressed me and put me to bed. Taking off his dressing gown he climbed into bed with me and held me closely in his arms, his soft hands gently caressing me as he told me how much he loved and missed me, how happy he was I had come back.

If he noticed my tears he didn't acknowledge them, but gently crooned his love and covered my face and throat with soft butterfly kisses. I felt the phoniness. The sham. He didn't mean most of what he said. He was a bad actor and I knew I couldn't trust him. But the warmth of his arms and the feeling of his strength along with words I like to hear, were enough to push my thoughts and fears away and allow me to take him on total face level, a human blanket offering me comfort without soul. Nevertheless, we fell asleep cradled together and I didn't wake till the bright sun and heightened sounds of mid-day life in Georgetown clattered enough to rouse me.

Tinkling silver and glass brought me to full wakefulness as Phillip came in with a breakfast tray of fresh fruit, juice and a beautiful white rose. A cloth floating in warm water and rose petals freshened my face and hands while Phillip brought the Venetian lace bed jacket I had purchased for our honeymoon and draped it across my bare shoulders.

Refreshed by my long rest I luxuriated in the peace and quiet of the town house. It wasn't till I was halfway through the glass of chilled fresh orange juice that I thought of Catherine. Nearly spilling the juice I hastily put it back on the tray, grabbed the phone and called Catherine in Connecticut. Nerves and guilt passed through me as I anxiously waited for Catherine's phone to ring.

The answering service picked up and I asked if Catherine had called in for messages. When the operator said "no", I told them to please track her down and tell her to call me immediately, it was urgent.

Panic spread as I turned to Phillip, calmly reading the Washington Post.

"Catherine isn't home." My throat was so tight my voice croaked. What ifs ran through me. Did I really see what had happened? Was it my imagination? Did I make it up? Maybe my thoughts in some mystical dark way caused her death. But is she dead? Why am I thinking like this? She said it could happen if anyone knew. Was she murdered? I made it happen. But maybe it didn't.

"Darling, what's the matter?" Phillip put his paper down.

"Catherine and I left each other late last night and she's not answering her cell phone or her home in Connecticut. She's supposed to be there."

"Maybe she's still sleeping. Or she changed her mind and stayed somewhere else," he suggested.

"She wouldn't do that. I have a bad feeling. We both had it. I wanted her to come back to Washington with me but she wouldn't. She said something about destiny. That worries me. I don't like this feeling. I can feel it happening. I can see it in my mind. She's left her body."

He chuckled. "Destiny hmm? Well I wouldn't worry darling, I'm sure she's all right. Maybe Destiny is a new hot stud she went to be with last night."

"That's not funny." I tried calling Catherine's private cell number again, then called her apartment and the NY office, but the answering service and her secretary gave me the same news, Catherine has not picked up any of her messages or come to the office.

I close the phone, certain my face is drained of color, my body quivering in waves of dread. "She's dead." My lips tightened and twist in the beginnings of sorrow and rage.

"Darling," Phillip crosses the room, arms outstretched like a bad Shakespearean actor. He takes my hand and sits on the bed beside me. "I'm sure she'll be calling as soon as she picks up your messages. Don't do this to yourself."

"This isn't like her. You don't understand. Last night when she was getting in the cab I felt like I was saying goodbye. Forever. I think she felt the same way. What if it's true?"

"Sweetheart," he stroked my hair. The phone is going to ring and all this anxiety will be for nothing."

I shrink away. I don't want him touching me and scoot close to the wall. "I pray so." I clutch the lace bed jacket close to my throat. "Do you believe that evil is the same as good?" I ask him.

"I think that without evil, we would not recognize good. It's part of the same vibration but causes different perceptions, positive or negative."

"So you condone evil in the interest of good," I continue, trying to keep condemnation out of my voice. "The taking of lives, adultery, and theft is acceptable as long as it serves what one perceives as the ultimate good?"

"Jenny. You're annoying me. "What are you talking about? I never said that, we're talking philosophically. In certain cultures murder is called religious sacrifice and therefore condoned. Look at the Bible, Abraham almost sacrificed his son Isaac because he said God told him to do it. Isaac wasn't going to be slain because his father hated him or he was a psychotic. The attempted murder so to speak is accepted universally among Christians and Jews because it was done as a result of Abraham's love of

God. Every society has its different taboos and standards, and in ours the things you named, murder and theft are on the negative side of the taboo line and not acceptable."

"And adultery?" I ask.

"I believe that when a person has sex with another behind their mate's back, and that act hurts the mate, it destroys the positive aspects of what could have been an intimate relationship. Everyone has to be a willing participant whether actively or passively. Otherwise it's adultery."

Pulling the jacket more closely around myself I got out of bed and headed for the bathroom. "I need a bath."

"Of course darling." Phillip got up and rang for the maid to clear the breakfast tray then went to his study.

The phone call I dreaded came through on Wednesday. In a tearful halting way, Westy, Catherine's assistant, had just come from the morgue where she had identified her body. Catherine had been found in the middle of an abandoned housing project in Brooklyn. The cab had been left a block away and by the time the police had gotten to it, it had been totally stripped of every accessory and every visible ID. They attributed Catherine's death to a heart attack possibly during a hold-up. Her clothes had been badly rumpled, but there was no sign of sexual activity nor were there any bruises that would indicate a physical assault.

"They think it was a heart attack," I said when Phillip came home. "After she left me. In the taxi. The driver deserted both her and the car. Why would he do that? Why? He could have taken her to a hospital that was probably close by."

"He was afraid to," Phillip answered. "He could be in this country illegally or without a chauffeur license. Maybe he was using a stolen or foraged license. They're easy to get. They make them in Puerto Rico and the Dominican Republic. You can buy official licenses and passports if you know the right people."

"You're just full of all kinds of information and answers, aren't you?" Not waiting for an answer I leave the room and slam the door.

I don't come out of my room till the morning of Catherine's funeral wearing a black Chanel suit. Phillip confirmed that he had made arrangements to take the smaller Landfield jet and arranged with security to keep me away from the press and public and tried again to convince me not to go. He said it would make me too upset.

The funeral was happening quickly because the autopsy had been done the morning Catherine was brought in. Catherine's family had suddenly emerged from America's woodwork and insisted that because she was Jewish she had to be buried within forty-eight hours.

Nearly a week had gone by since Catherine's disappearance. It had been estimated she died early Saturday morning probably before sunrise. There was no way I could interfere or help Westy's pleas to countermand the families' arrangements which were opposite the kind of funeral Catherine's friends knew she would have wanted and deserved.

I couldn't help emotionally or legally. The family had every right to do what they wanted. No will had been found, Catherine had left no instructions, nothing. She clearly had no intention of dying. I feel so guilty, so responsible for her death.

Going over every moment from the time we met for lunch, I suddenly remember the piece of paper Catherine had given me at the Italian restaurant and told me to read later. I rush to the closet but can't find the suit I was wearing that night.

Barging into the servants' quarters, I ask the startled maid if she had found anything in the pockets when she collected my clothes for the cleaners. The girl confessed that she hadn't checked the pockets. I called Fritz and asked where the dry cleaning was taken. When he replied it had been picked up that morning I had him drive me to the cleaners and wait in the car while I went inside. Negotiating with the clerk to let me look through the pockets of the clothing that had just begun its cleaning process, I nearly collapsed with relief when the suit was found and it had not been doused in chemicals. The crumbled piece of paper in the pocket had not been destroyed. Catherine's last message. She had said not to read it till later.

I unfold the paper and almost faint from the rush of blood sugar dropping. Crumbling the paper I put it in an ashtray and set it on fire, forever destroying the words: "Phillip is following us. Don't let him know, you know."

Catherine had been right. Phillip is dangerous. They all are. Phillip killed Catherine. I had burned the one piece of solid evidence against my husband if I am to turn him in. Why did I do that? How stupid it was. What other evidence do I have? They'll kill me and it will be a political and media bonanza for Phillip. He'll be a martyr, sympathetic. The media will keep him in the spotlight from the moment of the death of his beautiful wife. It will add depth to his worth along with the long term publicity of who he's dating, who is the most eligible to be his next wife after I'm dead.

Chapter Thirty-Three

Against Phillip's continuing protest I went to New York for Catherine's memorial service. She had been closer to me than my own mother. And her reward was her murder.

I prayed Catherine hadn't suffered. I've been trying to get her doctor to return my calls to find out if he knows anything about her death or if she had a heart problem. Anything to help me know what happened, but his office had cited the HIPPA law when hearing what I wanted to talk about.

Catherine had been forty-seven, fit and healthy. Stress was part of her success and she kept it in stride. Outside the office her lifestyle was solitary and comfortable. She had invested in a small Connecticut farm that was her sanctuary. No way did Catherine have a heart attack. There should be a minimal investigation. The death would be called, *natural*. But she was murdered. I know it.

I don't understand why Catherine's family insisted upon having a religious Jewish funeral, which meant minimum visitation and quick burial when Catherine was a practicing Catholic. They also broke Jewish tradition by having her body cremated. It didn't make sense. Nothing was making sense. A document had been produced that was supposedly signed by Catherine requesting cremation in the event of her death. That was the only document they could find. Nothing about her possessions, her beloved pets or the multi-million dollar business she had created were in any papers. That was a-typical of a woman who created a business based on detail and contracts. I worried about what was to happen to all she built and loved.

We invited everyone back to the penthouse apartment for lunch after the service. It had been Phillip's idea. I was grateful for that, but not blinded. Phillip was the person that Catherine had seen following us. He was the one who had fingered Catherine and signed her death sentence. Because of Phillip, and also because of me, Catherine is dead. I'm lethal. If I go to anyone for help, they'll be dead.

I have to get away. If I tell Phillip I'm leaving, he'll kill me and I don't want to die. First I have to try to see justice served in Catherine's death. Then figure out why I survived so far and what I should do next.

Chapter Thirty-Four

The pain started shortly before the last mourners left. Shooting, ripping, cramping pains shooting into my stomach, travelling between my legs that were too weak to support my body. Leaning and sweating, wet splashed down my legs and turned the white marble floor red. I was bleeding. I called for help and collapsed.

Feet ran, voices collided, the ceiling moved, straps dug across my body, a needle stung, a siren screamed, or is that me? Am I screaming? I can't tell. I'm no longer attached. There's a drill somewhere off in the distance then sudden thick and deadly silence almost like cotton is stuffed in my ears. Nothing remains. Am I flat lining?

A heated ray of sun pierces the window. Comfort pours over me. *Catherine? Are you here? Can you help me?*

Opening my eyes in response to a thick pungent small I see flowers in ornate vases and baskets covering nearly every space of a small room with an underlying *sharp medicinal smell. On the ceiling is an array of tracks and blinking lights that I guess are there to determine if someone can be fixed or die. A hospital room. But where? Is this where I'm supposed to die?* The too familiar feelings of panic start to approach.

Nauseous, my hand throbs and swollen where a needle is inserted on top of my wrist.

A rush of unpleasant cold sweeps into the room as Virendra materializes at the door.

If only it was an illusion and he'd go away, but he's doesn't. My sinking heart telescopes I have no escape. I'm always trapped when this man is around.

"How are you feeling?" his British accent fills the room with formality, the question protocol, v*erbal garbage*. Like a five year old I turn my head and shut my eyes to make the monster go away.

But it doesn't. Instead a tingle goes up my free arm as he lifts and touches his lips to my hand.

"I hope you're listening," he was saying. "I just want to tell you how sorry we are."

I opened my eyes and look at him. "Where's Phillip?"

"He has a pile of work. You've taken up a lot of his time."

"So have you." The bluntness makes me feel good. "When are you leaving?" I'm proud of myself.

"I'm not leaving, Jenny. My home is with you."

My bubbly, heady feeling falls away. Dread pours in.

"You're our precious star," he continues to hold my hand and kiss the fingertips. "We have to take care of you." He puts my hand down and walks around the room, checking the cards on the flowers.

"Did I lose the baby?" It galls me to have to ask him.

"Of course. Didn't you want to?"

His words are a blow. The reality and the cruelty of the question causes a heaviness to drop down on me as I feel the physical loss of that glowing life force that had been inside me, now gone. Anger replaces the hurt. "How dare you!"

"Next time I impregnate you I'll make sure you take better care of my baby," Virendra says in a flat, matter of fact way.

Head spinning I try to choose my words deliberately. "That was not your baby. I only allow Phillip to be with me without protection. You know that. I knew the moment that baby inside me had been created. I felt it — something you will never know. Phillip is my husband and from now on, he is the only one who can touch me."

"Whatever you say." He turned and left the room.

His words mean nothing. He will do whatever he wants. His promises are more fragile than dandelions turned to fluff. I feel so weary.

The rustle of clothing wakes me and the smiling face of my gynecologist, Dr. Violet, is looking down at me. "How are you feeling?" she asks as she takes my hand to check my pulse.

"Ok I guess. But, not really."

"Don't worry. You've been through a lot. You've lost blood, but you're *going* to be fine." The doctor went to the foot of the bed and lifted the sheet to examine me. I close my eyes to make the reality go away. Dr. Violet finishes quickly and comes back to the head of the bed. "You look good, but you've lost a lot of blood and have been stressed. So I'll give you another IV of glucose and vitamins and you can go home if you like, however it would be better for you to stay the night."

"Please. I want to stay. I'm not ready to go. Will you come back before you leave?" I mouthed the word, *alone*. Doctor Violet nodded. Then I drift back to sleep.

When I wake again its pitch black and very quiet. I reach for the light chord that should have been next to my pillow but it's not there. Everything feels different but familiar. I find the light switch and turn it on. I'm not in the hospital. I'm in Georgetown. How did I get here?

Cramped by pain but able to walk, I manage to get to the bathroom and look in the mirror. The face staring back is pale and drawn. Like the reflection in the store window days ago, I find it difficult to relate to the messy hair and the puffy red eyes. The image is a Halloween fright mask.

Dizzy and weak I pull my hair back into a ponytail then hold a cold damp washcloth to my face. It makes me feel better.

Get out yelled that voice in my head. *They'll drug you.*

Throwing on a gray cashmere sweat suit, I try to get out but the door is locked. The French doors to the balcony are open so I go out and check the moon soaked garden not too far below. I probably could have climbed down the trellis if I was feeling better, but I don't think I can make it now.

Are they going to keep me locked in? Bernstein and Kalman are expecting me at the office for Phillip's campaign. What would he tell them? From a publicity point of view the marriage is a windfall. Phillip had practically become a household name. Reporters and photographers follow us everywhere. Phillip and his people would never let me drop out of sight. They can't. They'd kill me first. They proved that with Catherine.

Virendra enters the room without knocking. "You're dressed," he said.

"How observant."

"Don't you think you might be better off in bed?" he asked with a gentle patronizing tone.

"I want the cook to make me something to eat."

"Why don't you call" he pressed the button on the intercom.

"Because I don't want to. I'm tired of being in bed."

"Jenny, you haven't been in bed that long and the doctor told you to rest."

"The doctor told me to spend another night in the hospital so I could stay on IV fluids. You took me out of there."

"Jenny," his mouth smiled. "The doctor said she was releasing you. That's why we brought you home. Don't you remember? They gave you a sedative for the trip. Phillip thought you should stay in New York at the apartment for a few days but you insisted on coming back to D.C. with him. You said you needed to be with him."

"DO you think I'm going to believe another ridiculous lie you throw at me. Do you think I'm a fool?"

"Jenny we'll talk later, I have guests waiting."

"Oh!" I couldn't hold myself back. "Am I to perform tonight or does the house whore get a break?"

I collapse in sobs on the bed, furious for having lost control, furious with him for having brought me so low. "Am I going to be locked in?" I'm screaming now. "A prisoner in my own home?"

"I'll have the cook make you soup. You'll feel better if you eat something. It will be brought up to you". He started to leave, "don't exert yourself, you need rest." He closed the door.

I waited for the click of the lock but it didn't come, then started toward the door. It wasn't necessary to lock me in. The house has a long staircase I have to transcend then a long walk across a huge marble foyer that echoes every step. Security cameras are mounted everywhere so if they want to keep me here they can.

With resignation I dampen my hair and pull it tightly away from my face. I lined my eyes with dark brown kohl and a smidgen of pink on the lids to try to offset the deep set unhappy eyes that are making me look more dramatic then I like. I wanted to change the image in the mirror, but I had crossed the threshold from a bubbling cute blonde to a streamlined femme fatale. I've been through too much. I look ready for anything.

Another wave of sadness suddenly comes over me. The way I look is a product, essentially created by my dear Catherine. A piece of my heart has died with Catherine. I knew it would be the last time I would see her. She knew it too. Nothing can hurt as much as saying good bye to her and feeling it was the last time I'd see and talk to her. There is no curse worse than having caused the death of someone you love.

The clatter of people ascending the stairway to the third floor shook my thoughts. What would they be doing in the ballroom? I obviously am not going to be involved. There's no way I can have sex for at least a month and the way I feel now, I'll never let anyone touch me again.

When I hear the last person go up the stairs, I start to go out but a terrible pain shoots through my belly and makes me stop. Is this repentance for having caused the death of Catherine? And what about Roger? A sinking, terrible feeling blasts through me. He hasn't answered my messages. He always does. Something has happened to him. He knows too much. Did they kill him too? Like Catherine? My fault. I killed them both. My mother! I have to protect her.

These are terrible people I thought I understood, but I don't. Somewhere in the schemata of my mind's standards and practices I had the impulse to sacrifice everything for the man I loved. I wanted to fulfill his wishes and prove to him the singular intimacy of love, its rapture. I could have brought magic to Phillip but instead I was his mindless sexual puppet. I had fallen in love with an image, made my bed with a nightmare, sacrificed my beliefs and traded them for the promise of love. I served a false master.

Chapter Thirty-Five

I watch the room grow dark as my place on this earth rotates away from the sun. I had slept through the day and have no intention of tasting the food set out for me. A luxury prison with an unlocked door doesn't matter because it's so hard to move. Physically I'm hurting but emotionally too. Not sure which is worse.

Most of my life I fought to be free. Then I met Phillip and willingly slipped through the cracks to follow delusion and become a prisoner.

Trying to hold on to the little pieces of will power left inside me I try to remember to obey my personal rules of survival. Stay positive, believe in survival. Escape to survive.

Carefully I get off the bed and go to the door. It's unlocked. Should I go down the stairs and out the front door or go up and find out what's happening.

I have to know what they're doing. Grasping the banister I hold on to it for support and pull myself up.

Pausing and holding the wall to breathe through a spasm, I chant, I'll survive, I'll survive. I survived childhood, I'll survive now.

Dreams and expectations brought me here, I was caught in my own myth; the gorgeous damsel and the perfect prince. Phillip's promises made my dream come true. It was the scenario of his campaign, life followed art. It had all been planned. Sex bartered for power. Thank God I've woken up.

I wouldn't have believed it if I hadn't been in the center of it as the new sex toy, the party favor passed around so Phillip could bond with people who would put him in the White House. They would be indebted to him. They would fear what he knew about them.

Finally making it to the top of the steps I see the ballroom is empty. However the screening room is teeming with people seated in the burgundy velvet chairs. I make out the face of a Senator, two Captains of industry, a well-known political biographer and the gay wife of a U.S. Cabinet member. I know them all intimately, very intimately.

Virendra ushers a distinguished looking man to a seat next to his own. I thought he was familiar, but like so many of the others it was probably from having seen him in the news or maybe in another state of dress, or undress.

The lights dim. Like a swarm of bees an expectant buzz fills the air, then abrupt silence as the room turns to black. Half hidden behind a door, my heart beats so loudly I fear someone can hear it.

Every seat is filled but no one is drinking Champaign or eating the caviar usually served at these screenings. There are no servants and when I search the room, Phillip doesn't seem to be here. It's very dark even with the tiny bit of light left in the entranceway. Suddenly the sound of a loud whoosh of wind fills the small screening room, leaping from speaker to speaker, building in intensity and surrounding the audience as bright white letters words bleed on to the black screen: SNOW GODDESS.

The noisy sounds of a market came up as a cavalcade of black cars drive through the narrow red cobblestone streets of Katmandu, the capitol of Nepal. Emerging from the lead car the glamorous figure turns out to be me, glowing and obviously enjoying every moment of the adventure.

Oh my God! Wishing I could sit down I feel light-headed. That footage was shot the first time I had been in Nepal. Footage from so many years ago. They have been targeting me for years. Was this why I became a success so quickly? Had it been planned?

The few stone faced profiles I could make out in the audience seemed unresponsive to the joy bubbling off of me on the large screen. However it was affecting me deeply, reactivating a chain of emotions that had once made me so happy. Sadly it was pure innocence only remembered, no longer a part of my psyche.

Something bumped into me, jolting me as I crashed to the present reality of lying on air bags in an American hospital, waiting for my life to end.

There were so many questions to ask. Two movies continued simultaneously in my head; the one in my memory and the conscious awareness of where I am. Or is this the future. I must go back and see my memory movie. I want to experience it again.

The audience seems restless, bored with the bubbling energy cascading off my screen image. Instead there seems to be restless anticipation. An anticipation that fills me with dread. Those golden days would follow with footage I had hoped didn't exist.

Clinging to the doorframe I watch as the image of a wagon comes into view. It's the wagon I had ridden in the first night of our honeymoon. The camera pulls back to include the breathtaking vista I had viewed with such wonderment, then darkness covers the screen for an instant as a man passes in front of the camera and climbs into the wagon. Staying slightly behind the man, the camera follows in close-up over his shoulder as he approaches me on my bed of fur. It captures him opening my clothing and exposing my pale breasts. Coming in closer the screen fills with the man's lips as I writhe and moan with sexual hunger whenever and wherever he touches me.

The man is Virendra. It hadn't been Phillip as he had said it was. Phillip had lied. At the time that little inkling inside me had not believed him, but I wanted to believe that my husband, the love of my life, would never let another man have me sexually. And I had been so hungry for Phillip's love I blotted out any doubt, any conception, that it was different than I believed. How could that happen keeps rolling like a tape in my mind as I watch, almost impassive, as the figure undulates on the screen in front of me.

Sickened by the exquisitely shot images as the camera explores the sensuality of the bend in my knee, the inside of my elbow, a close up of my tongue moistening my lips and his tongue joining mine, then withdrawing and tracing my body to the inside of my thigh. Back lit, in slow motion, a fountain of sexual juices flow into an abstract vision that fills the screen. A primal screen morphs to a laugh as the film cuts to me romping through the mountains carefree and happy. I remember how buoyant I had felt with the two men walking on either side of me that day. The men's faces are not recognizable because of computer - generated affects, however I'm lit so it looks like I have a slight halo. I had no recollection of a camera following us! It was well concealed, like everything else that I touched with Phillip.

It then cut to the women massaging and arousing me as they ready me for Phillip's initiation. Next cut reveals me as a compelling vision covered in gold, led by a young girl through the cavernous corridors of the sanctuary to the initiation.

From the moment I bow to Phillip, the gold Adonis on the throne, the movie shows every moment, passionate, aggressive, passive and powerful.

Phillip's courtship, our marriage, the precisely plotted and manipulated honeymoon, the reckless behavior on my return is all documented on film.

Through it all I had carried a deep knowing that I kept choosing to ignore - that inner voice telling me not to marry Phillip, not to give in to his demands. I ignored them. Why?

Those inner voices are teachers, I hear in my mind. *The culmination of experience to serve as an emissary for informed choice. The experience is giving you the choice to turn a positive learning experience into a nightmare. It's your perspective. A choice to be a student or a victim.*

Still, I feel betrayed. Guilt has taken me over. I'm now a porn star performing sex acts for potentially thousands, maybe millions of people, in a film that is visually and sensually spectacular. The SNOW PRINCESS is dazzling.

I'll always be known that way.

But why would Phillip lead me into this position when he wanted to be elected to the Presidency? He'd be ruined if this ever came out. Why would he do such a thing? Was it Virendra? What am I not seeing?

If only Catherine or Roger were here! I'll try calling Roger again. If I don't reach him, I'll hire detectives to find him.

The film is playing a segment in which I remember feeling dizzy and confused - probably because I was drugged with that sweet vanilla milk. On the screen my long bare legs are spread bigger than life as I'm being sucked and sodomized, pinched and massaged. I don't remember much of what happened.

The elite screening room audience watches silently, probably breathless with horror as they wait for their identities and their participation to be revealed on the larger than life screen.

Warm breath covers the back of my neck. My heart stops. Its Phillip. I try to push his hands away as he fondles a breast with one hand and travels up my inner thigh. I'm horrified he would even do this now. I've just had a miscarriage.

As he turns me toward him I feel my arm pull back practically on its own and slap him as hard as I can, raking my fingernails across his cheek, wanting to get at his eyes. Destroy him as much as he destroyed me. Immediately someone pulls my head back by the hair and hits me on the side of the head so hard I'm sent into semi-consciousness.

"Get her back to her room and lock the doors," I hear Phillip order Fritz. "Make sure her phone is gone. And make sure she's all right, we can't have anything happen to her. We need her to finish the film."

Groggy from the blow and the shock of Phillip's words as I'm carried away, I join in collective misery with the horror of the invited audience watching their futures potentially destroyed by their presence on the screen. The reaction is catastrophic, a frenzy of fury and despair as they see how they had been entrapped in a sinister plan to exploit and control them.

I can feel the hospital bed again as I live through the physical and mental pain of that horrible time. Betrayal seeded with promises of love. How needy I must have been not to see or even think it was all a lie to use me in such a perverted way.

The worst part is that in the beginning my body betrayed me, it responded even when my mind said no. But my body had a mind of its own, acting physically with no time for thought. My naïveté was used as a trap for financial and political gain.

Am I as guilty as Phillip and Virendra? I had joined the hunt not knowing I was the prey. I had loved the attention and not seen the danger, I called the sex love when it was just primal passion.

As an adolescent I hadn't smoked marijuana, taken drugs or drank alcohol. But on the threshold of my adult years I discovered a high that can be terrifying in its boundless proportions. I had become addicted to something that sent me into a hazy world where abnormality was normal and the only rule was to let convention go. I had gone to the farthest reaches to make myself and others feel passion. I *will never do that again.*

Chapter Thirty-Six

Using every bit of the self-help techniques I know, I take a hot shower then used makeup to arrange my image and keep it intact. In black cashmere leggings and a hoodie, I try the door and find it unlocked so go downstairs to the library where Phillip is multi-tasking in a green leather wing chair, watching stock prices and signing documents while talking to an unseen person from a nearly invisible speaker in his ear.

From the moment our engagement was announced, I accepted that I would not be involved with anything other than Phillip's political campaign and his personal comforts. Though I don't know much about his businesses, I thought Bernstein and Kalman would tell me what I needed to know.

My Prince of darkness looked up from his media screen, seemingly nonchalant about my presence, and flipped the switch to off on his earpiece. Smiling his version of a smile he swept his eyes over my body to judge me, checking for imperfections.

Tuned to reading thoughts through body language and reacting, I hide my cringing under Phillip's gaze.

Phillip's assistant appears out of the ethers clutching papers in her hand. Replacing them with others on Phillip's desk, she flashes me a capped smile and offers me something to drink as she scurries out of the room, not waiting to hear my answer.

Sitting down, I slide a little on the slippery oiled surface of the leather sofa. Phillip's eyebrows lifting and his smile broadening toward looking real.

It's that little jolt of reality that makes me grieve. If only he could have accepted what I could mean to him. He could have been so much more than this life he has chosen of sex, deception and depravity. He could have had pure love.

Leaning back in his executive chair, Phillip shifts his focus back to the media screen.

Not so long ago I had fantasized Phillip was the master and I should live to serve him. How could I have thought that way? And now he doesn't care if I'm sitting in his office or the reason for it. He doesn't care. I'm no longer useful, struck from the team, on the bench, sidelined for injuries and no longer needed till I can work again. The Thoroughbred is laid up for the moment.

Yet beyond all thought or reason I still wish I could have connected with this poster of a man behind the desk. There could be goodness there. But I can't reach it. It's over.

Pushing myself off the slippery sofa I say good-by to Phillip's bent head. There's no reply. I leave without hesitation.

With the exception of a slight wince of pain when I bend to put on shoes after changing to a Chanel jump suit, I'm able to dress without mishap. Putting simple essentials into my large Vuitton bag, I sling it over my shoulder and leave the townhouse.

Breathing comes easier out on the street. I hail a cab to Bernstein and Kalman's. I'll be safe there.

Chapter Thirty-Seven

A testament to stationery movement and a step back in time, little had changed at Bernstein and Kalman's office since I had left there.

"You've changed," Lew Bernstein confirmed as I stepped into his office. "Like good port, you've enhanced with time."

"So I've aged and look terrible." Laughing despite the jolt to my insecure feelings, I cover with a quick kiss and hug.

"You look great," Bernstein lied. "I'd marry you right now if you'd admit you made a mistake and get rid of that handsome rich hunk and replace him with me."

"Okay," I took his hand. "I admit it. I made a mistake." It took a breath to compose the emotion I'm feeling. "It was a big mistake." Emotion is welling up, I try to keep it down but it's overwhelming.

Culminating from weeks of solitude and despair, tears take over and start to pour down. "I need your help."

Bernstein seems embarrassed and ushers me toward Kalman's office.

I stop and lean weakly against the wall for support. "I need a friend. I need your help."

"We're friends. Let's talk to Bernie." Bernstein guides me away from gossiping eyes and ears.

I try to check my tears but they've crossed all bounds. I feel safe here, protected, permitted to cry. Bernstein and Kalman are my equivalent of a family. They've provided wisdom and direction, financial direction and companionship. I hope I can trust them, but I'm not sure. If I can't I have no one.

"So," Bernie is grinning broadly, choosing or maybe pretending to interpret my tears as those of joy. "We thought you were coming in on Monday," he pursed his lips and made a quick visual sweep across the large appointment calendar embedded in the media display of his desk.

"Bernie," Bernstein's voice was low, guarded, "Jenny came to ask for help."

Silence filled the room till Kalman whispered lethally, "What? The honeymoon isn't over, it's too soon."

I sat down carefully, not sure I liked the feelings beginning to permeate the room. Bernstein started to go to me, then at Kalman's look, pulled back and sat across the room, like I was contagious.

"Think about what you say before you say another word," Kalman barked.

"Believe me, I have," I answered quietly, trying to push the hurt that is building up. I thought I was among friends, surrogate *family*, but the annoyance in Kalman's voice, his obvious concern I may spoil Phillip's run for office along with Bernstein's sudden fear of contact set off an alarm that makes me see things in a clearer light that makes me angry which makes me strong. "A media bomb will explode if I say anything."

Bernstein pulls a chair close and takes my hand. Taking his cue Kalman's face changes from angry red to pinkish neutral as he manipulates his mouth into the semblance of a sympathetic smile still quivering with annoyance.

Pushing a button he tells his assistant to hold all calls, pushes a few more to lock the door and turn up the volume of a Mahler symphony. Leaning close he asks softly, controlled, "What happened?"

I gave them a brief description of the ordeal, the shoddy reality under Phillip Landfield's elegant veneer. Bad enough to have experienced it, the telling made me feel guilty, culpable in this reputation destroying material that was painting stricken and somber looks on the partners' faces.

Split in two as the distraught victim and interested observer, I watch Lew Bernstein mimic everything Bernie Kalman does or says. I hadn't realized till now that whenever one of them react to something, the other one adopts the same attitude. They live and work a mirror game.

Their truth is stark. It's crushingly obvious these men don't care about me or what I had been through. They aren't upset because I suffered. Their concern is with the work they had already put into Phillip's campaign and what the affect would be if any of this became public. The disappointment covering their silly-putty feelings exaggerated their attitude that I was responsible for screwing things up and possibly losing a lucrative account. Nothing more.

"Have you no concern for the morality of this and the potential to bring that consciousness into the government of the United States?" I blurted out.

They stared at me as if they didn't understand what I was saying. I could have been speaking in tongues.

Kalman shifts in his seat, his finger lightly hiding a smile creeping on to his face. "Are you sure you're not exaggerating?" he asks.

My heart stops. A verbal bomb just exploded in my face. Did he really say that? Does he think that's funny? I could scream.

"Sometimes honeymoons can get a little raunchy," Kalman was expounding. "You should have seen my first wife. She got hysterical when I wanted to kiss her," he interrupted himself and considered his words, "in places other than her lips," he continued carefully. "If you had been there you would have thought I was a sex maniac or rapist. Sometimes young brides can get hyper and exaggerate." He nodded to Bernstein who returned his assent.

"What I told you is no exaggeration."

"We understand," Bernstein pitched in. "Between us we've had quite a bit of experience with emotional women."

They both chuckle, oblivious to my reaction.

They could be the ones who set me up. They think I won't be able to compute what they're saying.

I close my eyes and waited till I feel their full attention. "Bernie, you're right. I'm a hysterical woman and I'll work it out." I nod to both of them and smile. "Thank you for your advice.

I got up to leave. "I guess I panicked about the nuts and bolts of being a politician's wife."

I smile at them with my practiced sincerity look. "It's a lot more difficult than modeling or taking directions from a director or someone like yourselves." I go to the door, "If I'm going to be a role model I guess public sex and starring in porno movies is what you guys want me to do." I blow them a Marilyn Monroe type kiss and glide out the door.

The two men sit, suspended. For the first time in a long time, they are not sure what to do.

Not risking the elevator, I run down the steps and exit before either man moved.

I had counted on them not alerting security as their reputations are at stake. They're strategizing before they do anything.

Across the street I see a magazine stand on the corner and I know what to do. The media is my haven. I buy a pair of fake Hermes sunglasses from the news kiosk and blend with the scores of well-dressed professional women in Washington's nerve center. Ducking into the lobby of a nearby Four Seasons hotel I pull out my phone and call the NEW YORK TIMES. I haven't gotten friendly with any of the political writers yet but the fashion editor knows me well and can connect me to someone in the Washington bureau.

The phone keeps ringing and finally a secretary answers. "The Fashion staff is in Europe for the Pret. They won't be back for ten days."

The "Prêt". How much has happened since that first walk down the runway less than five years ago and now, I hadn't realized it was on.

I was so innocent then, so excited about going on my first plane ride to France. I was going to accomplish so much. I had so many hopes and ideas.

I have to remember those ideals are still intact under these new layers of experience. I feel wiped out by these latest betrayals from Bernstein and Kalman and since I'm at the Four Seasons, I'll wait till I'm stronger and try to make a plan.

But scrolling through my contacts I can't find anyone to call. *Who can I trust?* I don't know where to go. I can't put my mother in jeopardy. I don't have Catherine anymore and Roger might be gone. I'm so alone.

A young guy in jeans and a tweed sport jacket just walked past me going to the registration counter sending a chill through me. He looks so familiar. I don't know if I should be scared. He doesn't seem to have seen me and he's walking away with a bellboy pushing a large stack of luggage toward the elevators.

His face is familiar. I think I know him and I feel more curious than scared. I hope by the time I reach him I'll remember who he is. Maybe he's a movie star or a politician I've seen at parties or on television, or, oh my god, what if he was at one of the parties!

I don't feel relieved as the elevator doors open and the young man and his luggage pushed by the bellboy, step in.

I hesitate, I don't know what to do. Should I push the button, try to get on.

It's too late. The elevator door is almost closed as the young man sees me and a quick, excited look of recognition crosses his face. In a freeze frame moment as he starts toward me, the elevator door shuts.

I watch the arrow point to the floors and see it stop at the Mezzanine. As it continues up, another elevator comes down and the young man comes out, his arms outstretched, a huge smile on his face.

"Jenny!" he gives me a quick peck on the cheek. "This is wonderful. I wanted to look you up but I wasn't sure if you would remember me."

"How could I ever forget you? We were going to Mustang." I want him to know I remember, but I can't remember his name.

"We shall go there, " said the young consulate worker, a strange look on his face. "Would you like a drink, coffee, lunch? I just arrived for an extended stay. I have to get my visa renewed and generate lots of meaningless documents for people to sign."

"I'd love to have lunch with you. Let's go to your room and have room service. It'll be private."

"Yeah, right."

Bill Farrow smiled as he reminded himself that having worked in the American consulate in Nepal with their share of celebrities he understood Jenny didn't want to be disturbed. He also remembered going to Swai Bodhinath and circling it three times asking to see Jenny again. And now he was with her.

"A monk once told me that joy is hidden in the crevices of disappointment, waiting to be seen and appreciated by those chosen. I feel that way now. Seeing you again," Farrow blurted out, his blush revealing he wished he hadn't.

Unable to suppress a giggle I settle into the sofa in the living room area of the large suite and finger the fringe on the embroidered Buddhist shawl Bill presented to me once we were settled inside.

After ordering lunch, he started to unpack, respectful of my reluctance to talk.

I was thinking if there was such a thing as divine intervention, it's showing its presence now. Bill is neutral. There is no way he could have been involved with anything that happened to me. I have to believe that not every person is against me. I can't live like that.

Tracing the gold threads of the Buddhist shawl I have to keep reminding myself that my life has been extraordinarily lucky so far, most of the obstacles have been surmounted even though they seemed impossible at their time.

This one is different. I've never felt the kind of heavy and total despair of losing the person I believed to be my true love and knowing I caused the death of my dear Catherine.

"Bill," I ask the young man, "do you think everything that happens in life has a reason?"

"I'd think you could answer that yourself." He closed a suitcase and sat down on the edge of the bed. "You have been living at a degree of fame and adoration that most people could never even imagine. Your beauty is so incredible it serves as a screen behind which you can observe. Don't you think you've been given all those gifts so you can use your objectivity to learn?"

"Yes," I replied slowly and carefully. "But sometimes beauty is a barrier that keeps good people away."

Thinking about Phillip I realize I had deceived myself. Even now I believe in some deep part of myself that together we could have changed the world to make it a better place. Head over heels in love I closed my mind to my instincts and accepted Phillip's strange needs and demands.

"You're human," Bill was telling me. "Your safety precaution, your shield, is beauty. We all have shields but they're mostly in our heads. We call them secrets and judgments and sometimes they help us build walls to keep us from seeing what is really there." He stopped then grinned shyly, "I guess I have to pull one of mine down, it would be hypocritical if I didn't."

"What do you mean?" I was surprised by his increased breathing and the red color creeping up his face.

"I thought I could never tell you this, but," he faltered a bit, "when I picture you in my thoughts, I see you as a Goddess." He dropped his eyes.

I search his face. Did he see the film? Does he know what I did? Relief is turning to misery.

Because of me, Catherine is dead and probably Roger. Until this moment I had forgotten my mother. She could be in danger. Why is everything falling apart?

"Bill, I feel haunted. I don't know what to do. I'm not sure I should trust you though I feel that I should."

He shrugged, a gentle smile on his face. "I can't tell you to do that," he said.

"I trusted some people and they betrayed me." Tears threaten again. "Their agenda is different from the one they sold me."

Bill shook his head. "You had the choice to examine the situation from whatever reality or aspect you could. You seem to have chosen on face value, ignoring signs and following what felt good."

"Isn't it right to act on the positive?"

'The forbidden fruit is a choice within us. Ultimately what counts is the understanding of the experience - good or bad. When an experience is enlightening, a new level of knowledge and awareness is achieved. If you don't learn from the experience, you return and take the lesson again."

"Reincarnation."

"You can call it that."

A knock on the door startled us.

"Yes?" Bill called, his voice shaken by the interruption.

"Mr. Farrow, I have an urgent message for you." came a breathy voice through the hotel door. "It's a secure message."

Bill opened the door to a young Ivy League intern from the State Department holding a manila envelope wrapped with enforced steel tape.

"I have to get your signature," apologized the trainee as he looked at me silhouetted behind Bill, trying to figure out why I looked familiar.

"Wait here." Bill slit the envelope as he closed the door.

Pulling out an average letter-size piece of paper, he read the words printed in the center of the page then turned to me. "There's been trouble. You could be in danger."

"What happened?" My lungs forgot to push as time, space and sound stopped. Waiting for his next words, a dreaded tingling is running through me. I'm cold. Shivering. Something terrible has happened.

Bill took a breath. "Phillip has been killed. He was shot in front of the Capitol. A professional hit. No witnesses and the shooter has not been found. He's probably out of the country."

I barely heard his last words. All I could hear was Phillip was dead. He was *killed*. It felt like a wrecking ball had knocked out my breath and contracted my heart. I waited for my body to take me somewhere, anywhere, scream, pass out, anything to get away from the crashing reality of words that seemed to be crushing my heart. No matter what had happened, my turmoil is a result of my inability to emotionally separate from him. I love him despite everything.

"Why?" I'm gasping, struggling to breathe. Sure my face is white, eyes red and round as a Kabuki dancer. A scream is building, threatening to demolish my discipline. In an emotional spin I don't know if I'm feeling horror or relief. I'm losing control, but I'm free.

"We don't know why," Bill was explaining. "We think it's the Kebar family who decided they couldn't control him. Maybe he was so in love with you they had to eliminate him because there was too much risk."

His words intensified my pain. *"Maybe he was so in love with you." How I wished it were true.*

"Jenny," Bill was saying. "I've been given permission to tell you that I know quite a bit about what has been happening. I'm with the U.S. Information Agency. You've been watched and investigated ever since you became involved with Phillip Landfield. The Landfield family has been high on the State Department and CIA watch list for a long time. We know their connection to the Kebar family, and we have enough information on them to keep their actions and whereabouts on as short a rope as possible."

"What list? What are you talking about?" I can't control my sobbing. All I have is a wad of soggy tissue to wipe my tears.

"Criminal elements in the Pacific Rim and Asia are controlled by Virendra's family, the Kebars. They head up a powerful drug ring that processes opium from Asia. Their operations include the sale of armaments, which puts them on a high priority National Security list. We think you know nothing about this and have not been involved in any illegal activities. We know you were set up and victimized."

Farrow started to speak but I interrupted him. "And you let it go on. How could this happen? Did Bernstein and Kalman set me up? Is the State Department or some other agency behind this? Did they think they could use me to get information?"

Farrow dropped his eyes. "You were targeted because Virendra fell in love with you and wanted you. Phillip was Virendra Kebar's Lieutenant. He did everything he was told. The Kebar family controls the Landfields as well as many other large family controlled companies. The Landfields know that with a flick or a nod they can be annihilated financially, physically or both. It's been that way for over a century. The Kebar family is one of the most powerful and dangerous criminal dynasties on the planet and we haven't been able to get them yet."

A chill like the devil walked near me. I take a deep breath to dispel it. "Tell me more."

"Virendra and Phillip were educated together. But the delineation of their positions had always been clear from their start. Virendra was the crown prince of the Kebar dynasty. Phillip could stay next to the top and enjoy all the luxuries and benefits as long as he maintained and respected their inherited positions. Phillip followed the rules. So did his parents and his grandparents before them."

I groped for more tissues and blew my nose loudly. I can't stop shaking. It makes so much sense. But why didn't I know this before? Why couldn't I have picked up on how Phillip had manipulated and used me. What a fool I was. All my training since childhood to sublimate my emotions and keep myself detached and objective had stopped when I met Phillip. I stopped thinking. I was only feeling.

Violation poured down on me. Phillip never loved me. He was the delivery boy handing me the right words and perks, images and feelings I wanted to have. I had wanted love so desperately I thought I could put down my survival gear and give in to the luxurious feeling that someone truly loved and cared for me. Like the places where I posed as a model, none of it was real. He lied to me and used me. I was a fool.

"Have I been implicated?" Dread and anger started to mix with the little layer of relief that Phillip was dead.

"We know you are innocent of any wrongdoing," Bill explained. "Virendra wanted you from the moment he first saw you. I think he still wants you. Our people just arrested someone in the hallway who had been following you."

"Why didn't Virendra contact me directly?" I asked.

"Because he knows you wouldn't be interested and that no amount of money can buy you." Bill answered.

"And Roger? He must be involved as well."

Bill nodded very slightly. "They paid him a huge sum to reel you in. The money has been traced to a numbered account in the Cayman Islands he hasn't touched yet. That doesn't bode well for his future."

I shivered again. The thought of Roger made me angry. I had trusted the little twit. All the time I had thought working for Bernstein and Kalman was my idea. What a good manipulator he was, or am I excruciatingly stupid?

"Phillip was Virendra's beard, his front," Bill continued. It was a lifelong position and it had nothing to do with you personally."

"From my vantage point it's very personal. It's my life."

"Falling in love with Phillip for what he appeared to be rather than what he actually was, cost you short-term.

With longer-range life lessons, this has given you some profound insight about surface and inner values. I doubt you shall choose on face value again."

"What about Catherine Pearl?" I asked. "If I was being used and you knew what kind of people the Kebars and Landfields are, why couldn't someone have warned her, saved her life?"

"We didn't see it coming. Didn't think they'd go after her. We're sorry. Very sorry. It was human error and misjudgment. We're trying to connect them to the hit but it was done very efficiently and I'm not sure the lab tests can prove anything. I'd be lying if I told you we can trace it to the Kebars, but we'll try. Catherine's case has been closed, her death attributed to a massive coronary. Unless someone comes up with a confession and visible proof, it's probably a wash, but we'll keep digging. Sorry, that's the reality." His mouth twitched with anger, his usually warm eyes had turned cold.

"I caused Catherine's death," I whispered huskily. "I'm toxic to those I love."

"Don't be ridiculous." Bill said. "You were the victim in this." He checked his watch. "We have to get you out of here." He opened the door to Mr. Ivy League who was slouched against the wall in his preppy version of attention. "Get us a copter," Bill told the eager young Patrician.

"Yes sir," he said, whipping out his cellular and punching in a number.

"Okay," said Bill, turning to Jenny. We can't leave you alone, but you do have a choice. We can bend the rules and go to the Justice department or the DC police. These local police don't want to get involved with international cases. They have enough to worry about here in Washington."

I can't stop shaking. "The State Department," I finally answer. "I'll do almost anything, but I don't want to go near Virendra again. What if he can still control me?"

"Remember the experience at Swai Bodhinath, the large stupa where you asked for knowledge, then went into the small temple and experienced yourself outside your own body? DO you remember the lesson that was put in your head? You were to bring the lessons of your past lives to the contemporary world through modern energy."

"I never told anyone what happened that day." I was barely breathing.

Bill smiled. "Then you saw me exhibiting fear of the two boys stalking me at the top of the Stupa, backing away, afraid they were going to grab my cameras. You silently projected to them they were doing wrong, connecting them to their higher understanding. It's your talent and that's why Virendra wanted to use you."

Everything stopped and I looked at him carefully. What was he saying?

He smiled. "You made the choice to learn a lesson from the dark side of the universe," he explained. Your justification for the lesson was you believed you had no choice and you gave up personal responsibility. Now you know you can never do that." He smiled mysteriously.

"Do you think you can handle the public exposure if things get messy?" Bill was different now, no longer shy but composed and confident, a total professional. "You forget that you received one of the greatest gifts you asked for years before, knowledge. Since that time you learned much about the Western world, the customs of judging on two dimensions, the power of the physical, beauty and wealth, and the need to think we have control. Don't worry," he continued. "You'll be surrounded with security. The media can be good protection."

"It didn't help Oswald," I was alluding to the man accused of killing President John F. Kennedy who was shot to death in the Dallas police station after his arrest.

"Don't trust Bernstein or Kalman," Bill continued. "We think they're controlled by the Kebar family. We can't prove it, but whenever there are vast sums of money and power like the Kebars, they control government and criminal elements.

A deep calm began to settle upon me. I was no longer shivering and took Bill's hands and looked deeply into his eyes. "Did our government assassinate Phillip?"

"I doubt it. He would have been a good information source if we had been able to get him. It's most likely the Kebar family killed him for that reason. It's also quite possible it was the work of a single unrelated crackpot. Anything and everything is possible at this point."

"I think some things are more probable than others," I answered as grief, relief, tears and expectation start to take control. I was seeing it whole. I know I would have made the same choices again if there was a lesson to be learned. Something big was happening. A major shift in my life is taking place.

Chapter Thirty-Eight

Photographers are waiting for me as I come back to the town house. Once again my life is a newsworthy event. A reality show. Paparazzi mobbed, reporters dissected, clothing is scrutinized and my face and name are all over social media.

Before the funeral I receive a polite letter from a respectable museum asking me to donate my funeral ensemble for one of their crime scene displays. I write back their timing is insensitive.

Virendra disappeared the day of Phillip's murder. His whereabouts are unknown. Farrell told me a jumbo jet took off without clearance from a private airport in New Jersey an hour before Phillip was murdered. The State Department could only assume Virendra was on that plane. If so it would be almost impossible to find him once he reached the Himalayas.

Many of the assets of the Kebar family as well as those of the Landfield's have been frozen in banks throughout the world. Financial records have been subpoenaed and confiscated. The massive operation, long in gathering evidence on the Kebars and Landfields, has catapulted into full action.

My heart nearly stopped when Bill Farrow told me the film had been found. He promised it would not be used for evidence and he would try to get it destroyed. However there is a probability copies were made. He would do what he could to find them.

The funeral received more notice in the media than any other newsworthy event. Slanted and choreographed in the pure public relations style of Bernstein and Kalman, it was being played as an example of crime growing out of bounds in the streets of the nation's capitol. News reported I was going into seclusion.

Seclusion was a safe farm in Virginia where I was debriefed by State Department's F.B.I. and C.I.A. officials. The first time I was led into the living room of the safe house where people from the Justice Department were waiting for me, I felt a familiar energy that I can't name but it made me feel safe. I trusted them and told them everything I had heard or seen with Virendra and Phillip along with the names of all the people I recognized who have been compromised by the Kebar family and Phillip.

Conversely, I learned during this time that the Kebar family ran an international pornography and sex slave ring as well as a drug cartel. They collected great sums of money from satanic and devil-worshipping networks that had been set up to enlarge their drug market along with snuff films and pornography. Using me as the star of a series of pornographic films set them in the forefront of international porn distributors. And most importantly, it gave them incredible material with which to control political and corporate leaders filmed in career ending behavior at the orgies.

From my detailed descriptions, police artists were able to draw pictures of the monastery and sanctuary where they kept me on that ill-fated honeymoon. I was told that because of the eclectic styles of the architecture, I could have been anywhere in the world because they had kept me lightly drugged with a form of Ketamine that can create out of body experiences. It was likely the structures had been newly erected and were movie sets and in my suggestive state and with my background, I accepted the environment as real.

After a few weeks when they were sure I was safe, I returned to New York with bittersweet feelings. There was nothing to do except have lunch with mom and shop. Coming from a life of glamour and high adventure, the reality of how empty life can feel, began to burn impatiently.

When Westy, who had graduated from booking agent to taking over Catherine's agency called me with an offer to do a commercial for HIMALAYAN HARMONY, a new soft drink to promote life-enhancing ingredients, I jumped at the offer. It was a chance to go back to Nepal, a country I consider magical and where so many pivotal moments in my life happened. I also liked the concept of the soft drink. Perhaps I can reawaken some primal truths in my consciousness when I'm there. And it will be good to go back to work. I missed it.

Suddenly thoughts turned into words, words becoming snowballs of ice. Pummeling, burying me. Once again. Thoughts, emotions, experiences - all rushing past. *The avalanche! Again! Am I dying?*

Chapter Thirty-Nine

The hard reality of my hospital bed brings me back to the present with an even harder reality. *I'm facing death. Would I have come to Nepal if I had known I would die here? Would I have been brave enough to test my trust in destiny?*

No, resounded in my head.

I want to live. There is so much more to do, to learn. Will I have to come back and face the same mistakes, even if I don't know what they were? What will it be like? Will I die today?

Panic took hold. I tried with all my will power to kick the covers off, but the sheets won't move. My legs are like wooden slabs. "I'm not ready!" I scream noiselessly. "I'm not finished. There's so much to do."

I need tears. Crying can give me *a chance.*

The hood of a dark maroon wool robe covers the shaved head of a Buddhist Nun coming out of the ethers and approaching me. Our eyes connect as if in a mirror and I know I'm seeing myself. *Nothing is changed, yet everything is different. This part is the unfinished business of my soul,* I'm told by that voice in my head. *Or is it the voice of the nun?*

Truth resonates within me as I accept *the person called Jenny had been programmed to experience success in order to pull down a vast network of dark energy; pornography, drugs and money laundering* that is permeating the globe.

Mixing thoughts with feelings I'm able to receive an irrefutable flow of knowledge that I know in my heart to be true. The Tibetan nun reminds me I had been trained for this work in the West for hundreds of years. It has been an ongoing process of consciousness that I've learned by living in different bodies during many lifetimes. The lesson is always the same; there is no turning away from the struggle between good and evil, darkness and light on Planet Earth. It is a proving ground for the gods. Those who can rise above it never have to return. "never have to" are the operative words.

"*FINALLY*," said that voice in my head. "*You got the picture. Go back to work.*"

"Please," I whispered. "Let me serve."

I can hear feet scurrying to change position. I'm back in the American hospital. Returned from the recollection of my life before I came here. It's cold. I wonder if it manifests in any way so the technicians can know how I'm feeling.

"*Her temperature is normal. The EEG has shown no signs of body* functioning shutting down."

"Will you shut the fuck up. What if she can hear you?"

"Then we're in big trouble."

There are a few nervous titters. Wish I could smile.

Tick. The clock on the hospital room wall ticked away another minute of this life. If only I could call out, wiggle a toe or a finger, let someone know I'm aware. I don't want to die.

What if I'm still alive when they bury me? Maybe all "dead" people are conscious but can no longer use their bodies. Billions of people buried or burned consciously, like Zombies! Is the true reward for our thoughts and deeds the way we experience our death?

The clock ticked again. The machines stay still. I can't understand why my brain activity isn't jumping all over the graph. Quite the contrary, it's registering almost flat. Maybe I'm almost dead.

But first I want to walk the earth on my own two feet, put my hand in water, touch soil, move my fingers, smell flowers, laugh and feel things.

I never had an inkling how much I would miss the world of touch, longing for silk instead of the harsh detergent and bleach-permeated hospital sheets that rub and burn my skin. I hadn't realized till a short time ago, how sensual and intimate my physical life had been.

A sob tried to work its way out. It couldn't. Nothing works, not even my tears. Only time and its messenger move with speed.

"OH SHIT!" came a cry, **"LOOK AT THIS! I DON'T BELIEVE IT!"**

"Keep it down, Doctor. What are you talking about?" an annoyed voice snaps.

"The EEG plug has been pulled half out." The voice is nearly hysterical. Jenny could only see hospital issue green and hear a blur of scurrying feet.

"Oh my God!" She heard someone else gasp. **"What should we do?"**

"You're going to put the plug back in the wall," ordered the stern older voice. "What is wrong with all of you? Don't you know these machines have battery backups when something like this happens? You should know that."

"Sir" came a hesitant voice, "the battery light has been flashing. It's flat. It was going to be changed but, well, we assumed the machine was plugged in."

"You assumed!" the older man's voice was low, deep, menacing. Then he exploded, no longer able to hold his temper. "Your assumptions nearly killed this patient. Don't you EVER let anything like this happen again!"

"You're right sir," someone called from the foot of the bed. "There's quite a bit of brain activity here!"

"Dr. Rubinstein, come quick," a high pitched voice was shaking with excitement, "LOOK!"

"What?" the man snapped. "Oh my God..." he drew in a quick breath. "A tear."

"Life and death are one. Only those who will consider the experience as one, may come to understand or comprehend what peace indeed means."-
~Edgar Cayce

THE END

About the Author

Since the age of five when she wrote, produced, directed and starred in her own musical J. has been involved in the entertainment business.

As a theatre major, J. studied in England then worked in television and theatre as an actor and later a TV executive. Writing came while researching a character for a screenplay and J. ended up as a feature writer for the LOS ANGELES TIMES, while starting two magazines, and writing for various publications

Involved in animal welfare, the arts and science, this is J.'s first book of the Jenny Webster series. "Between Body and Soul" is followed by the "Solid State Conspiracy".

Visit Author website at
www.jsilverstone.com

Made in the USA
Middletown, DE
05 November 2022

14099887R00195